"School starts day after tomorrow. You should go over there tomorrow morning and register. I've got everything you need." Tico handed Beth a manila envelope. "School records."

"But... I've never..."

"You went to a charter school. Defunct now. Had a thought to just say you were home schooled, but they keep testing records and I'm betting they don't have any on you— right?" He didn't wait for an answer. "Can't check this out too fast since it's defunct." He smiled at his own cleverness. "Gave you a B average—eleventh grade. They'll test you and put you where they want to anyway. They'd love to put you back one—love thinking they're better than Eastern schools."

It was all happening too fast for Beth. *Eleventh grade*? She wasn't altogether sure what that really meant. But *school*? She was really going to go to *school*?

"Getting you a driver's license," said Tico. "That's what the picture's for. Have it ready in a minute." A picture rolled out of his printer, and he did something with some scissors and a glue stick as he spoke and was now fiddling with yet another machine—laminating the license that already looked authentic.

"Get yourself a library card. You'll get a student ID at school. Got you a social security number. But don't use it. Won't get caught if you don't try to use it. That's all you'll need."

D0391294

Also by J.D. Shaw:

The Secrets of Loon Lake

Leave No Footprints

J.D. Shaw

Tiny Satchel Press
Philadelphia

Tiny Satchel Press
    311 West Seymour Street
    Philadelphia, PA 19144
    tinysatchelpress@gmail.com
    www.tinysatchelpress.com

Distributed by
    Bella Books
    P.O. Box 10543
    Tallahassee, FL 32302
    1-800-729-4992

Tiny Satchel Press Publisher: Victoria A. Brownworth
Art direction: Maddy Gold
Book design: Judith Redding
Cover design: Jennifer Mercer

Printed in the United States of America.
First edition.

ISBN 978-0-9845318-6-8

For my extremely supportive family—my husband, Dick, and our daughters, Cindy, Karen, and Amy. Your help, encouragement, and enthusiasm make it all possible.

It was 1:30 a.m. when Beth Watson left the house. She put the car in reverse and let it glide down the driveway before she turned on the engine and lights. Then she left the quiet, dark neighborhood and the city itself as fast as she could. She was old enough now to have a driver's license, but she didn't have one. She didn't have much driving experience either, and never in traffic or on a highway. Jack had let her drive around in grocery store parking lots, mostly. She was worried about the trip ahead of her, but she had to go, right away, and this was the only way to do it.

It wasn't until she was on the Schuylkill Expressway, the only highway heading west, that she began to breathe normally, but her hands were trembling as she held the steering wheel. There was no particular reason to go west, except that direction symbolized space. The whole country spread out west from Philadelphia, all the way to the Pacific Ocean. Plenty of places to hide. And Jack had always said he'd go to California if he could, said it was the only place far enough away for him. But she couldn't think about Jack. Not now, maybe not ever. He had come back for her. Nothing would have happened if he hadn't come back for her. If he had just joined the Army and stayed away, nothing would have happened.

Beth got on the Pennsylvania Turnpike and allowed the low hum of the tires and the rhythm of the road to push her onward. There was little traffic, trucks mostly, and after a while she got used to their noise and the pull of their weight as they passed. The night was dark and she was cocooned in the car, the ribbon of lane markers visible in her headlights, pulling her along. The driving was easier than she had expected, especially in the middle of the night.

Her adrenaline was high. Her fear made her stomach tense. She drove on and on. She didn't even turn on the radio. It did occur to her to wonder how long she could keep it up. She hadn't slept the last two nights, not since she had seen— *that*—and had made her decision to leave.

Strange thoughts filtered through her head. She'd need a name. But all that occurred to her were book characters. She needed to blend in. Keep her same initials, she had heard that somewhere. Belinda or Brenda. No. Those didn't seem like her, at least not the her she intended to become. She couldn't think about it anymore. Her thoughts were centered on her fear, on getting away, on creating distance.

Dawn broke before she reached the Ohio turnpike, a weak, end-of-summer sun painfully trying to make a new day. In Ohio she pulled into a rest center to get fuel for the car. Everyone was filling their own tanks. She watched them carefully so she could copy what they were doing. But they were all inserting cards in the pump machines. She knew they were credit cards, she understood that much. But she had never even held such a thing in her hand. How did you get gasoline with actual money?

Finally, she saw one person walk up to the booth in the middle of the car aisles and she thought she saw him hand over cash. She immediately followed him.

"I want some gasoline," she said to the man when it was her turn.

"Gasoline?" he laughed, looking at her oddly. "How much *gasoline* do you want?" He was pointing to a slot in the window.

"I don't know," said Beth. *What was she supposed to say? How would she know how much the car would take?*

"How much money's worth of gas?" he said the words slowly, like he was talking to someone who spoke another language.

She pulled out the bills she had stuffed into her jeans pocket before she left. She handed him a twenty-dollar bill, wondering how he would handle the change.

"Won't get you much," the man commented. The bill disappeared through the slot. "Pump four," he said. "I saw you standing there not doing nothing, wondered what was the matter."

Oh no, had she called attention to herself? That was something to be avoided at all costs. She hurried back to the pump and tried to figure out how to get the little door open on the side of the car. It didn't even have a handle.

Finally, the man filling his tank on the other side of the aisle came over.

"It's a lever inside the car," he said." He reached in the driver's side door and popped it open.

Beth still looked puzzled. She had no idea how to make the machine begin. The man gave her the same look the attendant had given her. But he got the pump started and stood there until it suddenly stopped.

"Hope you don't have much farther to go," he said. "You probably only got about a half a tank."

"Thank you," Beth said. She needed to get away from here fast. She had made herself very conspicuous with all the things she didn't know.

She had intended to drive over to the restaurant in the rest stop for something to drink, but now she was far too nervous. She had to get out of here. She had to hurry, had to gain more miles. She drove through a bit of Indiana and then, somehow, was in Michigan.

Later, she unintentionally followed a car off an exit. But maybe it was better, being off the interstate. *Had this car been reported stolen?* She didn't think so. It wasn't actually stolen, not like a stranger taking someone's car. Jack wouldn't have minded her taking it. But CJ might have reported it missing, just to catch her. She'd feel better if she could figure out how to get a different license plate.

As the day had progressed, the landscape had changed. Pennsylvania had been lush and green and hilly. Ohio was flat farm land. Here, there were still acres of field corn, the stalks jammed together, but now there were lakes and occasional towns, some villages that seemed closed up, forgotten.

Once again Beth followed a car, this time onto a country road. The landscape was more interesting.

A little after noon, it hit her. Quite suddenly, she couldn't keep her eyes open. She almost went off the road, caught herself as her front wheels started toward a ditch. She had just passed a pretty little lake and was coming into another small town, but this one seemed different. Once she passed the inevitable 25-miles-an-hour sign, there were white Victorian houses lining the shady streets. When she drove into the village itself, there were people going in and out of stores. No boarded windows here.

She looked for a motel, some chain that she would recognize—a Motel 6 or something cheap. She had to stop. She couldn't drive for one more minute. She felt sick with fatigue; her eyes were scratchy and her vision blurred.

But now the town was behind her and she had seen nothing resembling a motel. Several miles later, she spotted a vacancy sign with several letters missing. The place was a shambles, old and decrepit, a once-white building shaped like an L, with a rutted parking lot along the side. Beth almost didn't stop. It would probably be better to just pull off the road and sleep, but she would feel so exposed, and somebody might stop to see what was going on. Besides, there were beds and pillows in there. Did she really care about the peeling paint? It had to be inexpensive.

She pulled up to the entrance and wearily got out of the car. It was difficult even to stand up straight—she seemed locked into the sitting position she had maintained for so many hours.

The door to the office opened with a reluctant squeak. There were a man and a teen-aged boy, probably her age or a little older, sitting at a card table in front of a high counter. They were playing chess.

Beth almost turned and left then. The man looked scary. He was a caricature of a motorcycle biker, missing only the leather jacket. But he was already standing up, going behind the counter, nodding at her to come forward. His head was shiny bald and his arms tattooed from top to bottom, fully exposed in the tank top he wore. He had a flowing mustache and a neck that was as wide as his head. Another tattoo covered the back of that neck, a spider with legs crawling up onto his the back of his head.

This was, perhaps, not a good situation. She should turn around and get back in the car. Beth knew about bad situations.

She had her antenna tuned for them, recognizing them immediately. They rang alarm bells for her, and she could never understand why they didn't for everyone. But now, here, she wasn't feeling anything. She was too tired, too used up. She simply wanted a bed. She had to sleep. Nothing else mattered. At least not now.

"What can I do for you, miss?" the big man asked. His eyebrows hid any eyelids he might have had. His baggy shorts stretched across his big belly.

"A room?" Her voice came out in a timid stutter, from lack of use, or complete exhaustion, or that rising feeling that she should turn and run. They were both staring at her. Would the man tell her she was too young to check in? She tried to stand tall, look older. She had purposely made herself look dumpy in an effort to gain some years and to not be noticed. But would it work? She knew she looked older than she was. Her serious expression belied her years.

The boy was thin and had on Army fatigues and wore his hair cut very short. He was staring at her.

The big man looked at the clock behind him. "How long you checking in for? Odd time to be stopping."

This wasn't good. It was important not to be different,

not to stand out. "For the rest of the day and the night, I guess," she said. "I'm not feeling good, I need to stop and rest before I drive any more."

"That's good, that's safe," said the boy.

"You need a doctor or anything?" asked the big man.

"No, nothing like that. I just need some sleep. I want to pay cash. Can I do that?" Again her voice was too timid. She had never checked into a motel before. Didn't they always demand some sort of credit card? Didn't they demand a name?

"Money is fine," said the bald man. "I'll give you a deal, thirty dollars. Lasts you until tomorrow morning. Ten o'clock check out time. That all right?"

Beth scrambled for the money in her jeans pocket, bringing out wrinkled bills.

"Give you a room in back. Nice and quiet back there," said the man. It was the tone of his voice that seemed menacing, so deep and guttural. His words were innocent enough, weren't they?

Beth took the key and was very aware of them watching her walk out. But they hadn't asked for a name, she hadn't had to sign anything—that was good. She drove around to the back. There were no other cars pulled up to the rooms. Again she almost drove away, but the temptation of a bed was too much. She'd at least look at the room. After all, at this time of day there'd be no one else checking in. Would being alone always feel so vulnerable?

When she opened the door of the motel room, the smell of cigarettes almost choked her. She hated that stagnant stale smell, it reminded her of everything she wanted to forget. It reminded her of C.J.

There were stains on the walls, especially below the rusted air conditioner. But the bed that took up most of the room called to her like a siren. She closed and locked the door and threw herself onto the bed, crosswise, not even hitting the pillow.

She was thinking about an Oprah show she had watched one time, a man warning women, telling them to obey their instincts, that if a situation seemed dangerous, it usually was. She, of all people, should be aware of potential danger.

But she couldn't move. The bedspread was filthy, probably full of all sorts of germs. But that was the last thought she had before the darkness of sleep totally enfolded her.

2

Chief of Police Josh Winters looked down at the body. He was not supposed to have to deal with this kind of thing. Beaumont was a sleepy little town. It had been a one-policeman town until recently, when he finally was allowed one more officer, who happened to be the nephew of the mayor and, so far, pretty useless. In the summer, he was kept busy with loud parties on the lake and boating accidents. In the winter, occasionally, someone broke into a boarded-up cottage, but it was not a town where murder ever happened.

The body had washed up on shore, probably thrown off a boat. It hadn't been in the water long; it wasn't bloated or disfigured yet. But it made for a big contrast to the glimmering lake and bright sunshine of this early morning. And Josh knew the guy. Everyone knew this guy. There weren't many who would be sorry he was dead. It made for a suspect list that included almost everyone in town. And Bert Floyd had not died a natural death, not with the bullet hole in his forehead. A perfect shot. But there were a lot of good marksmen here in Beaumont. All the people Bert ran around with were good marksmen. They spent a great deal of their time practicing, wearing fatigues, playing soldier, and scaring each other with the idea that any minute some terrorist would aim his bomb at Beaumont. They didn't usually kill each other.

Josh knew he was lucky. Doc Purdy might be old and semi-retired, but he was a real doctor, which wasn't always the case for a coroner in a county as small as this. Purdy was bending over the body right now, examining the wound.

"He's dead," he said in that deadpan voice he used when being his sarcastic self.

"Yeah, I figured that," said Josh. "Like when?"

"You know better than that. This isn't *CSI*. You want to use the state lab?"

"Sure, I guess."

"They'll take forever."

"So what's the other option?"

"There isn't any." The doctor got off his knees with a groan. "I'm going to be losing a patient of mine and I couldn't be happier. Molly Floyd won't be coming to me anymore with her 'accidents.' No more broken bones and black eyes for that lady."

"Maybe she's the one who did it. Maybe she finally got fed up."

"Doubt it. Way too brain-washed. He did more damage to that little lady than just bones. Took out her spirit a long time ago. Bones heal. I'm not so sure about the spirit part. You going to be the one to tell her about this?"

"I guess that's part of my job," said Josh.

"Won't be the usual reaction. You'll be giving her back her life." The doctor gave a nod to the two men waiting with the gurney and the body bag. He turned away from the scene and put a hand on Josh's shoulder. "Been almost twenty years since anything like this happened around here. The last time started a bunch of bad stuff. I hope history won't repeat itself."

"My first guess is that it's tied up with that militia group. They gave themselves away with that perfect shot," Josh said.

"I don't know about that. This was pretty close range. But I agree they're a weird bunch. I wouldn't want to be the one to start asking them questions. Be careful, Josh. I don't want to be looking at *your* bullet wound next."

The doctor turned and climbed the hill to the street

slowly, carefully, walking like it hurt. He didn't look back.

3

Beth woke up, startled, not knowing where she was, not able to comprehend what had awakened her so suddenly, feeling vaguely afraid.

She raised her head from the rancid-smelling bedspread and looked around, then heard a car outside grinding to a start. The room was dark.

Her body felt sluggish as she tried to get off the bed. She remembered her fears checking in—that scary man. *Was it still night?* The window had a heavy shade.

She fumbled for the lamp beside the bed, but couldn't figure out how to turn it on. The stale air felt thick. She staggered to the window and raised the shade. It was daylight. Had she slept an hour or had the night come and gone? There didn't seem to be a clock in the room, and she didn't have a watch.

Feeling desperate for a breath of fresh air, she unlocked the door and quickly pulled it open. The boy from last night, still in fatigues, was walking along the side of the building, reaching for each door knob, as though testing to see if they were locked. He was only three doors away. She started to back into her room, but he called to her.

"Morning. You feeling better?" So it *was* the next morning.

"Yes, much better." And she *was* feeling slightly more human. "What time is it?" she asked.

He looked at his watch. "Nine-fifteen."

The motel didn't seem so threatening now that she had survived the night. She was a bit ashamed of her fears.

"Don't rush yourself," he told her. "Tico, he's loose about check-out time. Thing is, he won't know when you leave." The boy had found a door that wasn't locked. He reached in, fiddled with the mechanism and proceeded to the door next to her own.

"Quick shower and I'm gone," Beth said. "Where can I get some breakfast?"

"Back in town's your best bet. Nothing west of here for a lot of miles. Try Carter's Café. It's right on Main Street, you can't miss it. Best sweet rolls you ever tasted." He gave her a wave and sauntered back toward the little office.

The shower stall was plastic, as was the thin curtain that clung to her the minute she turned on the water, but there was nothing wrong with the water pressure. It felt wonderful. She could have stood under the flow forever. She would have loved to wash her hair, but there wasn't anything like shampoo or a hair dryer in this place.

Putting her dirty clothes back on made the shower almost worthless. Her next stop had to be somewhere to buy some cheap underwear. And a toothbrush. Oh, how she needed a toothbrush.

It was a relief to drive out of the motel's parking lot, but she felt like she was making a mistake in heading backward, even for a few miles.

The little town was pretty, with big trees that overhung the streets, adding shade to the sunny day. There was one traffic light, one intersection that was, of course, Main Street. She had never been on a "Main Street" before. It seemed too much of a cliché to be real. The town was bursting with activity. Merchants were putting things on tables and racks outside their stores. People were on the sidewalk in little groups, talking.

She spotted the café right away, in the middle of the

block of stores, bordered on one side by a gift shop and on the other side by a drug store. There was a parking place in front of the restaurant, a nose-to-the-curb parking place, in the middle of Main Street. There weren't many other cars parked on the street, and when she got out, she knew why. A hand-written sign was posted on the meter. *No parking after 11:30 Saturday—Parade Route.* It was only a little after ten. She'd have plenty of time for a quick breakfast. She checked the bills left in her jeans pocket. There weren't many. She had already gone through most of what she had. The price of gas had amazed her. The hotel, even if the man said he was giving her a bargain, was expensive. She hoped she had enough for at least a sweet roll and some orange juice. Crisp lace curtains on a brass rod hung on the lower half of the restaurant window, and the window itself sparkled in the sunshine. It all looked so clean. And, when she opened the door, it *was* clean—and empty. But then, it was mid-morning, and most people weren't looking for food. There were booths along the edges of the room, a few tables in the middle, and a long counter with seats across the back.

A woman was filling salt shakers behind the counter. She looked up at Beth and gave her a smile. She was pretty in spite of her haggard face and stringy blonde hair. Beth tried to guess her age and couldn't: older, like somebody's mother, a vast category she knew nothing about.

"Can I still get breakfast?" Beth asked her.

"Sure, why not? Except we're pretty busy. Something simple?"

Beth looked around at the empty restaurant.

"Well, we will be busy," said the blonde woman, whose name tag read Molly. "This is a very special day around here. Used to do it Labor Day, but now the kids have to be back in school before that. So we have our own celebration, except it's kind of sad. All the summer people will pack up and leave starting tomorrow. But by noon-time today this place will be jumping, believe me. So what'll it be?"

Beth sat down at the counter, thinking that would be easier for the woman, whose slumped posture made her appear exhausted. First Beth looked for a menu board and then noticed the stained menu that was stuck into the napkin dispenser.

Surreptitiously, she reached into her pocket and pulled out the remaining bills. She only had thirty dollars left and it had to last her. She wasn't going to be able to go much farther. Her gas money had pretty much run out.

Molly was watching her. "Got a special—scrambled eggs, toast, and coffee, a buck ninety-five."

"Okay. That sounds good," said Beth. She was starving, and in spite of the wonderful smell of cinnamon in the air, eggs would last her longer than a bun. She almost told her to forget the coffee, but she didn't. She was trying to appear older. She wanted no questions about what she was doing here by herself.

Molly called the order through the window behind her in a voice that was unnecessarily loud in such a small, empty place.

They were right across the counter from each other, the woman busy with her task, Beth sitting there, waiting. Molly kept taking quick furtive glances at Beth. It was making her nervous. It seemed necessary to say something.

"So what's so special about today? What happens?" Beth asked, finally.

"It's like the last day of summer. There'll be a kind of pitiful parade, right out there in front, about noon. They get out the fire engine for that and the kids decorate up their bikes and everybody with a classic car or anything like that all go down the street. And then there's Trudy, with her invisible band. That's the best part. That's worth you staying for. And there's the sidewalk sales and then a boat parade, which is pretty much like the kids and their bikes, only this time it's the grown-ups putting banners on their boats. After that there'll be sailboat races. Then there's the big picnic tonight and a band in the park and a big bonfire on the beach. And then it's over—the summer people leave. Town shrinks down to nothing."

"Do you like that? When they leave? It sounds kind of peaceful," said Beth.

Molly stopped filling the salt shakers and almost looked at Beth, but didn't quite make eye contact. Close, a glance toward the nose, a skim of the forehead, a quick dart, and then down, but no direct contact.

"It's peaceful, I suppose," she said.

"Eggs up," called a voice from the kitchen. Molly turned, reached for Beth's order, and placed it in front of her. She had finished with refilling the salts and was starting on the peppers.

"I haven't seen you here before. Are you a guest of one of the cottage families?" she asked Beth.

"No. Just passing through." Beth was now sorry she had begun this conversation. Would the woman start asking questions, ask her where she was going or where she was coming from?

The bell above the door jangled and they both looked toward it. Beth had her first forkful of egg in her mouth. She had an immediate reaction of panic: a big man in a uniform with a badge prominently displayed stepped in.

Beth made herself swallow slowly, so she wouldn't choke, made herself pick up the toast and take a nibble, made herself look away. But how had her face reacted when she first saw him? All those unconscious expressions that show fear— had they betrayed her? Had there been a rise of an eyebrow, a drawing in of breath, a widening of the eyes, a clenching of teeth? He had been looking right at her. She knew her face was utterly passive now—she knew how to do that. And besides, now she was turned away. But she felt his stare. She heard him walk directly toward her.

"Hi, Molly," he said.

Molly was smiling. "Hi, Josh. What are you looking so ornery about?"

"Could I talk to you? I mean alone?"

Molly gave Beth a curious glance. "Sure," she said.

"Maybe outside?"

"Sure." Molly came around the counter and Beth turned

enough to watch them walk outside. Now she was really worried. She looked around the room. There might be a back door through the kitchen. But then what? Her car was parked right there in front. Actually, the officer was leaning on it.

"What's that all about?" A large woman was leaning over the kitchen pass-through. "What does the police chief want with Molly?" she asked.

"I don't know," answered Beth, putting down her fork. Her stomach was twisted in a knot. She was no longer hungry.

"Probably something about that no-good husband of hers," said the woman in a soft, thick voice. She disappeared for a minute, then came out the kitchen door and walked to the front window, watching the two outside with obvious interest.

Without turning toward Beth, still watching, she spoke to her. "You here for all the goings-on today?" she asked.

"No, just passing through," Beth answered quickly.

"Nobody passes through this town." The woman turned and gave Beth the same curious look she had directed toward the pair talking on the other side of the window. She was a tall woman, with reddened cheeks and large, strong arms that were now crossed on her chest. Her hair, graying, was slicked back in an unattractive hair net. "We're so off the beaten track, it's like we're lost or something." She might have gone on, but Molly's return stopped her.

"Good Lord, what's the matter with you?" The large woman took a good look at Molly and then folded her in a hug, pressing her into her ample bosom. Beth wondered if Molly could breathe.

Molly mumbled something and was released.

"He's dead, Dee. He's dead. Killed. *Murdered*," Molly gasped.

"Who? Who's murdered?" Dee now had her hands on each side of Molly's face, making her look at her. "You're not talking about Bert, are you?"

The police officer had come in right behind Molly. He nodded toward Dee. "Found him this morning. Washed up on shore. He was shot."

Beth was ashamed of the sigh of relief that escaped her. The officer wasn't after her. He was here about a murder. Nobody was paying any attention to her anymore. Never had been. None of this was about her. This was high drama, but she wasn't involved. She reached inside her pocket for a couple of dollars to put on the counter, intending to leave. But would that make her conspicuous? Would it be better to just sit here and try to eat her eggs? She took another bite. They had grown cold. She wrapped the toast in a paper napkin, saving it for later in the car.

She started to get up, started to turn, but this time there was no mistake, the policeman was walking toward her. She sat back down and tried to pretend she was invisible.

But, again, he stopped before he got to Beth, if that was where he was heading. Dee had grabbed his arm. Beth could see their shadow shapes in the stainless steel in front of her.

"What's going to happen?" Dee asked him. "You going to need Molly? I need her here."

Beth couldn't help hearing what was being said by the three people behind her. She now ate as slowly as she could. Her eggs were almost gone, her toast down to a bit of crust. She sipped her coffee, hardly putting any into her mouth. She had never had coffee before. She didn't like the taste. Someone had left a paper on the counter; she picked it up and pretended to read.

"She'll have to come with me this morning, to the station," the chief was saying.

"I have to see the body?" Molly cried out in alarm.

"No. We need no identification. But we need to get

things straight, we need to write it all down, when you saw him last, what his plans were as far as you knew, who he might have seen last night, things like that." His voice was low and quiet and reassuring.

Molly's voice wasn't. There was panic in it. "Bert never told me anything. Never."

Beth could feel the woman's despair. She could identify with it.

"You wouldn't expect her to work today," the officer was saying to Dee. "First of all, people are going to be all over this. Even if she's not here, they'll be coming in droves, asking you questions. You'd better prepare yourself. It's kind of sick, that kind of curiosity, but it's a given."

"But what am I going to do?" Dee asked, alarmed. "This is my busiest day of the year. You can't leave me in the lurch like this. That silly Danielle already bailed on me. And Sally asked for the day off a long time ago."

The police chief tried once again to explain what had to happen. And Beth, fingering the few wrinkled bills in her pocket, suddenly had a very good idea.

4

When Maxwell Cummings looked in the mirror, he liked what he saw, more so every year. He needed the few streaks of gray that now grazed his temples for the distinguished look that a mayor should have. Always careful of his diet, he had nothing but contempt for those people who let themselves go. He stood artificially straight, soldier-like, although he had never served in the military. And he truly enjoyed standing next to people who didn't have his six-foot-two advantage. But most of all, he liked his smile. He had practiced it to perfection and he used it often. As his parting gesture to his image in the bathroom mirror, he gave forth with a blazing show of teeth, being careful to wrinkle his eyes at the same time. People noticed when you didn't get your eyes involved.

He walked out to the veranda where the breakfast table was set and aimed yet another smile at his wife, Lillian.

"Good morning, my dear," he said, as he did each and every morning.

She was still in her shorts and sweatshirt from her early-morning canoe ride around the lake, an event that happened every day, just after dawn, weather permitting. People told Max they could set their clocks by it. As far as Cummings was concerned, it sounded like the biggest bore on earth, but he didn't say anything. He tried to never criticize his wife. He owed her. He knew perfectly well he wouldn't be where he was today if it weren't for Lillian. She was, after all, a Beaumont. Her family had once owned Squall Lake and all the land around it.

Mrs. Roe, the housekeeper, came out from the kitchen and poured his coffee from the china pot on the table. Max enjoyed people waiting on him.

Their breakfast was relatively silent. It usually was. Mrs. Roe brought out his egg-white omelet and poured more coffee. Lillian gazed out at the water and Max read the various papers that were delivered to him early in the morning.

"Are you going to the parade?" Lillian asked him, finally.

"Of course, my dear. I judge the parade, remember?" He looked at her over the top of his paper.

"Perhaps I will go this year," she said in a small voice.

He put the paper down, folding it and placing it beside his plate. "That would be lovely, my dear. You could be in the reviewing stand with me."

"Oh no, oh no, I wouldn't want to do that," she said quickly, with a bit of panic in her voice. "I wouldn't want everyone looking at me like that."

"You'd feel more secure there. The streets are crowded, lots of milling around. It's inevitable that there's some pushing and shoving."

"Oh dear, I do remember that. Perhaps I don't want to go after all. But Mrs. Roe keeps talking about how funny the invisible band is."

"It is funny. But you know Trudy borrowed the idea from a parade farther up north. It's not original with us."

"Oh." Her eyes went back to the lake.

Max got up soon after that, gave her a quick kiss on the cheek, a quick "have a good day," and left her sitting there, still looking at the water.

He didn't go to the town hall where his mayor's office was or to his real estate office down the block. He parked in the spot reserved for him in the lot in back of the two buildings and walked down Main Street. It was bustling with people. There was excitement in the air, more so than he remembered from other parade days. That made him happy. This was a day both he and the town could take pride in. People came from all over.

Max prided himself on knowing the names of almost everyone in town. He couldn't walk down the street without shaking the hand of everyone he encountered, including young children. So it was a normal thing that he held out his hand to the first person he passed. But it wasn't taken up.

"A shocker, huh, Mayor?" Ted Mitchell looked even more bug-eyed than usual.

"Yeah, I mean, Bert Floyd, who'd dare mess with him?" asked Al, Ted's brother, who was walking with him.

"What are you talking about?" Max was perplexed. Something was going on and Cummings knew nothing about it. That wasn't supposed to happen.

Old Mrs. Williams now joined the group. "You mean you haven't heard?" She said it like an accusation and seemed pleased about it.

Max's irritation didn't register on his face.

"You must enlighten me," he said to her.

"Killed." Al Mitchell sounded almost gleeful, excited about being the one to give the news.

"This morning," added Ted.

"He was found washed up at the public beach," Mrs. Williams told him with a pursing of her lips, as though the place he was found was somehow the shocking part.

"This morning? Why wasn't I told about this? Where's Chief Winters?" Max asked, looking around, realizing that the special buzz in town didn't have anything to do with the parade.

"I saw Josh earlier, talking to Molly at the café, probably telling her the bad news," Al told him.

"Actually, I'm not so sure that was such bad news," commented Mrs. Williams. Then she turned toward Max. "We still going to have all the festivities?"

He hadn't thought about that, but he prided himself on never being ambivalent about anything. "Of course," he answered quickly and only then began to consider the repercussions. More people had stopped and gathered around them, listening. That wouldn't do.

"I need to find Chief Winters," Cummings said. He turned away and walked hurriedly down the street. For once he didn't stop and greet the people he passed.

What was Josh Winters thinking to put him in such an

awkward position? He was the mayor. He should have been the first one informed.

He glanced around as he walked. Main Street was ready for the parade. The reviewing stand at the edge of the park was already draped with the red, white, and blue bunting and the small set of bleachers had been erected. There were plenty of people already sitting on the curb, staking their claim to a good position. The side streets now had cars parked in front of the old Victorian houses. They looked out of place, spoiling the look the town was famous for, of going back in time.

It made him think about the ordinance—*All cars off the parade route by 11:30.* He looked at his watch. That was one minute away. So what was that car doing in front of Dee's café? What was happening here? He took pride in the fact that Beaumont was a town that worked.

And then he spotted the sign on the door. It had been turned around, from "open" to "closed."

Closed? Carter's Café closed on this day of all days? This, his favorite day of the year, was becoming one big irritation. He put his hand on the knob of the door and was surprised when it opened.

The restaurant was almost empty. Three people sat at

the table closest to the door. Molly Floyd turned to look at him. Dee Carter and Josh Winters were so engaged in an intense conversation that they didn't seem to notice him. A dark-haired young woman, who was a stranger to the mayor, was in the process of delivering cups of coffee to the table.

"What's this about Bert Floyd?" Max demanded.

Josh turned toward him. "So you heard?"

"From the people on the street. Last I checked I was still mayor of this town." The mayor never yelled. His words, more than his voice, showed his exasperation.

"I called your office. You weren't there. They should have informed you."

"This puts me in a rather embarrassing position, Josh."

"Sorry about that," said Josh, without too much concern.

"Well, I realize this is bigger than what you usually have to handle and I'm here to help you, Josh. We need to work together. He was actually killed? People are assuming all kinds of things. Was it an accident?"

"Not likely. Not with a bullet hole in the middle of his forehead," said Josh.

"Good God." The mayor turned and closed the door

behind himself. "And what's that car doing out there? Isn't it past the deadline?"

"Your car?" Dee asked the young woman Maxwell didn't know.

"Yes. I'll move it. Where should I put it?"

"Go around to the back—I have a couple of spaces back there," said Dee.

The young woman started toward the door, but Maxwell was blocking her way. She was really quite pretty in a natural, not trying, sort of way. He automatically put on a smile.

"I don't believe we've met," he said, holding out that ever-ready hand.

"Beth, please meet the mayor," said Dee.

Beth's handshake was tentative at best. The mayor shook hard, his other hand gripped her elbow and didn't let go.

"Maxwell Cummings, but everyone calls me Max," he boomed at her in his hearty voice. "And does Beth have a last name?"

"Wa... ter... man," mumbled Beth. She hadn't been quick enough. It sounded like what it was, a last minute fumble. Why hadn't she thought of another name altogether, even something besides Beth? She had been too quick with that too, with Dee. Why hadn't she been thinking of a really different last name? She made a motion to go around Mr. Cummings. "I'll move my car."

"Well, little lady, I see from your license plate that you're from Pennsylvania. Up for the big day, I presume. Who are you visiting?" Max's voice was too loud and too cheerful. Beth smiled a nervous smile.

Dee got up, pushed past the mayor and opened the door. "Hurry back," she said to Beth. "Come in the rear exit. It's open."

As soon as Beth left, the mayor walked over to the table and leaned down to take one of Molly's hands, as though suddenly remembering his mission here.

"I am so sorry, my dear, for your loss. Of course, if there is anything at all that I can do..." he allowed his words to drift off.

Josh stood up. "Molly and I were just leaving. We need to go to my office, get some information down in writing, establish a timeline on Bert's activities for the last couple of days. Leroy will be here any minute to handle the traffic control."

"I keep telling you," Molly said, her voice whiny, "I can't really help you. Bert never told me where he was going or when. If I asked, he got angry, so I didn't ask. I have no idea where he went last night, or any other night, for that matter. And I feel terrible leaving Dee in the lurch."

"Well, you don't have to worry about that anymore," Dee told her. "Except for Beth, I'd have been up the creek, but now we'll be just fine."

Josh knew what was happening here. He had seen it before. It hadn't really hit any of them yet—that Bert Floyd was dead—that their priorities were now very different. People clung to what they knew. They desperately wanted life to go on, just like it always had.

"Oh my God," Molly said suddenly, grabbing Dee's arm. "What about Bert's boat shop?"

"What about it?" asked Dee.

"This is the busy time. Everyone will be taking their boats out of the water and they'll want their docks put up. You know how it is. Who's going to do all that? Harvey's a good worker, but he's useless unless somebody tells him what to do. That's what Bert liked about him. No back-talk, just listen and do. But Harvey will spend three days trying to decide what to do first." Molly looked panicked.

"I'm not taking you away forever," Josh reassured her. "You can deal with Harvey later today."

"Can I even do that? Who does the marina belong to? Oh dear, what's going to happen? I mean that was really our income." Tears started to fall down Molly's cheeks. The reality of what had happened was starting to sink in.

"We'll straighten all that out," Josh told her, guiding her to the door. "These things take time, but they get straightened out. Don't you worry. You've got lots of friends in this town."

"Yes," agreed Dee. "You should probably concentrate on the boat shop. I think Beth will be able to handle things. You won't be able to do both, and I think maybe she needs this job."

Josh paused at the door and turned to speak to Max. "I'll let you know what we know. The state lab is handling things. This is not going to be easy, not with all the summer people leaving in the next few days. Floyd managed to tick off most of those people, too. And they won't be around to question." He shrugged his shoulders and guided Molly out the door, closing it behind them.

Max was left standing there with Dee, who had her

hands on her hips.

He smiled at her. Dee always managed to make him uncomfortable. She was one of the few people he had never been able to charm. He kept trying. And he would continue to keep trying.

"So, the young woman is a waitress?" he asked as pleasantly as he could.

"About to become one," said Dee. "Saving my life here. She heard me moan that Molly couldn't leave me in the lurch and offered to help. Nice. I accepted."

They both heard the back door open and close. "Turn that sign around as you leave," Dee told the mayor, heading toward the kitchen. "I've got some quick instructions to give."

5

The day raced by. Beth hardly stopped for a minute. She took orders, brought heaping trays of food, and cleared the dirty dishes, only to start all over again as the tables and booths filled and emptied and filled again. There was a reprieve when the parade went by. Everyone, including Dee, ran outside, leaving their belongings and even purses behind. Beth watched the parade from the window, wondering about the trust that seemed to exist in this community. It amazed her. It would be so easy for her to grab a few badly needed dollars from one of those purses. But she wouldn't. That wasn't her anymore. That had never really been her.

The parade started off with fire trucks. Beaumont's one truck had been joined by those from several neighboring towns, all shiny red, their volunteer name or town displayed on their sides, all giving an occasional blast of their sirens.

The high school band, which Beth decided hadn't practiced since the spring, played enthusiastically, if not well. It seemed like any group that could manage costumes could march. There were clusters of tiny dancers and baton twirlers and baseball teams, a couple of floats crepe-papered in no discernible theme, and a great many decorated bikes.

Then there was a lull, no people passing, no floats. But music could be heard coming their way, and a tall woman, perhaps in her seventies, dressed like a sexy drum majorette and wielding a long baton, came marching down the street. Behind her was nothing. But she kept turning and bowing to the empty space with encouraging gestures, until one could almost imagine a band following her. Somehow it was very funny. The music came from a boom box carried by a teen-aged boy running along the curb. The woman pranced and preened, did some high kicks, smiled a huge smile, and managed to wave at everyone. The crowd cheered and shouted. This obviously was their favorite part.

After the invisible band came a couple of convertibles with some pretty girls sitting on the doors. Banners declared they were last year's high-school homecoming queen and her court. When they had passed, as if on cue, people left their posts and mingled, covering the sidewalks and the street, many of them trying to get into Dee's café. It was a happy crowd, and Beth almost caught their joy, but it seemed a foreign language

40

to her. It was hard to tell if they were laughing at the events or laughing with them. Either way, everyone was outrageously friendly. She had been told by Dee to introduce herself, and she did so as she took their orders. But what completely befuddled her was that so many of them introduced themselves right back. People didn't do that in Philadelphia. And it wasn't fair—there were so many of them and only one of her. It had been a mistake to use her own first name, as she had realized too late, but it was helping her now, still being Beth. She at least was quick to answer when people called to her.

Only three people came in without friendly smiles— three big, burly men dressed in fatigues with scowls on their faces. They sat down in a back booth without saying hello to anyone. One was older than the others—he did all the talking. The other two listened and nodded respectfully to everything he said. All of them gave occasional, disapproving glances to the lunch crowd. Then the older man would make another comment, as if passing judgment. Beth waited on them and got away quickly. They made her nervous. But they didn't take long with their hamburgers and Beth didn't have time to dwell on them. They left a fifty-cent tip.

She continued to smile until her face hurt—unused muscles, perhaps. Her feet screamed; her thin sneakers lacked any support. There was no afternoon down-time. Lunch ran into early dinner. Beth knew if she so much as sat down, even for a minute, she'd never get up again.

And then, suddenly, the place emptied. The last few people all headed for the cash register at the same time. Beth glanced at the clock on the wall. It was seven-thirty. Where were they all going?

Dee came out from the kitchen, looking as tired as Beth felt. She collapsed into a chair.

"They're setting up in the park. The music's about to start," Dee explained. "I'm going to rest right here for a few minutes and then I'll take care of closing up. You go on over to the park, you've done a good day's work here and I can't thank you enough."

Beth collapsed into a chair beside her. "I don't think I could walk two steps right now."

Dee laughed, and Beth started laughing, and they couldn't stop for a minute—it wasn't funny, it was exhaustion.

Dee reached in the pocket of her apron and pulled out a wad of twenty-dollar bills. "We never did discuss money, but you did a good day's work," she said, handing them to Beth. "This is what I would have paid Molly. She won't be back for a while. I think you've made some good tips today. Would you consider this on a more permanent basis?"

That presented all sorts of dangers—a Social Security number, records, things Beth didn't want to deal with.

"Could we just try it for a while?" Beth asked. "Keep it kind of casual? Pay me cash, like this?"

Dee looked at her shrewdly. "You've got some kind of story, gal. I'm not nosy, but I know a good person when I see one. We'll do this on any terms you want. So what about tonight? You have a place to stay?"

Beth told her about the motel she had stayed in last night. She really didn't want to go back there.

"Oh, you're talking about Tico Zane's place. That old reprobate. He likes to think of himself as dangerous, living over the edge, slightly illegal. And he is, I suppose. He gets the kids fake IDs, he rents those rooms of his by the hour. He's on this kick where he doesn't believe anybody should tell anybody else what to do, including the government. Doesn't think there should be such a thing as an ID. But he's a softy at heart. Don't be fooled by him. He's got a heart of gold, as they say. He practically raised that boy, Slim Carry. Slim's mother is a mess—in and out of rehab and jail. So, every time the mother is gone, Slim just goes over to Tico's. He's harmless enough, but you're right, you don't want to go back there."

By the hour? Beth thought about that heavy shade. *Fake ID?* The ID part sounded really interesting. But Dee was going on.

"You could stay with me until you decide what you want to do. It would mean sleeping on the sofa, but you'd have a roof over your head." Dee got up and stretched.

"Oh, no. I couldn't..."

"Listen, girl, you helped me out when I really needed it, don't give me any of that *couldn't* stuff. But wait a minute. I might have a better idea. You sit tight and let me check something out. I might have the perfect place for you." She got up and went back toward the kitchen, a smile on her face as she yelled back to Beth, "Better yet, get yourself on down to the park. Find some grass and save me a place. You and I deserve a good time tonight and we're going to have it."

Beth left the restaurant. The streets were still crowded, but everyone was heading in the same direction. She followed them to a little park only a block away, in the center of town and right on the water, a picturesque place with shady trees and benches.

The park was already jammed. Blankets and beach chairs covered the grassy lawn. She walked carefully, trying

44

not to step in anyone's place or on their sprawled out hands and legs. Several people called out to her, people who had been in the restaurant. They knew her name, even if she didn't remember theirs.

She found a place halfway up a little hill and sat down. There was a gazebo in the middle of the park and a rather motley group of musicians were tuning up their instruments.

When they actually started to play, it surprised Beth because they were good and had the crowd clapping to the music in no time. At first it was patriotic tunes, which seemed like an extension of the parade. But then, slowly, they started playing a bit of everything, from rock that made the teenagers get up and dance, to show tunes that had the older people singing along. Little kids surrounded the bandstand and jumped and wiggled to every kind of music. There was a pretty girl singer in a flowered sundress with a nice, if not overpowering, voice.

Beth leaned back on her elbows and enjoyed the weakening sun on her face, the noise around her, and the music. She was tired, too tired to move, but she felt a sense of contentment. She wanted to stay right there, let the world just go on without her, not think, not worry. Oh, how tired she was of worrying.

45

She was pulled back into reality when Dee came up, struggling with two beach chairs and a big picnic basket.

"I don't do grass-sitting anymore," Dee said as she got the chairs settled.

Beth could hardly get up, but the chair was definitely more comfortable.

"The band's called the Raggedy Rascals," Dee said. "You see your friend Tico there, playing the drums?"

Beth hadn't been looking at the band, just listening. The large man from the motel banged away at the drums as if he had some score to settle. She thought again about what Dee had said. He could get a person fake identification. But how would you approach something like that?

Dee began grabbing things out of the basket, chips and dip and a can of beer. At first it looked like she was going to hand it to Beth, but she paused.

"How old are you? Did you tell me?" Dee asked her.

"I don't like beer anyway," said Beth, trying to avoid an answer.

Dee continued to look at Beth, but she reached back into the basket and got out a bottle of Coke. She wasn't buying Beth's evasiveness, not really. This was a smart and observant woman, and Beth needed to be careful around her. She had been asking questions all day, just simple questions, asked on the fly, questions anyone would ask a new acquaintance, not nosy, not intrusive. But Beth couldn't answer questions, and if she couldn't continue to avoid them, maybe it was time to move on.

The crowd didn't sit still. People wandered around and they all greeted Dee as they went by, and many of them stopped for a minute of conversation. Beth was grateful when Dee's attention turned away from her. She watched the band, and she particularly liked watching the children around the bandstand. They never stopped moving, and Beth could tell they enjoyed what they believed was dancing. They were so free and uninhibited. She didn't believe she had ever felt like that.

Elaborate picnics took place on the grassy slope, with bottles of wine and interesting food being passed around. Beth was intrigued by the whole scene. The band gave up on the soft music, playing to the more raucous young adults. The children finally tired and sat down to eat with their parents, and day turned into twilight and then into a creeping darkness. Beth slipped down in the chair and put her head back and watched the stars come out. There seemed to be millions of them over the lake.

Finally Dee nudged her. "It's bonfire time. Let's go down to the beach."

Beth was surprised that so many people had already left and she hadn't noticed. She followed Dee the few yards to the beach, helping her carry the chairs. They put them in the rear of the already-assembled crowd around the fire—kids up close toasting marshmallows, everyone else farther back to avoid the heat.

The atmosphere had changed. Now voices were low murmurs, everyone gazing at the mesmerizing fire. Somebody started singing John Jacob Jingleheimer Smith and others joined in, especially picking up on the chorus lines. The water lapped against the shore. The moon was bright.

Beth stared at the fire, almost in a trance. This town, this peace—it seemed unreal. She didn't want to leave, yet she didn't see how she could possibly stay.

Suddenly, she became aware of movement beside her. The police chief was lowering himself onto the sand right next to her.

Beth's stomach tensed and she made an involuntary move toward Dee.

"So, I hear you played Molly all day at the restaurant. Not so easy on parade day," Chief Winters said to Beth.

She took in a big breath.

"That's a good idea, you staying with Molly. She needs someone right now," he continued.

"What?" Beth turned toward Dee.

"I didn't want to say anything until it was a sure thing. I only left a message. So?" Dee turned to the chief, "She agreed?"

"Absolutely. And it's a good idea. She's going to meet you at the diner in about twenty minutes to drive you to her house." Now he was talking directly to Beth. "You know, she was really afraid to be alone. She said she never had been, went from her parents' house to Bert's. I know I'd feel more comfortable with you there. Bert had some weird friends and there are some strange rumors getting started. She shouldn't be alone."

The chief was looking at Beth as some kind of protection? Beth couldn't get that thought to even begin to work in her mind.

The fire was dwindling, people were getting up and leaving.

"So, you're going to stay around awhile?" the chief asked in a conversational tone.

"Maybe, for a little while," Beth answered. She

couldn't look at him. She knew her hands were starting to shake.

"It's a nice little town. You'll like it. Not much to do, but a nice place. Small-town America at its best."

"It's beautiful," said Beth, looking at the embers glowing from the fire and the blackness of the lake beyond.

"Anyway," the chief continued, "I'm glad you're staying with Molly. This isn't going to be easy for her. It hasn't really hit her yet. Her life is going to change. Losing someone is never easy, no matter who it is and how they've treated you. It will take time, and it would be better if she wasn't alone."

He got up in one smooth movement, testifying to his fitness. He held out a hand each to Beth and Dee, helping them up from their beach chairs.

Chief Winters grabbed the chairs and Beth took the basket as they walked out of the park, letting Dee walk up the hill unencumbered.

6

Stan Jones was not a nervous person. In fact, he had no patience for such a thing as nerves. But his latest client made him nervous and this assignment made him nervous. He tracked people down —that was his job. It wasn't his problem why someone wanted his services. It was usually a long-lost cousin or a birth mother or someone who had lost contact over the years. It was usually pretty satisfying, bringing people together who wanted to be brought together. Occasionally, as with adoption cases, the outcome didn't please everyone, but truth is truth. That's what Stan believed.

This case, however, seemed different from the very beginning. He didn't like the client and wished he had said no right off the bat. But bills had to be paid. And he had a bunch of them, stuck under his paperweight—the dud grenade he had smuggled back from 'Nam. And those bills weren't going to wait much longer.

But there were no leads, no trail to follow, no nothing.

No explanation why the girl ran away, and no idea of what was going to happen to her when she was found. Just a bad feeling in his gut.

Most clients went on and on about the whys. He got their whole life stories, more than he needed, more than he wanted. Not this time. Just a name, Beth Watson, age sixteen, height 5' 6", weight 115, dark brown hair, brown eyes. She had taken a car that didn't belong to her. But she wasn't supposed to be arrested. The only thing the client wanted was information. Where she was. That was unusual. Normally, the parents wanted runaways returned; normally, they got the police involved. But none of that was happening here. And even weirder was that when Stan found her, he wasn't even supposed to approach her. No questions to make sure he had the right one. No talking to her. Nothing. Just the information relayed back.

And if that wasn't weird enough, the entire case had been over the phone. Stan had never seen the client. All he knew was a gravelly voice and the name, C.J. Watson, not even much of a name. There had been an intonation in the voice that made him wary.

When clients came in, they underwent his own scrutiny.

He had been a cop long enough to judge people pretty quickly and pretty well. And there was Harry, his dog, also retired from the force, sitting under his desk and warming his feet right now, who also passed judgment on the clients. Harry loved most people, but occasionally his sniff detector said no, and Stan paid attention to Harry.

"She did something she shouldn't have done," the voice on the phone had said. And it had been delivered with such finality, such judgment, that it had made Stan's skin crawl.

The next day there had been an envelope dropped through the slot of his office door, no stamp. Harry hadn't liked the smell, but it contained five one-hundred-dollar bills and a photograph of a pretty girl, serious looking, slumped a bit, not a happy camper. But then, happy campers don't run away. But why drop the envelope? Why not come in, as most people did? The vibes were all wrong, one too many warnings about not getting the police involved. Why not?

Normally, Stan could get a lot of information via the computer, even Social Security and credit card numbers, but this time he came up empty. The client wouldn't even give him a phone number to call or to trace. Stan could call an old pal in the department, get him working on the license plate, check with the highway patrol. He knew people; he wouldn't make it official. He could do that—he'd been a cop for a long time before he retired and started his agency. People owed him plenty.

He'd get the word spread. But which way did she go? Stan had a map spread out on his desk. South? Along the Atlantic seaboard? Toward Florida? Kids headed that way, looking for the TV Miami. They'd heard of South Beach, all of that. Or would she head up north, toward Canada? Was she street-wise enough to get across the border? Wise enough to hide in another country?

That was the trouble—Stan lacked information, the most rudimentary information. With any other client, he'd know who he was looking for, know her personality, her quirks, her ambitions, and—especially—her faults. Kids run away for a bunch of reasons, but perfect parents aren't usually one of them. There's usually trouble in the household, big trouble. Mostly Stan had found that it was a too-strict parent who demanded too much. And such parents were the most eager to state their case, tell him what was wrong with the kid, how right they had been, what little appreciation the kid had shown for all they had done, that sort of thing.

But this client said very little.

"Just find her. She took a car without permission and she doesn't even know how to drive, so somebody else must have driven her. Look for two of them," C.J. Watson had told him, "probably some guy, the little tramp." C.J. didn't think she'd get very far, was sure she didn't have much money. "Not even enough to buy gas, so there has to be somebody else with her."

Stan had asked about her computer use—Facebook, My Space, Twitter—you could find out things that way. But C.J. said that Beth had never used a computer. That was way more than odd. And it cut Stan's chances of finding her way down. What he usually searched for were the digital footprints. Anyone who used technology could be found with enough time and patience. And who didn't use technology these days? Beth Watson, it would seem.

Stan had been looking at the map as he let his thoughts wander, his way of getting started. *If it were me,* he thought, *I'd go west. The whole country stretches out that way. And kids do aim for California. Don't make it, most of them, but they aim there.* He let his finger trace the route he would take—out of the city, onto the turnpike, and keep driving.

He'd waste a lot of time if he guessed wrong. C.J. said Beth wouldn't use a credit card—had no access to one. But what if the someone else she was with had a card? That would help. Anyway you looked at it, this was going to take a lot of luck.

Normally, Stan would start with New York City. A lot of kids headed that way. Easy to lose yourself in a big city. But Beth wouldn't have taken the car, she'd have hopped on a train or a bus and, besides, C.J. Watson seemed sure she wouldn't head that way. Seemed to indicate that she'd be afraid of a big city like that. Stan wasn't sure he was buying that. In his experience, sixteen-year-olds weren't scared of very much. Or maybe they were scared of everything and had to pretend so that fear wouldn't eat them up.

What did he know? He couldn't even begin to remember what it was like to be sixteen. Had he ever been that young?

His fingers were still tracing across the map. Which way did she go?

This was getting him nowhere. He had to know more about the girl.

What followed were several days of what he thought to himself as the grind—visiting records departments, plowing through computer sites and even microfiche. But he came up empty. There was nothing there.

Beth Watson had no birth certificate in Philadelphia, so she must have been born somewhere else. But there were no school records either. And the address C.J. had given turned out to be a vacant lot. Beth Watson didn't seem to exist.

When C.J. finally did call in, things turned even more weird.

"No questions. Just find her. I don't like questions," said the angry voice.

"No questions, no kid," Stan said. "I can't operate like that."

"I'll send some more money in the morning. Find her."

Stan knew he'd take the money. He knew he'd look for the kid. He had always told himself that he was neither judge, nor jury. He'd find her. He'd give C.J. the information. But he had a really bad feeling about this whole thing.

7

Molly was waiting for Beth in her car in front of the café.

It started off with more lies, more cover-ups. Molly asked Beth if she wanted to follow her home in her car—she'd need her things in order to stay the night, wouldn't she? Once again, Beth felt that panicked clutch in her stomach. It would look suspicious, wouldn't it, her not having anything, not even a toothbrush? Beth quickly made up a story about almost being out of gas. That was true, but Molly didn't look satisfied with that, so Beth went on about having had her suitcase stolen when she stayed in a motel. That sounded pathetically untrue even to her own ears. But Molly wasn't paying close attention; she had, after all, lost her husband that day.

So they got into Molly's pickup truck and drove away from the center of town, winding around tree-lined streets, past neat lawns. To Beth's eyes, it all looked so planned; even the flower beds were orderly. The old Victorian houses, painted in pastel colors, looked like houses in a child's picture book.

Once they were away from the lake, the neighborhood changed—more space between the houses, overgrown lawns, no street lights, an occasional mobile home set into the middle of a lot. The paved road became dirt.

Molly pulled into a driveway, behind another pick-up. The headlights revealed a small, white-shingled house, totally dark. Once the headlights were turned off, the darkness was as complete as anything Beth had ever experienced, broken only by weak glimmers from far-away neighbors' windows.

"There should be a floodlight, but the bulb's been out for a month or so. I kept telling Bert to fix it. Guess I'll have to do it myself. Guess I was always going to have to do it myself," Molly grumbled as she grabbed a flashlight from the console between them.

Beth got out of the truck and followed Molly up the dark driveway, through an unlocked back door, and into a kitchen.

Molly flipped a switch and the sudden glare of fluorescent light made Beth blink.

The kitchen was small, with a torn linoleum floor. It was hard for Beth to determine what the floor's original color had been—gray or beige. Everything seemed crowded together, the sink alongside a chipped enamel stove, a refrigerator that was making a loud hum, and a small table with three chairs. Molly led her quickly through the room. She turned on lights as she entered the hall and then the living room.

The living room was overwhelmed by a big leatherette recliner that faced a large TV. There was a coffee table in front of the chair and an end table beside it, both crowded with magazines and overflowing ashtrays. The tables were marred with cigarette burns. A sofa sat against the front window, affording only a side view of the TV.

"There's an apartment above the garage. I'm sure that's where Dee thought you could stay, but it's all dusty and dirty. And besides, I'd really like you to be here in the house for a little while. I don't like being alone."

"That's fine. Anything's okay with me. I really do appreciate you letting me stay..." Beth began.

Molly interrupted her. "None of that—you're doing me a favor. And I've been trying to rent that apartment for quite a while."

Molly had stopped and was staring at the recliner. "We're going to get rid of that," she said, almost to herself. "First thing tomorrow morning, we're going to get rid of that."

Beth followed Molly up a narrow staircase. There were two bedrooms and a bath upstairs.

"You can stay in Holt's room until he gets back," Molly said, opening a door and turning on another light.

"Holt?" But Beth hardly needed to ask. The room was a splash of red and black, the walls covered with posters and pennants, and a few shelves with more trophies than books. A magazine photo of a boy's room.

"My son. He'll be a senior this year at the high school. He'll be back next week. This was his third summer as a sailing counselor at a camp on Lake Superior." Molly had a special smile on her face when she talked about her son. "He and some of the other counselors decided to go to Chicago for a couple of days. I thought about calling him on his cell phone, but now I've decided I'm not going to spoil anything for him. No point in him knowing about his father until he gets back, don't you think?"

"I... guess." Beth was hardly the person to give advice on family protocol.

"By the time he gets back, we'll have that little apartment all cleaned up." Molly left the room, still talking. She returned with clean sheets and started to make the bed, but

Beth stopped her.

"I can do this. You've done enough."

Molly nodded and started for the door, then stopped and turned back. She looked seriously at Beth. "You know, you look about the same age as Holt." She waited as though that were some kind of a question. "Are you still in high school?" Molly was looking at Beth more intently than she had before, as though she were really seeing her for the first time.

"I... um... I was home schooled," Beth confessed. It came out sounding shameful.

"All the way through high school? You done with it?" Molly stood still, her hand on the door knob. She was paying attention now, the dreamy note she had had all day gone from her voice.

"Yes, I guess I am... done with it." Beth said. She was trying to stay busy with making the bed, but she had finished the job.

"Your parents know where you are?" asked Molly. "It's okay, you being here?"

This was a conversation Beth had dreaded. It was bound to come up. But she had shoved it into the back of her mind and things had happened so quickly today. She didn't have any answers ready. She realized she was just staring at the floor.

"Hey, don't look like that," Molly said, still at the door. "I never graduated from high school myself. Sorry later, of course. Went and got my GED, but it's not the same. Best years of my life were in high school."

Still, Beth could think of nothing to say. Molly was being so kind, as Dee had been kind. Beth had no experience with kindness. It made her want to cry.

Molly continued to talk, not looking at Beth so intently now. "I don't know what reaction Holt's going to have about his father. They didn't get along. That's why he left every summer, every chance he could. It was getting really bad. Holt got bigger than Bert, see. That didn't work. Bert couldn't stand that except for the football. Holt was good, really good, and Bert finally approved of something someone in this family did. But then Holt just quit. Couldn't stand his father's interference, telling the coach what to do, yelling from the sidelines, all of that. And nothing Bert could say would make Holt go back to it. He could have had a scholarship. I tried to tell him that. But he's stubborn—not like his father stubborn, but still stubborn. Maybe now he'll go back to it. Maybe now he can get that scholarship."

Molly stopped talking, sighed, then said, "But I'm blabbering. It's just such a relief to talk to someone who hasn't pre-judged me for years. The rest of the town has, I'm afraid. And you look young, but there's something about you that isn't young at all. Still, I shouldn't be laying all this on you and you need some sleep. Let me get you some PJs. I think mine would fit you." She turned to go, and then stopped. "You know, I always wished I had a daughter as well as a son. Boys, especially teenaged boys, don't talk to their mothers very much. Holt would have never let me blab on like this."

She left and came back a minute later and handed Beth a cotton nightshirt.

"Anyway, you get some sleep," said Molly. "We'll talk more in the morning." She wished Beth a good sleep and closed the door.

The clean pillow was beckoning. But maybe Beth shouldn't be here in the morning. There'd be more questions about school and parents and all of that, questions she couldn't possibly answer. But Beth didn't have her car and she had no idea of how to find her way back into town anyway. She had tried to pay attention, but it was too confusing. Everything was just too confusing.

Beth wandered around the room. Everything was clean, dusted, neat. She didn't imagine it was a high-school boy who had kept it like this. The room shouted out that somebody cared. She remembered a small gesture Molly had made as she handed Beth the sheets, how she had rubbed her finger along one of the wall shelves, touching one of the trophies affectionately, a mother who loved her son. It made Beth uncomfortable. She didn't belong here; this was territory she knew nothing about.

After visiting the bathroom across the hall and rubbing some toothpaste over her teeth, Beth returned to the room and slipped out of her clothes. The clean nightshirt felt good against her skin. She had more money now. Tomorrow she'd buy some underwear and some T-shirts and a toothbrush. She got into bed but, as exhausted as she was, she felt restless.

She got up again. She knew she was intruding, but here she was, in a world she had always wondered about. This place, this room, the boy who lived here—they were *normal*, that word that had always so intrigued her. She wanted to crawl inside Holt's head, see the world through his eyes, and know all the little, everyday things he knew. This room held answers, like the lighted windows in houses she had passed in the night that looked so cozy and which she had always wondered about. Here she was, inside.

She went to the desk and opened the center drawer, feeling guilty, but consumed with curiosity. It wasn't neat like the rest of the room. This was a place where Molly didn't trespass. There were papers stuffed every which way, an assortment of pens and pencils, a half-eaten candy bar, and lots of pieces and parts of unidentifiable things.

Beth didn't touch anything. She opened the first of the three drawers on the side of the desk. There were stacks of papers, stapled or paper-clipped together: school assignments graded A+, A, a couple with B+, and some notations: "excellent," "well written," "great insight into the subject."

The next drawer held copies of the school newspaper. Holt Floyd, Editor. She meant to just look at the first one, but so many of the articles were written by Holt that she found herself reading one after another. He wrote about everything—sports mostly—but he had articles about the dress-code issue, about the seniors' right to leave campus during the school day, about the war against graffiti, about the students' parking lot, and about bullying. Her eyes were growing heavy, but she felt, just for a little while, a part of that world. High school, normal. It was heady stuff.

Beth didn't look in the bottom drawer. Her eyes refused to stay open a minute longer. She closed the drawers and crawled into bed, barely aware of hitting the pillow.

She was in a deep sleep, beyond dreaming, the sleep that people speak of as dead sleep, when, suddenly, the bedroom door burst open, the light came on, and a voice startled her into consciousness.

"What the... Wow! Who are you? Come home and find a pretty girl in my bed? You must be kidding! Maybe I didn't wake up from that little zone-out I had on the road back there. Maybe you'd better pinch me."

Beth bolted into a sitting position, grabbing the covers up to her chin. She had a moment when she had no idea where she was. Her eyes took a few seconds to focus. A tall, broad-shouldered boy was staring at her, his mouth open, ready to say more. He had a huge duffel bag slung on one of those shoulders, and beside him were all sorts of things—a tennis racket, a football, swimming fins, and another duffel. He had several baseball caps on his head, one on top of the other.

Beth wanted to laugh. He was a ridiculous sight.

He dropped the duffel with a thud.

"Holt? Holt? Is that you?" Molly's footsteps pounded down the hall. She reached him and hugged him from the back before he even had a chance to turn around. "I didn't expect you for another week." Her voice was high with excitement.

"Hi, Mom," he said, turning, and giving her a kiss on the cheek. He towered over his mother.

"Don't you think some introductions are in order here?" he said, nodding toward Beth.

His mother hugged him even harder, and then started to cry. No tears had been shed up until that moment. Beth had wondered about that. There hadn't been any tears for the dead husband. But there wouldn't be, would there? Not from what Beth had heard that day. How strange: she knew more about these people from her few hours in town than she had ever known about C.J.

8

Beth slept in Holt's bed that night. She tried to protest. It wasn't fair that Holt had to sleep on the sofa on his first night home. But both Molly and he insisted she stay where she was. And she didn't feel she knew these people well enough to argue.

In the morning, she woke to the smell of coffee and bacon and to soft voices from downstairs. Had she overslept? Hurrying into the bathroom, she took a quick shower and dressed. She'd get out of their way as soon as she could. But, once again, she hadn't thought ahead. How was she going to get back into town to go to work? She should have brought her car. But even if she had, she could never find her way back. All those twists and turns and little gas.

She made sure they heard her coming down the stairs. She didn't want to interrupt what could be a personal conversation. Molly would be telling Holt about the death of his father. That was a scene that shouldn't include strangers.

"Good morning, Beth," Molly said when she looked up the stairs. "We've been waiting breakfast for you. I'll get the eggs going. You two sit."

"I hope I didn't scare you last night," Holt said with an awkward smile.

"Well, I'll admit to being surprised," said Beth.

"Me, too. As I said, I don't usually find pretty girls in my bed." He looked only slightly embarrassed by what he had said.

That was the second time he had called her pretty. That had never happened before, and Beth didn't know what to say. "I feel really bad about putting you out."

"Forget it. Even the sofa here is more comfortable than the bunk I've been sleeping on."

Molly called them from the kitchen. "It's ready. Come on."

They sat at the little table, the sunshine streaming through the window, making the room much more cheerful than it had seemed the previous night. The eggs were scrambled to perfection. Molly had added some cheese, and Beth thought this was the nicest meal she had ever had. It was what she had imagined was happening in those houses she had driven by.

At first they didn't speak. Holt was shoveling the eggs into his mouth as if he hadn't eaten in months.

Finally, Molly spoke. "You can have your father's pickup if you want."

He looked directly at his mother. "No. Sell it. We could probably use the money."

"But your car's always breaking down. I worry about it."

"I know how to fix it. I'll be all right. I don't want anything from him."

Beth squirmed in her seat. She shouldn't be hearing this. Wasn't it odd for them to be talking about these things in front of her? Or did all people in this new world act like this? She was used to a life of secrets. Everything had been a secret where she came from.

There was silence again. Then the doorbell rang.

"I'll get it," Holt said. He scooped the last bite of his eggs into his mouth.

"What do you want?" Holt demanded at the door. Molly hurried from the table.

"Leroy?"

"Officer Conner. I'm here on official business."

Beth turned around in her seat and watched a thin, young man walk into the house. He wore a blue uniform and a gun belt that looked too big for the rest of him.

"Oh, come off it, Leroy," Holt said. "So you've been a cop for what... ten minutes? But it's what you always wanted, isn't it? I guess I should congratulate you."

"Don't need your congratulations, just your cooperation. I didn't know you were home. The chief will be very interested in that. No secret about your feelings for your father." He stood in the middle of the room, legs spread, and gave a hitch to his gun belt as he spoke.

"He just got home last night," Molly jumped in. "Very late last night."

"From where?" Leroy asked.

"Chicago," said Holt, "but what's it to you?"

"Chief Winters seemed to think you wouldn't be home for a week." Leroy's face implied more than he was saying. He seemed pleased with himself.

"Well, I left early." Holt's response sounded angry.

"Hmm." Leroy took out a small note pad from his shirt pocket. "And exactly when did you leave Chicago?" he asked.

"What business is that of yours?" Holt moved his feet restlessly.

"Very much my business." Leroy hitched his belt again.

"Yesterday, probably about five o'clock," said Holt. "But my car broke down, so it took me longer than it should have."

"Exactly where did your car break down and do you have a witness? Some garage who fixed it?"

"No. No garage. I fixed it myself. But it took me a couple of hours. And I was in the middle of nowhere."

"So you really can't account for yourself from midnight yesterday to the early morning hours?"

"No. I can't."

"And what about the day before that?"

"Look, I left the camp on Lake Superior, I drove almost to Chicago but I decided I wasn't going to stay. It was too expensive. I called the guys I was going to be with and bailed. I headed home. So, no. I didn't see anyone. Nobody saw me."

"Interesting." Another hitch to the belt. "I came to tell you, Mrs. Floyd, that the chief wants to see you sometime today. I know he'll be even more interested to see you, Holt." Leroy had a smug look on his face.

"I would think that would have taken a phone call," said Holt.

"Good I didn't do that, isn't it? I might not have caught you here," said Leroy.

"Come off it, Leroy," said Holt with disgust. "You sound ridiculous."

"Be careful. You don't want a charge of interfering with an officer."

Holt threw up his hands and was about to say something, but Molly intervened.

"We've had a terrible shock, Leroy. I'm sure you understand. We'll be more than happy to see Chief Winters. Tell him we'll drop by later today." She started to lead Leroy toward the door. Right then he spotted Beth sitting at the table in the kitchen, trying to be invisible.

"Who are you?" he demanded.

"That's Beth Waterman," Molly said. "Beth, this is a high-school acquaintance of Holt's."

"Not quite, Mrs. Floyd. *I've* finished high school. And I think it would be more accurate to introduce me in my professional capacity. Officer Leroy Conner at your service, Miss." He walked toward her.

Beth wondered if she should get up or something. She didn't like talking to anyone representing the law.

"You visiting? Haven't seen you around here before." He was standing over her, a little too close.

"She's going to be staying here," said Molly, again trying to guide Leroy toward the door. "And I'm afraid she must be going. She's working at Dee's café and she doesn't want to be late on her second day."

"So, exactly when did you get into town?" he asked Beth, not making a move toward the door.

"Yesterday," said Beth.

"Interesting," said Leroy. He added to the writings in his notebook. "All kinds of people arriving in town right about the time of a murder, it seems." He paused and took another long look at Beth before he finally went out the door.

9

Molly insisted that Holt drive Beth into town, which made Beth feel like a total nuisance, but Holt didn't complain. They left after Beth finished her breakfast. He helped her into his car—a necessity, since the passenger door didn't open in the normal way. It had to be lifted somehow and placed back. The car was a rusted blue. Beth looked at the shiny black pickup sitting in the driveway and thought again about how Holt had refused to accept his father's car. There had to be a lot of strong feelings there. Bad feelings. She had listened when Molly told her of Holt's relationship with his father, but the refusal of the car brought it to a new level. Had he felt about his father like she felt about C.J.? No. Such hatred was not something normal people had.

The engine was noisy and made talking difficult. Beth didn't know what to say anyway. What did normal kids talk about? She kept glancing sideways at the tall, good-looking boy. And he finally caught her at it. He gave her a smile that crinkled up his eyes and made her smile back. He was so at ease with himself—so normal—a different universe about which she knew nothing.

"How old are you, anyway?" he asked.

That wasn't a question she wanted to deal with, but she quickly blurted out "Sixteen." C.J. hadn't believed in birthdays. No celebration, no mention of it. Beth had been five and then C.J. had suddenly started arguing with her that she wasn't, she was only four. And it happened again when she was twelve. One day C.J. insisted she was wrong, that she was thirteen. Now, according to C.J., she was sixteen and Beth figured that was about as good an age as any.

"What grade are you in?" he asked.

"Um, I was home schooled." She said it in much the same tone as she had used with Molly.

"Some kind of religious thing or something?" asked Holt.

"No. I'm not sure why." She tried to think of something else to talk about.

"You going to go to school here?" he asked

"I need to work," she answered.

"You can do both. You can work after school and on

weekends."

Beth thought about that. School. In the car with C.J., she had driven by schools, she had seen kids pouring out of them, laughing and looking like they were having a wonderful time. When she was smaller, she had been fascinated when she saw little girls holding hands with other little girls and had wondered what it would be like to have a friend, someone you could talk to about everything. It had become a fantasy of hers—having a best friend. Of course, she had Jack, but that didn't count and she couldn't let herself think about Jack. Those were images she couldn't handle.

The morning was a bit cool. Beth tried to roll up the passenger window only to discover there wasn't any glass there. She shivered.

"Sorry about that," Holt told her. "There"s a sweater of mine in back. Grab it, if you want.

She looked in the back seat. There was a sweater on top of a heap of clothes. She reached back for it and pulled it over her head. Instant warmth. And she loved the smell—laundry soap and something else. She guessed it was Holt himself, but not sweat or anything disgusting like that. She snuggled into it. It gave her such a cozy feeling. No, more than that—somehow, it made her feel safe.

They were going around all the turns and twists that Molly had driven. Beth tried to pay attention, tried to notice the landmarks. She would have to drive herself back after work tonight.

"Where are you from?" Holt asked, making conversation. But those simple and ordinary questions were a danger zone. She needed to direct the conversation, but she didn't know how.

"From Philadelphia," she answered. "What was being a counselor at a camp like?" she asked, quickly.

"It was fun, but I should have gotten a better-paying job. Now I'm going to be scrimping all year long again. How long are you going to be around?" he asked.

Again, the questions. "I don't know." Beth tried to think of something else to talk about. But she didn't need to. Once started, Holt had a lot on his mind.

"What happened to my Dad? I mean, how did he die? My mom didn't want to talk about it."

"He was shot," said Beth, wondering if she should have just blurted it out like that.

"Shot? My dad? I would have expected him to be the

shooter. He's a big militia freak. He *was* a militia freak," he corrected himself. "You probably think I'm terrible, not being upset about my own father being killed, but I couldn't stand the way he treated my mother. I will never understand why she took it. Why do women do that? Just keep taking it and taking it? Even some girls at school are like that, they let their boyfriends insult them and push them around, and they just take it. Why? I don't get it."

Beth almost laughed. She was not the person to answer that question. Or maybe she was. She could describe the fear, and the helplessness, and the feeling of deserving what you got, all the things that kept someone frozen in place. But she couldn't explain the why.

"Leroy Conner is such an ass... jerk," Holt went on, not expecting an answer to his question. "I can't believe he's a cop. It's only because he's related to the mayor. He'd love to make trouble for me. So he thinks I snuck into town and killed my father? He would love to pin this on me. Make himself feel real powerful and put me down. But Chief Winters knows me. I can't believe he would take anything Leroy told him seriously." Holt was looking straight ahead, like he needed to talk but he couldn't look at her when he did.

"It sounds like you and Leroy never got along," Beth offered.

"He's a total loser. Always was and always will be. Give a guy like that a little power, a badge, and you've created a monster. No, I never got along with him. My dad was like him."

Beth loved the fact that Holt was talking to her like this, like they were old friends. Again, she thought about how open he was. So different from the world of secrets she came from. A world of not telling, of keeping quiet. She would never have dreamed of telling anyone her feelings about C.J. or anyone else. "Nobody's business" was C.J.'s mantra.

They had reached the outskirts of the town. Beth would be sorry when the ride ended. She liked sitting here next to Holt, liked him talking to her like she was a real person.

He pulled up in front of the diner.

"You've got a car, I hear. You'll be all right getting back after work?"

"Yes. I'll be fine." She hoped she remembered the way.

He had to get out and open her door and place it back. He laughed. "What would I do with a car that actually worked? It wouldn't be any fun at all."

"Thanks for the ride," Beth said.

"Anytime." Again he smiled that great smile and gave a little wave as he drove off.

Beth was still smiling back as she entered the restaurant.

Dee greeted her with a big sigh of relief. "Thank God you're here. This place has been jumping. I don't know why so many people are in town this morning."

Dee introduced her to another waitress, Sally Web. "Sally handles the counter mostly. You'll do the tables." Sally was an older woman, thin, with a huge amount of teased, bleached-blonde hair. She gave Beth a cursory glance.

Dee hurried back into the kitchen, and Beth got right to work. She'd have to get there earlier tomorrow. She didn't want to lose this job. All the time she was scrambling around the tables and booths, she was thinking about the money she was earning, and the tips continued to be good. Everyone was so friendly. They asked questions, which she didn't like, but they were just trying to be nice, not nosy. She realized that. Not everyone reacted to personal questions like she did. And a friendly smile and a little laugh was all she needed, the answers didn't matter.

It was almost four o'clock, and there weren't any customers when Molly came hurrying into the diner. She flung herself into the first chair she came to.

"I think I'm going to go crazy," she said. "Nothing's making sense and it's coming at me way too fast." She was very agitated, close to tears. "I just can't believe what's happening."

Dee came out from the kitchen. Sally was out in back having yet another cigarette.

"Get some coffee," Dee told Beth as she sat down beside Molly.

With nobody else in the restaurant, Beth could hear the conversation just fine even as she went behind the counter for the coffee.

"They think Holt did it. At least that stupid Leroy Conner thinks Holt did it."

Beth brought the coffee.

"He didn't do it. He couldn't do it," Beth heard herself saying.

"Of course he didn't do it," said Dee. "And I can't believe Josh thinks he did."

"Oh, Josh. I don't know what to think about him. One

minute he's giving me so much support, called the funeral home and the lawyer for me, made appointments and everything. Told me things I had to do. Then the next minute he's letting that nasty Leroy fling all sorts of questions at Holt and he's not saying a word in his defense."

"But he knows Holt. He has to know he wouldn't do anything like this," Dee said, moving her chair close to Molly and giving her an awkward hug. "Murder his own father?"

"That's what I keep telling myself," Molly said. She shuddered.

"Josh has a lot of common sense. You can trust him," Dee assured her.

"That's not even all. I went to the lawyer. He said he could see me right away. Irving Lewis. You know, the old guy who doesn't practice much anymore. But I guess his younger partner, Tom Morgan, was Bert's lawyer. Anyway, Josh insisted both of them be there. He says I can trust Mr. Lewis. I guess he's not so sure about the other one. Anyway, I didn't even know Bert *had* a lawyer. And it wasn't like criminal stuff, like DUIs or some gun violation or anything like that. This guy handles business stuff, like property and investments. Bert had investments. Lots of them. He owns property all over the place.

He had so much money socked away, you can't believe it. And he didn't make a will. Mr. Morgan said he tried to get him to, but said Bert couldn't stand the thought of giving away anything. I have no trouble believing that. So I'm going to get all the money, Holt and me. They used words like 'intestate' and they tell me I get the first $150,000 and half of the balance and the rest goes to Holt. The rest? What rest? What $150,000? Here we lived in that crappy house and he wouldn't even get me a new fridge, and he's got all this money. Can you believe it? Now Holt can go to college and everything. Unless he's in jail for something he didn't do. My head is swimming. I'm going crazy."

Both Dee and Beth were staring at Molly. Even Dee didn't say anything for a minute.

Finally, Dee sat back. "Well, Mrs. Rich-bitch, I don't guess you'll be waitressing anymore. I hope you'll still talk to your old friends."

Molly laughed an unsettled laugh.

"It's all too unreal. I feel like I'm Alice and I've fallen down the rabbit hole."

"Where did he get it?" Dee asked. "The marina can't make that much money."

"I don't know. He never told me anything. But I don't have a good feeling about it." Molly looked like she would cry.

Beth was still standing there, coffee pot in hand. Nobody had taken even a swallow.

Sally came banging back into the room. "What's going on?" she asked. No one spoke, and Sally walked away.

"Don't say anything to anyone, okay?" Molly asked, in a whisper. "Let me absorb this all before the rumors start."

Dee nodded her head and patted Molly's arm. She looked up at Beth.

"Of course not," said Beth, feeling flattered for this bit of trust they were putting in her.

After Molly left it was time to get ready for the dinner crowd. That was busy, too. When Dee finally decided to lock up, Beth was exhausted. But the money that Dee handed her, along with her tips, made a very nice feeling in her jeans pocket.

Beth went out the back door to her car. Now she had to remember the way to Molly's house. The first part was easy, down Main Street, turn at the light onto Fishers Road, then continue past all the Victorian houses with the pretty lawns. She tried to imagine what some of those rooms must look like, the circular ones, or the ones with a peaked ceiling.

When the pavement ended, she began to get nervous. She remembered the first turn, by a big white house. And she was pretty sure about the second turn, at a red barn. But when she came to a fork in the road, she wasn't a bit sure of herself. She decided to go right. If she didn't recognize anything, she'd come back and take the other way.

This was the part of the trip where there weren't many houses or farms. It was very dark. Her headlights illuminated only a few feet ahead of her, allowing her to keep on the narrow road. But other than that, the darkness hovered all around her.

And there wasn't, for these few minutes, anything to recognize. She didn't remember such a big space of nothing. But had she just not been noticing? She grew more and more unsure of herself. Maybe she should turn around right now. She certainly should have paid more attention this morning, instead of gazing at the too-good-looking boy who was driving.

She drove several more miles down the road and finally decided to turn around, go back, and take the other fork. The turn wasn't easy with the road as narrow as it was. There were ditches on each side of the road and she had to ease the car back and forth to make the turn. She drove what seemed to her a much longer way back. But where was the fork? Had she missed it? She was coming at it from a different direction. She became more and more convinced that she had missed it, but then, wouldn't she be coming back into town?

Once again she turned around. Now she was completely lost. No fork, nothing familiar. She just kept driving for what seemed a very long time. Thank goodness she had bought gas before she had left town.

Finally, there was a car coming toward her. She gave out a big sigh of relief. She could ask them where she was and how to get to the Floyd place. But they were coming up fast, driving recklessly, veering from one side of the road to the other. And how did you even pass on such a narrow road?

When they were closer, she could hear people shouting out the windows, sounding crazy. Maybe she wouldn't ask them after all.

They were almost up to her. She slowed down and clung as far to her side of the road as she could. But they seemed to be coming right at her. At the last minute they swerved around her, missing her by inches. The car was full of boys, jammed in on top of each other. One raised a beer bottle to her.

Then, they screeched to a halt, pulled to the side, and let her pass. She didn't look at them as she went by. They were all yelling, drowning each other out. She caught a "hi baby," and a "hot chick."

Suddenly, with squealing tires, they did a quick turn-around and were following her.

She pressed her foot down on the accelerator. It seemed only a few seconds before they caught up to her. She slowed down, in case they wanted to pass. But they hovered just behind her. A minute later she felt the first bump, a nudge from behind, then a bit more of a bump. *What were they trying to do?* Now she was really frightened. She held the steering wheel as tightly as she could. The next bump was more of a jolt and she heard the sound of metal crunching.

What could she do? C.J. had told terrible stories of what happened to young girls alone. And here she was, out in the dark in the middle of nowhere.

Were they trying to force her off the road? They pulled up level with her again and yelled some more. Then they drove past again and this time they stopped, angling the car so it took up the whole road. She had to slam on her brakes to stop.

Immediately, her car door was jerked opened.

"Hey there, pretty girl. You're not hurt or anything, are you?" said a voice. She couldn't see who was speaking to her. He was shining a flashlight right into her eyes.

"Hey guys. This one is hot," he called over his shoulder. "Come on, get out of the car. We need to make sure you're all right. Wouldn't want a pretty little thing like you to be hurt." There was drunken laughter behind him.

She sat still, barely breathing, caught in the cold grip of fear.

She felt his hands pulling at her, trying to get her out of the car. She fought against him, holding onto the steering wheel for dear life.

Now someone was helping him. One of them pulled and the other pried her hands off the wheel. She fell to the ground just outside the car.

The flashlight was still aimed at her. She was spotlighted and everything else was dark.

She heard someone else say, in a mumbled voice, "Let her go. She's really young. I think you're looking at jail bait."

Beth had a moment of hope.

The flashlight veered away from her and she caught one

glimpse of a boy, standing apart, a cigarette dangling from his lips.

But then the light was back on her and they were all talking to her at once, teasing, taunting.

"You're not from around here, are you?" asked one of the boys.

"We don't grow them that pretty," said another.

"License plate's from Pennsylvania," said still another.

Suddenly there was more light. A car was coming down the road. Beth felt her heart begin to beat again.

It pulled up behind her car and the flashlight turned that way. Holt Floyd got out of the car.

"Thank God," said Beth.

"What's going on here?" Holt asked.

"Let's beat it," said one of the boys. She thought it was the one who had spoken before, the one who had given her that moment of hope. "We don't need this kind of trouble."

Holt seemed to know everyone. "I was sent to find her," Holt was telling the boys. "She's staying at my place."

"Hey, don't get the wrong idea here. We were just fooling around, you know. Nothing bad was going to happen," said the boy who had pulled her out of the car.

"Yeah, I know, I can see that." Holt's voice was friendly enough, if a little strained. "Let me pull around you so I can lead her home," he said, in that same passive voice, as he helped her up from the ground.

The boys had started to saunter back to the jeep.

"How did you...?" Beth began. Her heart was pounding.

"My mom and Dee were worried about you. It was taking you way too long to get home. They sent me to look for you. They figured you were lost."

"I was," she said, thinking it was true more ways than one.

10

Beth followed Holt's car down the road. It didn't seem to take him long at all to get to his house. She couldn't believe she had been that close, but she was still totally confused. She'd have to write it all down before she set out again.

When she parked behind him in the driveway, he came around quickly to her door and opened it.

"Come on," he said. "I want to show you the apartment."

He led her over to the garage and climbed an outside staircase, waiting at the top for her. Then, with a flourish, he opened the door.

She stepped past him and tried to control a gasp. It was so absolutely perfect—cozy and warm and welcoming. She would not have allowed herself to even imagine such a place. But she mustn't get attached, she mustn't like it too much because she knew she'd have to leave just as soon as she got enough money to move on.

There was a little sitting room with a sofa, a chair with a footstool, and a small TV. Behind the sofa was a table with two chairs, and a little kitchen area beyond that. Then, partitioned off with a screen, was a bed and a small dresser. The only other door led to a tiny bathroom with a shower.

"So?" Holt asked. "Do you like it?"

No. She didn't like it, she *loved* it, loved everything about it: the sofa, upholstered in blue, the pretty white curtains at the windows, the chenille bedspread. It looked so much like what she imagined would be inside when she had seen those lighted windows in the houses she had passed.

She had paused too long.

"You don't like it?" Holt asked again. "I did a lot of work up here today. Mom had all these people to see and she had me clean it. I thought it looked pretty good." He was obviously disappointed by her reaction.

"Oh, it's wonderful," she said, still trying to push down the enthusiasm bubbling up inside her.

"What don't you like? I mean, Mom said we could change anything you needed changed."

"No, no. It's perfect." She allowed a bit of what she felt into her voice. "It's so much better than anything I expected.

It's wonderful." She wanted to run around the room, touch everything, turn on the little stove and open the little refrigerator. She wanted to lie down on that clean white bed and put her head on the pillow. But she didn't want Holt to leave. Not just yet.

"You cleaned this?" she asked him.

He gave her a strange little smile, a little embarrassed. "I'm a good cleaner. My dad would never let me help my mom, he said it was women's work. Yet he always complained about how she did it. So, of course, I helped her a lot, whenever he wasn't around. Got good at it. You won't find a speck of dust in this place. I washed out all the cabinets and stuff too."

"It looks wonderful," she told him. "But I thought you had to go to the police station with your mother. How did you do all this?"

"When that part was over, I came home. She had other people to see. I still don't know what that was all about. Here, let me show you how to work the TV. It's a little tricky," he said, handing her the remote and sitting her down on the sofa. The idea of having a TV of her own, to watch anything she wanted to, seemed impossible. Holt sat down beside her and showed her the buttons and explained the fact that you had to wait a minute for the picture to appear and you had to double click the start button and push hard on the channel-change button. The picture was a bit grainy, bur she had never expected a TV at all, so she was delighted.

He switched through the channels. "Hey, that's one of my favorites," he said, as a cartoon called "The Simpsons" came on.

She looked at him, surprised. He watched cartoons? Weren't they just for children? She had never been allowed to watch them. But maybe he'd stay and watch it with her.

"Oh, it's a rerun." he said, getting up. "And I bet you're tired."

She *was* tired. She was exhausted. But she still hated to let him go.

"You've got to tell me about those boys," she said. She couldn't believe she had put that scary experience into the back of her mind with her excitement about the apartment.

"They're just a bunch of really stupid loser guys. Get a few beers in them and they go insane. I don't really think anything bad would have happened. I mean, they have to live in this town, they've got parents. They would know you'd report it to the police if they did anything really criminal. They probably just wanted to scare you and act tough. A couple of them are friends of Leroy Conner. So that shows you just how much respect you should give that guy. The problem is their parents all have a bit of influence and so they never have to suffer any consequences."

"Leroy wasn't one of them, I'm pretty sure of that," Beth said, but it had been very dark and that light had been shining in her eyes.

"Probably not now that he's graduated. The rest are still in high school. Maybe they're worse now. Maybe Leroy kept them under a little bit of control. He does like control."

Holt walked toward the door and handed her a key as he left. She held it in the palm of her hand and stared at it. A key. Her own key to her own place. She felt tears pricking her eyes.

After he left, Beth went around the apartment, touching things, claiming them. But all the time she kept telling herself, *This is temporary.* She'd be leaving it all soon. She couldn't become attached.

She opened the little refrigerator and found a bottle of orange juice and a carton of milk. In the cupboard there was a box of cereal and a bag of chocolate-chip cookies. She had to believe that was Holt's idea. It, too, was so warm and welcoming.

She tried out the shower. There was even a new bar of soap for her. She wrapped herself in the big white towel that hung on the rack and washed out her bra and panties. She couldn't stand the thought of putting on any of her dirty clothes again and she crawled into bed without any. At first she felt vulnerable and strange, but the pillow was soft, the bed smelled so clean, the sheets were crisp. She wanted to stay right here forever, but she couldn't, could she? She mustn't. But she was here right now. She closed her eyes in complete contentment, thinking of this new life she had fallen into. She loved it. She loved the people and the place and everything.

11

Beth woke the next morning to someone pounding on her door.

"Who is it?" she shouted out, startled and instantly wary.

"It's me, Holt. Mom says you're to come over to the house for breakfast."

"But I have... you left me... in the fridge..."

"Aw, that's just for emergencies or a late night snack. Mom is a big believer in breakfast. She won't be happy if she doesn't feed you. She won't believe you can make it through the day unless she does. She says twenty-five minutes."

Before Beth could even answer, she heard Holt's footsteps going back down the stairs.

Her underwear was dry enough to go ahead and put it on. Today, no matter what else happened, she was going shopping. She had enough money for a couple of things, unless Molly wanted some rent right away for the room. They hadn't even discussed price. And Beth was afraid to mention it, because she had no idea of what people should pay.

She looked at the clock by her bedside. It was less than twenty-five minutes, but she walked over to the house anyway.

Again the breakfast area was bathed in sunshine; there was an old-fashioned waffle iron on the counter, syrup was heating on the stove, and Molly was busy stirring blueberries into a bowl of batter.

Beth watched Molly pour the batter onto the waffle iron, clamp the lid, and raise it a few minutes later to reveal the perfectly formed waffles. Beth had only ever had the frozen kind, and those rarely.

"Dee called," Molly told Beth. "She's got some business over in Keene today. She's closing the diner."

"No work?" Beth asked, picturing her pile of dollar bills shrinking rather than growing.

"You get the day off," said Molly. "I always thought about it like a surprise holiday. She does this about once a month. Never any warning."

"Where's Keene?"

"Next town over, around the lake. It's a much bigger place. They've even got a Wal-Mart."

"Oh?" Beth was interested. "I can go shopping." She could get everything she needed there. This time when she asked directions, she wrote them down.

"But this is too pretty a day to spend the whole time shopping," Molly said. "Holt, why don't you take Beth for a boat ride? Show her our lovely lake."

Beth looked quickly at Holt to see how he was taking this. To be ordered by his mother to take this girl he didn't know for a ride made her feel awkward. But he smiled at her and seemed to like the idea. Her heart took a leap forward.

"Sure, I haven't had the boat out since I left, and there won't be many more good days."

Beth's heart settled back down. So, it wasn't about taking her, it was just about the boat. That was all right. At least he didn't seem to mind her tagging along.

But Beth had never been on a boat in her life and suddenly the thought of it seemed terrifying.

"I don't know how to swim," she blurted out.

"That's something I've never understood," said Holt. "I mean it's natural, like walking. You just move your arms and legs and you're swimming. How can someone say they can't do that?"

"Holt, every place is not like here," Molly said. She turned to Beth. "Kids around here learn to swim about the same time as they learn to walk."

"Everyone can't swim. People drown, don't they?" Beth asked, trying to keep the fear out of her voice.

"Yeah, but unless you get a cramp or are unconscious or panic, I don't see how it can happen," Holt insisted.

"Ye of little understanding," Molly said to her son, with a smile.

Everyone had finished eating. Beth got up and began gathering up the dishes.

"You leave that," Molly insisted. "I'll tend to those. You go off to your boat ride. It's really nice in the early morning, before the other boats come out."

Beth and Holt left a few minutes later and drove to the marina. It was a ramshackle building of gray siding with what was once white trim. But the weather-beaten look seemed appropriate. Boats were stacked up on the shore and more were tied to the three big docks that protruded out into the water. There were some sailboats moored off shore.

Beth watched one boat filling up its gas tank at the end of one of the docks. Suddenly, it drove off in a roar. A lean African-American man hung up the pump and sauntered down the dock toward them.

"Hi, Harvey," Holt called. "This is Beth. We're going to take the speedboat out."

Speedboat? That sounded a little scary to Beth. Holt hadn't said anything about a speedboat.

"It's all gassed up. Your mother called, and said you were on your way," Harvey said, as he came up to them. He had a furrowed face and an abundance of white hair. "It's my pleasure to meet you, Beth. And it's good to have you back, Holt. I'm real sorry about your father."

"Yeah," said Holt, obviously uncomfortable.

"You two go on, it's at the end of the dock. Get out there while the getting's good."

Holt led the way to the end of the longest dock. A glistening white boat with a huge outboard motor was tied up.

Beth took a step backward. "I really can't swim, and in spite of what you say you believe," she said trying to keep the fear out of her voice, "I don't want to drown."

Holt reached into the boat and handed her a life jacket. "Here. Put this on. If you fall into the water, which is highly unlikely, you will bob up like a cork. You can't sink. It won't let you."

Bob up like a cork. Beth liked that. She put on the jacket and he showed her how to fasten it. She had an immediate feeling of safety. She would bob up like a cork, she reassured herself. She stepped gingerly into the boat and sat in the middle seat, as Holt instructed.

Holt got in, jarring the boat dangerously, as far as Beth was concerned, and fiddled with the motor for a few minutes. Then he released the rope that held the boat to the dock and pulled a cord, and the boat roared into action. It was beyond the dock in a flash and seemed to make the middle of the lake in only seconds.

Beth was not breathing. She clung to the sides of the boat. She could see Holt was laughing at her and she tried to relax. They roared along. The water shimmered around them; it was as still as glass until they broke through it, leaving a pathway of foam in their wake.

Finally, she began to relax and dared a look toward the shoreline. The trees came almost to the water, but there was always a small border of sand. There were stretches of what looked like wilderness and stretches of cottages, some built close to the water, others with wide lawns going up the hill. They all had docks with at least one boat tied to it. Some had several boats and even little boathouses.

Suddenly, Holt turned off the motor. Beth looked at him in a panic.

"I like to drift," he said. "Listen."

At first Beth didn't hear anything at all. It was peaceful

and quiet. But then, subtly, she noticed little sounds—the hum of insects, the calling of a bird, a splash as a fish jumped out of the water. She liked this drifting much better than the speed and the loud motor.

As they floated toward the shoreline, a canoe that had been hugging the bank approached them. A woman sat in the back, paddling leisurely.

"Hi, Mrs. Cummings," called Holt.

The woman put her hand to her forehead, like a visor, and then called back, "Hi, Holt. Nice to see you."

"This is Beth. She's new in town." He turned to Beth. "And this is Mrs. Cummings, the mayor's wife." He seemed proud of his introduction.

"Welcome, Beth," said Mrs. Cummings. "We're very glad to have you on the lake. You'll like it here. It's a little bit of heaven."

In the peace of the early morning, Beth could agree. "I think it's very beautiful," she said.

"At least it usually is," said Mrs. Cummings, in a voice that was barely audible. "Not always, not the other morning. Sometimes people see things they shouldn't see. And they should tell. But if they do, won't something terrible happen?"

Beth looked at Holt, puzzled.

"That's all right, Mrs. Cummings. I'm sure everything is all right," Holt said in a reassuring voice. He gave Beth a quick warning look, silencing any question she might ask.

Immediately, things went back to normal. Mrs. Cummings talked some more about the lake, and then she looked at her watch nervously.

"I'd better get back in time for breakfast," she said and turned toward a dock that was in front of a lush lawn that led up to a stately white house on the hill.

"What was that all about?" Beth asked Holt when the woman was gone.

"She's a bit strange, a recluse. You never see her except early in the morning on the lake like this or later, sitting on her porch. She doesn't like to be with people, though she doesn't seem to mind kids. But I've never heard her go off like that, I mean, not make sense like that. Maybe she's getting some kind of dementia or something."

Beth looked up the hill from where Mrs. Cummings had docked the boat.

"Wow," said Beth. "That's some house."

"By far the biggest on the lake. It's funny. The Beaumonts used to have a log cabin kind of cottage there. But the mayor tore it down and built this. I always thought the other one went with the lake a lot better."

Beth actually enjoyed the ride back, speed and noise and all. Holt said they'd do it again and she knew she'd be looking forward to it, and not just because it was another opportunity to be with Holt.

After he drove her back home, Beth wasted no time getting into her car and heading for Keene. The road she took wound around the lake and she caught glimpses of the shimmering water. She passed a lot of cottages, each very different, some built of logs, some small with shingles, some that looked like permanent homes. Many of them even had signs with names on them: *Up North,* or *Paul's Paradise,* or *Reilly's Retreat.* They were all surrounded by shady trees.

Beth hadn't realized that such beauty existed. She thought of the house where she had lived and it appeared in her imagination to be black and white, while here the houses and the landscaping were in brilliant color.

It took about twenty minutes to drive to Keene. The Wal-Mart was one of the first buildings Beth came to.

The store was busy. She got a toothbrush, toothpaste, and shampoo and then, immediately, picked up some new underwear and a new pair of jeans. She found a bin full of T-shirts on sale and plowed through them—so many colors, and the choice was all hers. It was potent stuff, making these decisions on her own. But it was almost too much. How could she decide?

"That blue one would look really good on you," said a voice.

Beth looked across the bin. A very pretty girl was standing there, looking at her. She was blonde, tall and thin, and wore very short shorts. She threw her hair back in a gesture Beth wished she could copy.

"The lime-green one, too," said the girl. "I can't wear green. People tell me I look sick. My skin is so pasty except right now, at the end of summer." She tossed a green T-shirt over the bin to Beth. "Hold it up. It's good on you. Look in the mirror over there, you'll see."

Beth walked over to the mirror and held up the shirt. It did look good. She loved the color. C.J. had never allowed anything but plain white.

"See, I told you so." The girl smiled, a beautiful smile, her teeth white against her sun-bronzed face.

Beth still hadn't said a word. She wanted to talk to this girl, but she was almost afraid to. She epitomized the friend Beth had fantasized about as a little girl, the one she would share secrets with, talk and giggle with. But what if Beth said the wrong thing? She didn't know how to talk to kids her own age—Holt had been the first.

Beth knew she had to say something fast or the girl would go away, thinking she was either rude or an idiot.

"You're really lucky—with your skin you can wear any color you want to," the girl went on. "You'd even look good in pink, and hardly anyone can really wear pink. Not that you'd want to, of course. Not cool."

Beth had to say something. "I think you're right about the blue and the green," she said, trying too hard to sound casual. "Thanks. I couldn't make up my mind."

"It's buy two, get one free," said the girl. "Let's see…" She started sorting through the T-shirts. "My name is Samantha. What's yours?" she asked, not even looking up.

"Beth."

"You live here in Keene?"

"No. Beaumont."

Samantha stopped what she was doing and looked up "Me too. But I don't know you. You a summer person?"

"No. I'm going to be here for a while."

Samantha handed Beth a coral shirt. "That's not pink, believe me. That's a pretty cool color. But maybe you'd better have something that looks more like fall, like that dark tangerine over there."

"Yes, I really like that one," said Beth, still nervous.

The girl was studying her. "You're not from around here, are you?" she asked.

"Why? Do I talk funny or something?" Beth asked.

"No, nothing like that. We took a trip to New York once, and you remind me of those people up there. They got that same look when I came right up to them and started talking. I guess we people in the Midwest are disgustingly friendly."

Beth laughed. "You caught me. I'm from Philadelphia."

"I knew it," said Samantha. "Want to go over to the food center and have a pop?"

"A what?"

"A Coke or something. I'm dying of thirst."

Beth knew she had a smile on her face that probably looked silly. But this was exactly what she had imagined having a friend would be like.

They sat down next to each other at the counter. Beth needn't have worried about keeping up the conversation. Samantha talked about clothes, the town, some of the people who she knew, and what she had done that summer.

"I know I talk a lot," Samantha said at one point. "It

used to drive my dad crazy. I guess he's used to it by now. Anyway, where do you live?"

"I'm staying in a little apartment over the garage at the Floyd place."

"Holt Floyd?" Her voice changed, sharpened.

"Well, it's his mother who rents the apartment."

"But you know Holt?"

"Yes. He's very nice."

"He's back in town? How long has he been back?" Samantha asked. Her voice definitely had changed. Gone was the chipper little tone.

"He came back Saturday night, my first night there," said Beth.

Samantha finished up her drink. She got up, grabbed her bill, and started walking toward the cash register. "See you around," she said, and she was gone.

Beth sat there for a long time. She had done something very wrong. Her fantasy of a friend had shattered and she had no idea why.

Before she left the store, she picked up a big T-shirt to sleep in and a new hairbrush. She had spent nearly all her money. But she had a job. She could do this very same thing again.

12

It was so great to put on fresh clothes the next morning after her shower. Molly even told Beth she could use the washing machine anytime she wanted. Never again would Beth have that filthy, sordid feeling she'd had since she had left Philadelphia.

Beth got into the café early. Sally was there and had already done all the setting up. She wondered if Dee even needed her in the mornings. But there was a steady flow of customers. Beth and Sally both stayed busy. After the breakfast crowd was gone and Sally went out for her cigarette, Dee emerged from the kitchen and told Beth to sit down at one of the tables.

Oh no. Dee was going to let her go. What had she done? Or was it that Dee didn't need her with Sally there? But Sally left after the lunch crowd was finished. Didn't Dee need Beth for the dinner hours? Had she found somebody else?

To make matters worse, Dee just looked at her for the

first few seconds.

"I know you have a story to tell," Dee started. "You don't have to tell me if you don't want to. But I'm here if you ever do want to..." She held up a hand to stop Beth when she started to say something.

"The thing is, you remind me of me. I was pretty much on my own when I wasn't much older than you. I could have used some help. And it wasn't anybody's business what had happened to me. I'm thinking you're running away from something. And that's okay with me. Sometimes you need to get out of a situation. I can understand that. Boy, can I understand that.

"Anyway, I want to help. I know you've given yourself a new name. You need to learn not to stumble over it every time you say it. And you need some new ID. I know somebody who can do that too."

"Is that possible? Is that legal?" Beth asked, a little stunned by what Dee was saying.

"Well, that's another subject we'll get into at some point," Dee said. "For now, I'll just say that legal is one thing. Moral—ethical—that can sometimes be something else altogether. Our justice system does a pretty good job, but people fall through the cracks all the time. If a jury decides you're guilty, you're guilty, even if you're not. You stay in jail because you don't show remorse. How can you show remorse for something you didn't do in the first place?

"And my standards can sometimes be higher than the justice system. So I go with me. You need help. If you obeyed the law, they would send you back to what you are escaping from. Does that make any sense? Or they'd put you in the foster system, which I guarantee wouldn't be out for your welfare as much as I am. So we fudge a little here. We get you a new identity. You stay here, where you'll be safe. What's so bad about that?"

"Nothing," Beth breathed, focusing on the word *safe*. What a lovely word.

"Leave it up to me. I'll get working on the ID. And remember, if you ever want to talk, I'm here. I don't set myself up as judge and jury."

Long after Dee went back into the kitchen, through the dinner hour and beyond, Beth mulled over Dee's words. It was like a boulder had been removed from her back, like she could take a big breath. *Safe.* She'd be safe. Dee would make sure of that.

After dinner, Molly came in. Just to chat, she said.

Dee hurried out from the kitchen and the two women hugged.

"I miss you," Molly told Dee.

"Me too," said Dee.

"I miss working, staying busy. I feel at loose ends," said Molly, her voice shaky.

"You'll be plenty busy soon enough, handling all your money," Dee said with a smile. "Or maybe you can just pile it up and keep counting it."

Molly sighed. "It is so unreal. I haven't seen any of it yet. And I'm not cut out for that kind of life. Can't you just see me at the country club? I'd make a fool of myself every time I opened my mouth. You haven't told anyone about this, have you?"

"You asked me not to, so of course not. But, Molly, it's nothing to be ashamed of. And there's no way to keep it a secret. That stuff has to go through a court. Probate. It gets published."

"The lawyer mentioned that. I didn't know what he was talking about more than half the time."

"Anyway, you'll be busy handling it and the marina.

Get yourself involved." Dee called out to Beth. "Get us both a cup of coffee, would you?" Dee got up and turned the sign to "closed." The two women sat down at a table in the middle of the room.

When Beth brought the coffee, they were talking about the murder.

"I know it's to do with the militia," Dee was saying. "They're a crazy bunch. It's that Hank Crowell's doing. He's always been a loony."

"I think so, too. Especially with that perfect shot. But that Leroy Conners, he wants to pin it on Holt so bad he can taste it."

"But Holt didn't do it," Beth heard herself saying. She couldn't help it. Holt couldn't have done anything like that. It took so much to murder someone…

"Of course he didn't," said Dee. "We know that."

"Well, then," said Beth, "we'll just have to find out who *did* do it." She didn't have much faith in the justice system either, probably less than Dee. She had been brought up to distrust it.

Dee looked up at Beth, standing there with the coffee pot. "Not a bad idea. Not a bad idea at all. We know everyone in this town."

"But how?" Molly asked.

"We'll have a meeting," said Dee. "Tomorrow, we'll have a meeting. Right here. You, me, Holt, and you, too, Beth. This was your idea. We'll put our heads together. We'll figure this all out. If the police are only looking at Holt, then they're not looking for who really did it."

"Well, I don't think Josh thinks Holt did it," said Molly.

"But he's considering him," said Dee. "That's too much distraction. And although I think highly of Josh, this isn't his thing. He doesn't usually deal with anything like this. He'd be the first to tell you. I hear he asked the county sheriff to help, but that lazy old bum doesn't want anything to do with it. He'd have to get off his duff and he doesn't like that idea. So, poor Josh is left to play detective. I don't see anything wrong with us putting our heads together to give him a little help."

13

The meeting at Dee's lasted most of the afternoon. Scheduled between lunch and dinner, it hadn't ended when it was time for Dee to start dinner preparations.

"To heck with it," said Dee and kept the "closed" sign on the door.

Beth wondered if all meetings were like this one: everyone talking at once, nobody listening, spending as much time veering off the subject as on it.

Holt kept insisting it was somebody in the militia. "That Hank Crowell, who's in charge now, he's got everybody riled up. It's like there's a North and South and they're fighting the Civil War all over again, right within the militia."

"What are they fighting about?" Dee asked, but she agreed that Hank was the problem.

"It kind of seems to me it's the good guy against the nut cases. Like Slim Carry against my dad and that bunch."

"Don't call your father a nut case," said Molly with

some anger. "Show a little respect to the dead."

"I'm not a hypocrite," said Holt. "He doesn't become a saint just because he died."

Dee kept intervening between the two of them, mostly by changing the subject, which sent the meeting off in yet another direction.

Finally, when it was nearly five o'clock, Beth spoke up with something that had been on her mind for a while.

"Holt," she said, "remember when we met Mrs. Cummings on the lake? Remember what she said about seeing something she shouldn't have seen? I keep wondering about that. You tell me she goes out canoeing every morning. What if she saw what happened to your father? What if that's what she meant?"

"She said that?" Dee asked, all excited. "She actually said that?"

"Words to that effect," said Holt.

"We need to talk to her," said Molly.

"If we all descended on her doorstep, we'd scare her to death." said Dee. "You know how reclusive she is."

"She likes me," said Holt. "I could talk to her."

"I think she liked me, too," said Beth. "Holt says she's not threatened by kids."

"Then both of you go," said Dee, still filled with excitement. "Go right now."

"We'll take the boat," said Holt. "That would be more normal for her. I've driven up by boat before, never by car."

"Get, both of you. Maybe we'll actually learn something Josh never would. Mrs. Cummings certainly wouldn't tell him anything. She would be much too shy," said Molly. "I'll call Harvey and have the boat ready."

They were practically pushed out the door. When they got to the marina, the boat was ready and Harvey saw them off.

Beth, secure in her life jacket, felt much better about this boat ride. She had survived it once, and this time she was thinking more about what they might hear when they talked to Mrs. Cummings than the dangers of the deep.

Holt aimed the boat right for the Cummings' place, so the journey didn't take long. Holt turned off the motor and guided the boat forward with what seemed to Beth to be perfect timing. The boat lost its momentum as it pulled up alongside the dock. Holt hopped out and tied it to a post.

"Mrs. Cummings?" he called out. "She's usually sitting on the porch reading this time of day," he said to Beth.

Beth looked up at the big white house sitting so stately on the hill. A porch spread across the entire front, with boxes of blooming flowers suspended over the railing. There were white wicker rocking chairs, a table, and a big chaise lounge. But Beth couldn't see anyone on the porch.

When Holt was finished with the boat, they started climbing up the steep hill. He called out once again, but no one answered.

They reached the top. By now the porch was above their heads. At the foot of the porch stairs, Holt again called out for Mrs. Cummings.

"Maybe she's in the house," Holt said. "She never leaves. And they have a housekeeper. I can't understand why she hasn't answered us."

He started climbing the stairs, and Beth followed him. When he reached the top, he stopped so suddenly, she bumped into his back.

"Don't come up," he said in a choked voice. "Go back down."

He took a few steps forward and she continued to follow, trying to peer over his shoulder.

Then she saw what he was seeing and she gasped. A woman was lying on her back in a pool of blood, her arms and legs at awkward angles.

"Oh no... Is it Mrs. Cummings?"

"Yes." Holt's voice was soft and low, as if he didn't want to disturb the dead woman.

The back of her head had been smashed. It seemed like such an affront to have happened to the shy, quiet woman who had been so sweet. Beth felt tears coming to her eyes. She had only met Mrs. Cummings that once, but this was so wrong.

"That poor woman," said Beth, her voice cracking. The scene was making her want to run and hide.

"We need to call the police," said Holt. He reached in his pocket for his cell phone.

"No," Beth instinctively grabbed it. "No. Call Dee first." Her fear of the police outweighed everything else.

Holt gave her a puzzled look, but he nodded and pressed a button.

"She's dead," he said into the phone. "Mrs. Cummings is dead."

Beth wished she could hear the other side of the conversation. He was pausing too long.

"No. Murdered. Her head is bashed in." Again, the long pause. And then he hung up.

"What did she say?" Beth demanded.

"She said we should leave. Get out of here," he said. "But that's wrong. We should call the police. It isn't right to leave her here like this. And why shouldn't we call the police?"

"I can't be involved in this," said Beth. "I can't be involved with the police."

"Why not?" asked Holt.

"Never mind that now. We need to leave. Dee's right. Someone else will find her. We don't have to have anything to do with this." She turned and started lunging down the hill, going so fast that she was tripping. She had to get away. She knew the police could be looking for her. Holt was right behind her, still mumbling about the police. But Beth wasn't listening as she careless plunged down the hill, toward the boat.

She had almost reached it when they heard the scream.

"Stop. Stop, you two. Murderers. You've killed her."

Beth did stop in her tracks. She turned briefly. A stout woman was leaning over the porch railing waving her hands frantically at them.

"I know you, Holt Floyd. You stop right there. I'm calling the police." And she was. They could see the phone at her ear.

"Now we've done it," said Holt. "We can't run away now. She knows me. It's Mrs. Roe."

"You get up here right now," the woman yelled. "The police are on their way."

"Call Dee back," Beth said, feeling panicked. "Quick, call her back."

Holt once again got his phone out and pushed a button.

This time Beth grabbed it away from him. "Dee, somebody saw us. She's calling the police. What can we do?"

"I'll be right there. Don't say any more than you have to when the police get there. I'm on my way." Beth was sure when she hung up that Dee would know what to do.

Beth handed the phone back to Holt and they slowly started back up the hill. Beth didn't want to see that body again. She didn't want to be anywhere near this place. It reminded Beth of everything she was running from, and that she needed to move on.

"Who is that woman?" Beth asked Holt. She was still yelling at them.

"She's the housekeeper. Mrs. Roe. I wondered where she was."

They reached the steps to the porch. The woman had continued to watch them, shouting at them all the time.

"How could you do that to poor Mrs. Cummings?" she wailed. "She never hurt a soul in her life."

"We didn't do anything," Holt shouted back. "We came to visit her, we found her like that."

"She never has visitors," said Mrs. Roe.

"She doesn't mind kids," Holt tried to explain. "She talks to me out on the water."

"Don't you come up those stairs. Don't you make a move," Mrs. Roe insisted.

That was fine with Beth. She stood there, her arms hanging at her sides, looking up, feeling awkward. But things were much worse than that. She was waiting for the axe to fall, waiting for the police, and the end of everything she was beginning to want.

Then Beth heard them: sirens in the distance, growing louder with each minute as she and Holt stood waiting at the bottom of the steps.

How Beth wanted to run, to jump into the boat and roar away, run to her car and drive away. With Holt. They'd go westward. They'd get to California. She wasn't sure what would happen after that, but they would be away. And with Holt at her side, she wouldn't be alone.

The sirens were very close now. Then they eased off into their dying moan. The police had arrived.

If she couldn't run, then why couldn't the earth open up and swallow her? She never should have stayed in this town. She should have kept on going. Now *she* was going to get caught.

"Don't you move. Don't you dare move," Mrs. Roe called over the railing. Then she disappeared. They heard the doorbell ring and there were voices, then heavy footsteps, several of them, coming back through the house and stomping onto the porch.

"Oh, my God," said a voice.

"Chief Winters," Holt said.

"It's them. It's them that did it," Mrs. Roe said and she was once again at the railing, pointing down at them. "They were trying to run away in that boat down there. I stopped them."

Now there were three faces looking down at Beth and Holt.

"Holt Floyd?" Leroy Conner sounded very pleased. "I knew it. I told you," he said as he turned to the chief. "Didn't I tell you?"

The chief ignored him. "You two, go around to the front door. Mrs. Roe, go let them in. Maybe there's a room we can use to ask some questions?"

"I'll put them in the library. I'll see to it that they stay right there," Mrs. Roe said in a firm voice.

Beth and Holt walked slowly toward the front of the

house. Or *was* it the front, Beth wondered when they got there. This side had stately white pillars. Definitely a front. But the other side, toward the lake with the great porch, also looked like a front. She'd have to ask someone about that, although she wasn't sure why she cared. It was not her most urgent concern at the moment.

Mrs. Roe already had the door open. She stood with arms folded, waiting for them. Her lips were tight and her frown deeply etched into her forehead. As Beth and Holt eased past her, she drew away as if afraid of contamination.

She led them silently into a small room with floor-to-ceiling bookcases. Once they were seated, she left, closing the door firmly behind her. They kept hearing voices and footsteps back and forth. Finally, the door opened, and Mrs. Roe showed Chief Winters and Leroy into the room. She turned to go.

"No. You stay, too, Mrs. Roe," said the chief.

"But I do need to put my fish away in the refrigerator," she complained.

The chief sat down across from Beth and Holt. Leroy stood by the door. He got out his pencil and a small pad from his shirt pocket. Mrs. Roe eased herself into a chair in the corner.

"Now then," said the chief, "You start, Holt. What were

you doing here?"

"Murdering my lovely Mrs. Cummings. That poor, poor soul," said Mrs. Roe from her corner.

The chief held up his hand, stopping her. "It will be your turn soon enough, Mrs. Roe. Holt?"

"We just came to talk to Mrs. Cummings. We found her like that."

"Talk to her about what?" asked Winters.

"She said something yesterday..."

Just then the doorbell rang. Mrs. Roe hopped up immediately. They could hear her footsteps and the door opening.

"Oh, Dr. Purdy. I haven't seen you in such a long time. You were always my favorite doctor, you know," Mrs. Roe was gushing.

The doctor's response was muffled.

The chief got up and left the room, Leroy following at his heels.

"We have to stop meeting like this," they heard the doctor say to the chief. Then there were more footsteps, more talk, and the three men went back out to the porch.

"Well, I don't care what happens, I'm going to put away the fish," they heard Mrs. Roe say to herself.

She was still mumbling to herself when she came back into the library and sat down. The doorbell rang again. She got up and let some more people into the house.

Holt and Beth had not said a word to each other. Beth wondered if they weren't supposed to or if Holt was really angry at her for not letting him call the police. He had every right to be. It made things much worse for them. And it hadn't done any good. She was now in the very situation she had dreaded. She was terrified. She wondered if it showed.

Finally, the two policemen returned. The chief started in again with Holt. *What was he doing here? When had he arrived? What had they seen or heard?*

"Mrs. Cummings never saw visitors," Mrs. Roe interrupted at one point.

"We already told her that she talks to us, to kids. I guess we're not threatening," Holt explained again.

"Harrumph." Mrs. Roe obviously didn't believe that for a minute.

"But why, exactly, did you decide to visit her right now?" the chief asked.

Again the doorbell rang. Leroy stopped Mrs. Roe from getting up. "This is a crime scene," he said with authority. "There shouldn't be anyone else allowed to come here." He hurried out of the room. The chief stopped asking questions. He, too, was listening.

"This is a crime scene," Leroy was repeating in a loud voice. "You need to leave."

"I certainly will not." It was Dee. "You can't question those kids without an adult, and we are the responsible adults. Come on, Molly." Dee and Molly obviously pushed past Leroy, appearing suddenly in the doorway.

"Dee, what are you doing here?" asked the chief, standing up.

"What's going on here?" Dee demanded.

"Holt, what's happened here?" Molly rushed over and hugged her son.

"Mom, Mrs. Cummings, she's been killed. We found her like that. But I don't think anyone believes us," Holt said.

"First of all, we think it's odd that they were even here," said the chief.

"Odd? We sent them," said Dee.

"Sent them—here?" he asked.

"Yes. We're trying to find out who really killed Bert, because we know full and well that it wasn't Holt and you people don't seem to be looking at anyone else," said Dee in a voice that brooked no disagreement.

"You're trying to *what?*" asked the chief in disbelief.

"We had a meeting," said Dee. "It was Beth's suggestion. And a smart one, at that. None of us think you're looking for who did do it, because you're fixated on Holt."

"You had a *meeting?*" Again, said in disbelief.

"Yes," Dee answered. "And you know good and well you shouldn't be interrogating these kids without us here."

Now the chief stood up. "Number one," he said. "This is not an interrogation. I was simply asking some questions. Number two, just who do you think you're responsible for? And number three, you are *not* some kind of super crime solvers. I don't try to cook in your kitchen. So please don't try to do my job for me."

"Number one yourself, Josh," replied Dee, "It sure looks like an interrogation. Number two, I'm responsible for Beth here, and number three, admit it, you've zeroed in on Holt and I don't see you questioning anyone else."

"A woman was murdered. We question the people who were here." Now the chief was getting angry.

"Why would anyone kill Mrs. Cummings?" Dee asked, her voice more reasonable. "That would be like killing Bambi. That woman never did anyone any harm."

"We all agree on that," said Chief Winters, now talking

in a softer voice as well. "But what responsibility do you hold with Beth here?"

"I'm her cousin," said Dee. "Third cousin twice removed."

"What... what does that mean?" asked the chief.

"Oh, I know all about that," said Mrs. Roe from the corner. "It means that they have the same great-great grandmother. Twice removed means different generations, like Dee would be of the generation of Beth's grandmother.

Dee gave her a look.

"No, I don't think that's right," said Molly. "Twice removed means..."

"Enough," said the chief. He turned to Beth.

"So who are you? And what are you doing here? Where are your parents, anyway?"

Beth had her mouth open to respond, but Dee was already talking.

"Her mother's sick, that's why she's here. Beth's going to stay with me until her mother gets better."

"You have never in your life mentioned having any relatives," said Chief Winters.

Molly looked over at Dee as if she was wondering about that, too.

"You don't know my business, Josh Winters. Nobody in this town knows all my business and I intend to keep it that way," said Dee.

Chief Winters threw up his hands. He turned to Mrs. Roe.

"So, where were you when all this happened?" he asked.

"On Monday we always have fish. Charlie Gray always catches fish on the weekends and he gives some to the mayor. I went over to get them. Nice perch this time. When I came back, I found poor Mrs. Cummings like that." Suddenly she put her hand to her mouth. "Who's going to tell the mayor? Oh, dear. That poor man. Who's going to give him this terrible news? I don't know how I can tell him." She was wringing her hands.

"You don't have to, Mrs. Roe," said the chief. "That's my job."

"Thank heavens. I would never have the words," said Mrs. Roe.

Chief Winters doubted that. He had never known Mrs. Roe to lack for words on anything.

There were more questions. But it seemed obvious that the chief was not aiming his suspicions at any of the individuals there.

The same was not true for Leroy. He hadn't taken his eyes off Holt the entire time.

14

Stan Jones sat at his desk, fiddling with his paperweight grenade, picking up the telephone and putting it back down, gathering up papers into a pile, and then pushing the whole mess aside. He didn't like this case, not one little bit. And he would tell C.J. Watson exactly where to go the next time he called. Except that there would be another envelope full of nice green bills shoved under his door and he'd use it to pay some more overdue bills and he'd talk to the weird SOB and wait for the next envelope. But he hated himself for the whole thing. Stan didn't cheat clients. He did a good day's work for a good day's pay. And he'd be willing to do it here, except C.J. Watson wouldn't tell him anything and he had no direction to go in. He had tried the usual methods—these days you could find people without ever leaving your computer. Big Brother really was out there watching. Everyone kept records—every company, every agency, even every grocery store. He had used his sources, called friends on the force, the state guys as well. They had done the basic searches. No missing teenager fit the description, no teenager suddenly showing up anywhere around here. He had reached farther afield, called some guys he knew in other states, but nobody was any help.

Just then the phone rang. *Let it be another client, let it be a case where he could actually do something.* But it wasn't. The raspy voice of C.J. Watson came over the telephone like fingernails on a blackboard.

"Any good news for me yet?" he asked.

"No, and there won't be unless you give me some information," Stan said, not trying to hide his anger or his frustration.

"Find her. Just find her."

"Look. We're going to have to meet, face to face," said Stan. "I can't and won't operate like this."

"You quit, and you owe me all the money I've paid you. You haven't done one thing." The voice on the phone was a monotone, never raised in volume. In fact, the softer it got, the more menacing it sounded.

"And if I did find her, how would I even let you know?"

"I am going to give you a number to call. Only use it if

it's to tell me you've found her. It can't be traced, so don't try."

Stan wrote down the number. He knew the guy was right. He couldn't trace it if he didn't use it. But maybe he would use it, and then it was a whole different story.

That gave Stan an idea. Suddenly, he had a direction. He couldn't find the girl, not without knowing anything about her, but maybe he could find this creep. He could track C.J. down. And he would. And once he did that, he'd find the girl. He'd know where she had lived, he'd know who she was, and he would be able to talk to friends and teachers and all kinds of people. He started to think of what he could do. A camera mounted outside the door so he could see C.J. leave the money? Or stake out the door and follow the guy? That would be time consuming, but that would be best. Or maybe both.

He hadn't been paying attention to the conversation. And C.J.'s voice was very low, almost inaudible.

But now Stan had a reason to keep the guy on the line—the more they talked, the more chance something might slip. And now Stan wanted this case to continue.

"Probably not important..." CJ was saying.

"No, tell me, you were mumbling, I didn't hear what you said." Stan sat up straighter in his chair.

"She'd stand out. She's not like other kids. She's... innocent."

"Innocent?" Stan thought that was a strange word to use.

"Yeah, not like other kids, all that music and TV, getting ideas way before they should. She's not like that. I made sure that she'd never be like that."

The statement was made with absolute authority. In Stan's experience, parents didn't always know what their kids were up to. This Watson character was delusional.

"She's not equipped to deal with the world," CJ continued.

"Well, she seems to be doing a pretty good job of staying hidden," said Stan.

"It's whoever she's with—somebody is helping her. But I kept her away from people like that. I don't know where she would have met someone like that."

"Parents don't always know all their kids' friends."

"That doesn't apply here." said C.J. simply.

"Okay. Look, I need some more money to put an idea I have into action. Not much more—let's just say another couple hundred. I need to pay somebody for some information. And I need it right away, maybe even tonight or tomorrow."

"Who?"

"I don't reveal my sources," Stan said quickly.

"I can get you the money, but I want some results."

"Tonight?" asked Stan.

"Perhaps. We'll see," said the voice, followed by an abrupt hang-up, as always.

This was crazy. Stan had spent sleepless nights on stakeouts before, but never on his own territory. He had some work to do to get ready, he didn't want to miss the guy. He'd need surveillance, ears and eyes in the hallway, a good parking space so he could have his car ready to follow. But at last he had something to act on. This was good.

15

When they were dismissed by the police and left the Cummings' house Dee, Molly, Holt, and Beth all stood on the steps and breathed a sigh of relief. They didn't even glance up at the sky; too much had just happened. Murder is not easily absorbed. They didn't notice the clouds that were already rolling in.

The two women got into their cars, and Dee called to Beth and Holt that they'd meet them back at the marina.

Beth followed Holt back down the hill without saying a word. He untied the boat and they got in, still not speaking. What was there to say? Beth grabbed her life jacket and put it on quickly. She was reassured by its snug fit. She sat facing forward as Holt started the motor. She had made trouble for him by not letting him call the police. He had every right to be upset about it. If only he knew what trouble it could cause her; if she had happened on any other town, maybe it wouldn't be turning out like this. No, she had to stop at the one town where there were two murders, the one town where the police would look at everyone suspiciously. She couldn't be associated with murder. *Not again.*

It was only about five in the afternoon, but it seemed much later as the sky darkened. The waves tossed the little boat up and down and created a constant spray on both Beth and Holt. Beth turned around to look at Holt, to ask him why it was so rough. She turned just in time to see him putting on a life jacket. He hadn't worn one before.

Glancing toward the shore for some reassurance, Beth found it was obscured in mist. She didn't know where they were, she hadn't been on the lake often enough to recognize any of the cottages, and the shoreline all looked the same to her, sand disappearing into trees. Now, in the mist, it looked eerie.

The first drop of rain came just as she turned back to Holt.

"It's going to get rougher," he said. "Hold on."

Within a few minutes the rain began to pelt Beth's face. The boat was bouncing from one wave to another; water splashed in. Now the rain was coming in a steady torrent, and she could barely see any shoreline at all. How could Holt know where he was going?

Beth must have looked at him with desperation. He tried to reassure her with a smile.

"It won't be long now. We're almost there," he shouted over the rain and the motor.

He was soaking wet and she could feel water squishing in her sneakers. She looked down at her feet and noticed how much water there was in the bottom of the boat. That couldn't be good, could it?

A streak of lightning lit up the sky and the thunder seemed simultaneous. It was night-dark now.

The waves crashed over the bow of the boat, which tilted way over to one side, then the other. Beth clung onto the gunwale, but her hands were slippery and numb with cold.

She wondered if she was crying. She couldn't tell, her face was so wet with rain.

Another flash of lightning. The water was black with great foaming waves crashing against the boat. What had she heard about water attracting lightning? Nothing good, nothing good at all.

"We're going to drown," Beth cried out, suddenly afraid she'd never lead her new life away from C.J.

"No, we'll be all right," Holt shouted back at her, but he looked worried.

It seemed forever before the boat began to make a slow turn toward shore. Holt pointed at something Beth couldn't see. The rain stung her face as she tried to look, but the waves were crashing even harder against the bow and the boat seemed unable to move in the water.

"Damn," she heard Holt yell.

"What? What's the matter?" Beth asked desperately.

"We're going against the wind and the current," he said.

"It's pushing us backward?" Beth asked.

"Not exactly, but it's going to take a while." He had to shout.

Beth peered anxiously at the shoreline. When the next flash of lightning came, she thought she saw the gray-and-white outline of the marina.

They inched their way toward the shore, and sometimes they did seem to be going backward. Beth could definitely see the marina now, and she could see three people waiting for them on the end of the longest dock. They had on slickers and were under huge umbrellas, but the wind was buffeting them around, and it looked like their umbrellas were turning inside out. They were waving frantically and shouting, although the wind took away the sound of their words.

Inch by inch Beth and Holt closed in on the dock. They would almost reach it only to be forced backward.

Finally, Harvey, teetering at the very end of the dock, held out a long pole and Holt told Beth to grab it. She tried, but it was waving in the wind, escaping her grasp each time she reached out.

When Holt cut the motor, there wasn't the usual quiet; the storm sounds only seemed more frightening. But Holt was beside her now and he managed, with his longer arms, to grab onto the end of the pole.

After that, Harvey was able to pull them in much like landing a fish. Then he reached out and grabbed Beth and lifted her onto the dock. She was instantly encircled by the arms of both Molly and Dee. They were as wet as she was. But she could hear them now as they shouted above the wind and rain.

"What were we thinking?" Dee exclaimed. "To let you go out on the lake in this weather?"

"You could have capsized," Molly added. "You could have been killed." Beth thought she was crying.

Beth knew it was Holt they were worried about, but

standing there, soaking wet, shivering in the rain, and feeling the warmth of their wet hugs gave her a sensation she had never experienced before. She didn't want it to end.

When Holt climbed onto the dock, the two women, without letting go of Beth, gathered him up in the big group hug as well.

He, however, was having no part of it. "What are we doing standing out here in the rain?" He released himself and led the way by running into the marina shed.

"You're shivering, Beth," said Harvey, once they were all inside. He handed her a ratty blanket. It didn't help much over her wet clothes.

"Yeah, there's not much we can do for ourselves here. Let's get home and take some hot showers," Molly suggested.

That sounded good to Beth. She could already imagine the warmth creeping back into her bones. She was shaking and her teeth chattered—as much from fear as from cold.

Holt and Beth followed the other two cars, caravan-like, to Molly's house. Beth was still shivering. Holt's heater didn't seem to produce much more than air, and rain blew through the glass-less window. They didn't speak. It was still raining hard and Holt was concentrating on the road, or at least that's what

Beth told herself. She knew he had reason enough to be angry with her. He had wanted to call the police and that would have worked out so much better for him. That would have been what an innocent person did. Not calling made him look suspicious. But she couldn't let him. It was asking for trouble for herself. The trouble had happened anyway; the police had come. Now they were suspicious of Holt and Beth. And she couldn't explain, couldn't tell Holt her reasons.

Holt got out of the car as quickly as she did when they got to Molly's house and ran inside. Beth made her way up the stairs to her apartment. She was so wet already, there was no point in running.

The shower felt as wonderful as she had anticipated. She stood under the hot water for a long time, thinking that very few things in life met up with expectations. At least they hadn't before. Now, these last few days, with one unexpected thing after another, Beth hadn't even had time to anticipate. It was all too new, too strange. There had been two murders, but most of what she was experiencing was quite wonderful. The people she had met were so different from those she knew, so nice and so... she didn't have a word for it other than *comfortable*. These people made her feel comfortable. She had never felt comfortable around anyone before, except, of course, Jack. But she shut out that thought quickly.

Beth put on her old pair of jeans and another T-shirt. She'd have to buy a sweater next. And sneakers, she'd have to buy another pair of sneakers. Hers were soggy inside and out. It would take her a long time to start saving her money if she kept needing to buy things. But she needed so much. She had left with nothing. She'd had to.

Just then the there was a knock on the door. *Holt,* Beth thought. Should she apologize? She should say something, she knew that much. She didn't want him to be mad at her. Her thoughts were whirling as she opened the door.

But it wasn't Holt; it was Dee. "I called Tico and he's got some stuff ready for you. We're going out there right now," she said, collapsing her umbrella and walking right in.

"Now?" Beth asked. She looked down at her feet. "I don't have any dry shoes."

"Molly will have something for you. Stay here for a minute. I'll run over." Dee was out the door before Beth could protest. But it gave her time to run her new brush through her wet hair. Eventually—maybe—she could buy a hair dryer. She had never had one of those either.

147

Dee returned with a pair of slippers and a sweater.

"Molly said you can keep the slippers. Bert gave them to her and they're too small. She said she never dared take anything back that he had given her. He'd get real insulted-like. If anyone ever needed anger management, it was Bert Floyd. She said hold onto the sweater for a while. But come on, hurry. Tico is doing us a favor and we don't want to keep him waiting."

Dee held the umbrella over both of them as they went down the stairs, across the grass, and into Dee's car. It made for an awkward progression.

As Dee started out to pull out of the driveway, Beth let her toes wiggle around in the fur lining of the slippers. They were so warm and soft. She never wanted to take them off. The slippers, the people—it all made her feel comfort.

It was still raining, but not as hard, when they approached the motel. The few remaining letters on the "No Vacancy" sign were dimly lit. The whole place was dark, and Beth wondered how she had ever convinced herself to stop here. It was menacing, and shouldn't she, of all people, have been aware of the menace? It showed how desperately tired she had been. Yet, it had been a lucky stop. It had led to the town and to the people she had met there. So much had happened these past few days. She was beginning to understand things she never had before, like that people and menace were not synonymous. She glanced sideways at Dee, busy steering the car up alongside the building, maneuvering in the mud.

Dee got out of the car quickly and hurried into the office. The door was unlocked, but the office was dark. Beth followed with some trepidation.

Dee didn't hesitate. She walked through the small reception area, seeming to know where she was going, even in the dark. She opened the door at the rear wall, behind the counter, and a beam of light greeted them.

"We're here," said Dee, disappearing into the room. Beth quickly followed her.

The room was a mess. There were boxes and stacks of papers on every surface and all over the floor. Tito Zane sat in a chair behind a desk, both normal size but made small by his huge dimensions. In addition to the boxes, the desk, the chair, and the man, there were other things: cameras, copy machines, computers, all stacked on other chairs, tables, and the floor.

"Sit," commanded Tito, not looking up.

"Yeah, sure," said Dee sarcastically.

With a swipe of his enormous arm, Tito flung the papers and folders from the chair nearest to him onto the floor. He still hadn't looked up. He was pounding away at a computer; his fingers seemed too big to hit one key at a time, yet the clicking was fast and efficient.

"Almost ready," he said, still busy. "Got everything figured out." His voice boomed out in the small, crowded room.

Finally, he heaved himself out of the chair. When he stood, the room seemed even smaller; he took up a great deal of space.

"Need a picture," he bellowed at Beth. Putting a meaty hand on her shoulder, he led her over to one of the cameras. She looked at it, a small camera on a tripod.

Beth stood in front of it, feeling self-conscious. She couldn't remember the last time her photo had been taken. There was a sudden flash that made her blink, and then Tico was again pulling her in another direction.

"Now then," he said as he threw the contents of another chair on the floor and sat Beth down, "school starts day after tomorrow. You should go over there tomorrow morning and register. I've got everything you need." He handed her a manila envelope. "School records," he said.

"But... I've never..."

"You went to a charter school. Defunct now. Had a thought to just say you were home schooled, but they keep testing records and I'm betting they don't have any on you—right?" He didn't wait for an answer. "Can't check this out too fast since it's defunct." He smiled at his own cleverness. "I'll get any mail they send. If they call, that's being handled too. Named it the Susan W. Brace School, my mother's maiden name. Good woman, my mother. Old Dee there reminds me of her." He gave Dee what was supposed to be a grin, incongruous on his wide face, making his already small eyes fold into mere slits. The effect made him look a bit demonic.

"Gave you a B average—eleventh grade. They'll test you and put you where they want to anyway. They'd love to put you back one—love thinking they're better than Eastern schools."

It was all happening too fast for Beth. *Eleventh grade?* She wasn't altogether sure what that really meant. But *school?* She was really going to go to *school?*

"Getting you a driver's license. That's what the picture's for. Have it ready in a minute." A picture rolled out of his printer, and he did something with some scissors and a glue stick as he spoke and was now fiddling with yet another machine—laminating the license that already looked authentic.

"Get yourself a library card. You'll get a student ID at school. Got you a social security number. But don't use it. Won't get caught if you don't try to use it. That's all you'll need." He waved the license in the air for a minute and then handed it to her.

"So here you are, Beth Waterman. All nice and legal— well, depends on what you call legal, of course." He laughed low in his throat.

Dee and Beth stood up to leave. As they approached the door, Tico gave Dee a little shove.

Dee laughed and gave him a shove back. Somehow, to Beth, it seemed like an affectionate gesture, not like what she knew. These *normal* people, in this *normal* world, were certainly very strange. Would she ever understand them?

16

The red brick building loomed large as Dee pulled into the circular driveway in front. "Beaumont High School" was etched into the facade above the doors. It looked like so many other schools that Beth had seen from the car window. The scene was lacking the usual bustle of yellow buses and swarming kids; school would start tomorrow. Still, it was fascinating, if a bit frightening. She had always wanted to see inside, see what went on in a school and be a part of it. But here it was, and here she was, and it didn't seem like such a good idea after all. The kids who would all be here tomorrow, and every one of them would know what to do—except her. Beth didn't think for a minute that she could pull this off.

They got out of the car, went up the steps to the double doors, and walked into the dim corridor beyond.

"The office is this way," said Dee. "I remember that. I was sent there often enough."

"You went here? To this school?" asked Beth.

"This very school. Just about this time for me too—transferred in the twelfth grade."

"What's it like?"

"Like every school anywhere, I suppose. Good kids, bad kids, nice kids, mean kids. But most of the kids are medium—getting medium grades, doing medium things, leading medium lives, which isn't all bad. In fact, I'd recommend it." Here Dee stopped and looked at Beth. "In your situation? Stay below the radar. Don't call attention to yourself. Don't be too smart or too dumb, know what I mean?"

Beth nodded. That's what she had been doing all her life.

As they walked, Beth looked at the closed doors, one after another, down the long hall. Tomorrow they would be full of kids. She peered in the window of one of them. Desks were lined up in rows, waiting, ready. How did they know where to sit? How did they know which room to go to? What happened in there day after day?

She had always loved learning, reading, finding out about things. She had always wanted to go to the library, a big building that C.J. told her was full of books, just for the taking. But that had not been allowed. C.J. went and got them for her. Still, the learning sessions were the one time that C.J. had almost praised her. *Almost.* There had been no yelling or fury. Not so with Jack; the learning sessions were a horror to him. He had not cooperated. It had always ended badly.

Dee turned into the one room that was lighted. A big counter cut the room in half: on one side, chairs were lined up against the wall; on the other side of the counter, two women were bustling around.

"I'd like to register a new student," Dee announced.

Both women stopped, turned, and stared at Beth. She shrank from their gaze. That's what was going to happen tomorrow, wasn't it? Everyone would be looking at her like she was some kind of a bug, and a new species of bug at that.

"This is Beth Waterman," Dee was saying. "Here are her records." She handed the big envelope that Tico had given them over the counter.

As they were standing there, two more people came in, women busily talking, obviously excited to see each other.

"Hello, Gwen, hi, Sue," they called, almost in sync, to the women behind the counter.

"Long meeting," said one of the women, "I need to get busy setting up my room." She took some papers from one of a series of cubbyholes set against the wall and hurried out.

The short woman behind the counter had been taking a

cursory look at the papers in Tico's envelope.

She looked up, a bit puzzled. "You're the guardian, Dee? I thought you didn't have any relatives." And the other woman, curious, came and looked at the place on the paper the shorter one was pointing to.

"Come on, Gwen Keeler, this town doesn't have to know all my business," Dee said in the disgruntled voice she could do so well.

"Of course it does, Dee," said the other woman, Sue. "But I do understand. I have a whole line of relatives I don't discuss."

"That would be her Uncle Carl," said Gwen, turning to Dee. "Kept losing his get out-of-jail-free card."

Suddenly, Sue looked at Beth, embarrassed. "I don't mean that your family is anything like my Uncle Carl. I was just being silly."

Beth tried a tentative smile; it didn't work.

"You'll be wanting to see the guidance counselor," said Gwen. "She'll have some placement tests for you to take. Nothing to worry about. They just help put you in the classes where you'll be most comfortable."

Beth still couldn't quite smile. It wasn't so much the tests. It was everything. Her feeling that this simply wasn't going to work was growing.

"Miss Jensen is the guidance counselor," Sue told Beth. "She'll be back from her meeting by now. She's five doors down, on your left. You can stay here," she said to Dee. "We'll get the necessary information from you. The tests will take a couple of hours. You can pick Beth up about noon."

"That's your busy time," said Beth. "I'll just walk to the café when I'm done."

Gwen handed Beth Tico's envelope, and there was nothing for Beth to do but walk back out the door and down the hall to the fifth room. She, who had traveled so far on her own, who had planned to travel so much farther, felt a deep sense of anxiety at being forced to walk down the hall by herself.

A woman was just entering the fifth door down, a tall, thin woman with glasses perched halfway down her nose. She looked up and over them when Beth stopped beside her. She didn't speak.

"Miss Jensen?" Beth asked in a small voice.

"That would be me," said the woman, now advancing into the room. "Come on in."

"I'm a new student," said Beth, not knowing what else she was supposed to say.

Miss Jensen went behind the desk and Beth sat down in

the chair in front, shoving the envelope she was carrying across the clean surface.

Miss Jensen nodded, opened the envelope, and carefully and silently read the contents. She glanced up periodically over those glasses, looking at Beth, who was trying very hard not to fidget. The idea of going to school was feeling more and more like a very bad idea. Beth should just get in her car and keep on driving, get to California, although what she would do there she didn't know. Someday, somehow, she was going to have to enter the real world. Was now the time?

Well, here it was. And it was probably going to blow up right in her face, right now. Beth felt trapped, not only here in this small room, but totally trapped. She couldn't go back to where she had come from, and she seemed ill-equipped to go forward. It wasn't just the test or even the idea of school—everything was becoming increasingly overwhelming.

"This all seems in order," Miss Jensen said, putting down the last of the sheets of paper, straightening them into a neat pile. "We'll begin the placement tests. You'll be tested on several subjects. It's not a pass/fail thing, it's a timed test, but they give you ample time. Just do what you can. And it's nothing to worry about. There's a desk in the corner. Sit there and make yourself comfortable. I see Dee Carter is your guardian. Good old Dee. I just love her apple pie. It's my favorite indulgence."

Miss Jensen got out several stapled forms and a pencil and handed them to Beth. "You get started while I go down to the office to say hello to Dee and gather up some things I need."

Beth picked up the pencil. What would Dee be saying about her? They hadn't really gotten their stories straight, not the details. But there was nothing Beth could do about it now. She eased her feet half out of her still-damp sneakers and began.

The test was easy. Beth sailed through the English and history. The math was harder. She had never been good with math and neither had C.J., who had left her on her own, given her textbooks, and told to figure it out for herself.

The next two hours went by quickly. Beth was aware of Miss Jensen leaving the room and returning several times.

"Time's up," Miss Jensen finally announced. Beth had been unaware of her most recent return, but she had done all she could do on the test.

"I don't think I did very well on the math part," Beth said, handing her the papers.

"Just between you and me, math was always my Waterloo, too."

Beth wasn't sure what that meant. That was a battle, wasn't it? She smiled, hoping that would cover the expected response.

"I'll have your schedule all set for you tomorrow morning. You come here first thing." Miss Jensen stopped and looked at Beth, studying her.

"Now don't you worry, dear. I know a new school is a traumatic experience. But we're not ogres here. You will come to love Beaumont High, I know you will. And if you need anything, anything at all, even someone just to talk to, you come right to me. Anytime."

Beth nodded and hurried out of the room, because once again she felt that urge to cry. She could take pain, humiliation, abuse. But these little darts of kindness, that was something she really couldn't handle.

17

Beth didn't sleep that night. She tossed and turned as she pictured herself going into school the next morning, walking down those hallways, lost and in trouble for being late for everything as she fumbled her way through the day. The kids would mock her, laugh at her, point at her. They would know she didn't belong there. She would stand out like a mouse in a cage of cats. She wasn't one of them. And there was so much she didn't know. What was worse, she didn't know what she didn't know. There were signals and signs all around her between people that she didn't understand. They said words that made no sense, words she knew the meaning of, put together with other words that she knew the meaning of, and together they made no sense at all.

Beth knew how ill equipped she was for what awaited her tomorrow. And, once again, she felt like she was about to walk off a cliff. Danger bells were ringing. She shouldn't do it. She would be a fool to do it. She could finally get caught.

At some point she slept. But when the alarm went off, she woke with scratchy eyes.

Holt drove her to school. They left a little early. Holt said he had a lot of people to see. But when he pulled up into the parking lot and stopped, he sat there, looking puzzled.

"Those are my guys over there and they didn't even give me a wave," he said. "In fact, they looked away. Do you suppose they've bought into Leroy's idea that I'm a killer?"

"Don't they know you?" asked Beth.

"Well, they'll have to say it to my face," Holt said, getting out of the car. He turned before he slammed the door. "You'll be all right? You know where to go?"

"Yes," Beth mumbled, "the guidance office." He seemed relieved and hurried off to a group of boys who were standing in the yard. She walked tentatively toward the building.

Beth remembered her way, but the halls were certainly different now. It was the noise that bothered her the most, the shouting, the too-loud laughter, the little screams. There was a lot of pushing and shoving. It was difficult to wiggle through the crowd.

Miss Jensen's door stood open and Beth made a final

dash for it, relieved to get out of the turbulent hallway. Once inside, she stood still for a minute.

"Right on time," Miss Jensen said, getting up and coming around her desk, smiling broadly. "I have your schedule right here." She handed Beth a slip of paper. Beth looked at it, but had no idea what it meant.

"Oh, don't worry," said Miss Jensen. "I have someone coming to be your escort today. She'll take you around to all your classes and show you where everything is. She should be here by now. She is usually very prompt." A small frown appeared on Miss Jensen's face.

Beth wondered if she should just stand there or sit down or what. She was already wishing this day was over.

"You know, you did extraordinarily well on the tests. In fact, I've put you in several advanced placement classes. And you shouldn't have worried, you did well in math, too, but since you seemed hesitant about your math skills, I decided Algebra II would give you more confidence." The bland smile had returned to Miss Jensen's face.

Suddenly the door slammed against the wall and the girl from Wal-Mart stood there. Beth smiled. Was this to be her escort? Maybe today would work out well after all.

"Samantha?" said Miss Jensen. "What may I do for you?"

"I'm going to show Beth around," stated the pretty blonde girl, almost defiantly.

"But... that was supposed to be Denise. Denise was supposed to do that."

"Well, I traded with her," said Samantha. "I already know Beth. She'll be more comfortable with me."

The frown was back on Miss Jensen's face. She hesitated a minute. "Well, I suppose that would be all right. It was all right with Denise?"

"Sure."

Miss Jensen still appeared doubtful.

"Come on," Samantha said, pulling Beth's arm. "We'll be late for homeroom." Samantha had them out of the room before Miss Jensen could say anything else.

Beth could feel a too-big smile on her face. She tried to control it, but she couldn't have asked for anything more perfect. This was the very girl she had wanted for a friend. She was so pretty and seemed to know so much—Beth's perfect fantasy of a friend suddenly coming true.

"How did you even know I was here?" asked Beth, as

Samantha hurried her down the hall.

"I saw you this morning, getting out of Holt's car," said Samantha. She gave Beth a sideways look, and the pressure on Beth's arm increased.

"Oh." Beth suddenly remembered that it was Holt's name that had turned Samantha off in Wal-Mart. She really didn't know how to act with kids her own age.

"What's with you and Holt anyway?" asked Samantha. She stopped and stepped in front of Beth, looking at her intently.

"I told you. I'm staying in the little apartment his mother rents out."

"Why?"

"Because it's where Dee Carter arranged for me to stay."

Samantha frowned. "What's Dee Carter got to do with you?"

"She's... my cousin," said Beth, voicing the lie for the first time and hating herself for lying to this girl who she wanted for a friend.

"So where are your parents?"

"My mother's sick. I've never known my dad."

165

"I'm a one-parent kid, myself," Samantha said with some understanding. "Only with me it's my dad. Anyway, we're late. We'll talk more later. We're in the same homeroom. Waterman, Winters, and here it is." She gave Beth a little push toward an open door.

Beth hesitated just inside the room. She had no idea what she was supposed to do.

"No more seats in the back," said Samantha with disgust. "You take this one." She pointed to an empty seat right up in the middle of the front row. "I'll sit over by the window." She aimed for the last seat in the second row.

A large man was standing in front of the room, arms folded, waiting until everyone was seated. He walked over and closed the door right after the two girls sat down, but the din of conversation continued.

"Quiet!" the teacher's voice boomed out. It made Beth jump. "You all know me. I do not, I repeat, *do not*, tolerate anywhere close to this level of noise. You will be on time and you will be quiet." He looked right at Beth, who was sitting directly in front of him.

Then he started listing rules and regulations, none of which had any meaning for Beth. But his voice was loud and filled with authority. She wished she could see the other students, see how they were reacting but, stuck in the first row, she couldn't see anything.

The loud speaker suddenly boomed over the teacher's voice and there were more announcements. Then it was over. A bell rang and everyone immediately jumped to their feet and rushed out the door, pushing and shoving and speaking all at once.

"He's such a twit," said Samantha before she had even ushered Beth out the door. Beth turned back quickly. Had he heard her? He was glaring their way.

Samantha grabbed the schedule out of Beth's hand. "You have history first period. Oh. It's AP. You have a lot of AP classes. Well, I certainly won't be in any of those. Come on, hurry it up. I need to get you there and get to my own class." She practically pushed Beth down the hall, up some stairs, and to a classroom at the end of the hall. The noise and kids rushing continued all around them. It seemed like mass confusion.

"Wait here. I'll pick you up after class," said Samantha as she hurried off.

Now Beth was really on her own. She walked into the

classroom and, this time, chose a seat in the back. That seemed to be what she was supposed to do.

This teacher had written her name on the board. Mrs. Herman. She immediately handed out several papers, all stapled together, outlining the course study of U.S. history from 1870 to the twenty-first century. She didn't yell, and the classroom was relatively quiet. Beth felt herself relax slightly. But it went by fast, much of it in a blur. As did the next class, chemistry, and then the next, English. Then was gym, which Beth found the weirdest of all.

Beth was puzzled about everything she had experienced, and it made her feel strange and different. There were so many kids, always moving, even while sitting. They didn't seem to pay attention, they sprawled in their seats, and they laughed at things Beth didn't think were funny. Would she ever get what was going on? There was no comparison to the lessons with C.J. She couldn't even imagine what would have happened if she had sprawled in her seat or appeared bored. The very thought made her shudder.

Finally, it was lunch time and Samantha led her to the cafeteria. If the day so far had been noisy, this was out of control. The din of voices, shouts, scraping chairs, clattering trays, and stomping feet seemed to bounce off the walls and the ceiling.

"I only get a salad," said Samantha. "If you want to go through the line, meet me at the salad bar."

"I'll have a salad," said Beth. She wasn't about to leave Samantha's side. She was trying hard not to look as confused and frightened as she felt.

Some tables were crowded with people wedged in together; others were almost empty.

Beth copied Samantha's choices at the salad bar. The lettuce looked a little brown and the cucumbers tired, but Samantha covered the whole thing with a lot of creamy dressing, and so did Beth.

Picking up her tray, Samantha turned and looked around the room. She paused for what seemed to Beth like a long time.

Some girls from one of the crowded tables were waving at her. Samantha waved back but then turned and walked the other way, to an empty table by the wall.

They sat across from each other and Samantha, moving her salad around with her fork, rather than eating, started talking.

"So, you're here all by yourself and although you're related to Dee Carter, you're staying with the Floyds?" asked Samantha.

"Weird, isn't it? But Dee doesn't have room for me. She told me she sold her house to buy the land and the building where the restaurant is, and now she lives in the little room above the café. She says she'll have a house again someday."

"I didn't know she hadn't always owned it," said Samantha.

"She's always owned the business, but she says the mayor owns the rest of the property on that block. When she heard he was trying to buy her land and building she just beat him to it."

"Yeah, well," Samantha was obviously not interested. "So about you and Holt. What's going on?"

"Nothing." Beth was suddenly getting it. "Is he your boyfriend or something?" she asked.

"We dated last year. I don't get why he hasn't called me since he's been back."

"Well, his father just died," said Beth. "And then we found the body of the mayor's wife and the police seem to think he had something to do with both those things." Beth was explaining fast and furious, not wanting this new friend to be mad at her, but total disappointment was whirling around in her head at the same time. Obviously, Holt had no interest in *her*, not when he could have beautiful Samantha for a girlfriend. What had she even been thinking?

"My father *is* the police. I can't believe he thinks Holt had anything to do with his father's death."

"Oh, of course, Chief Winters, and you're a Winters. But I don't think it's him as much as the other officer."

"You mean Leroy? Don't worry about him. My dad thinks he's a twit, which he is. He wouldn't even be working for the police department if it wasn't for the mayor. Mayor Cummings is always doing things like that—insisting my dad hire someone, or do something for someone for political reasons. So, you're not interested in Holt?"

"He's not interested in me," Beth said, realizing it had to be true. "He's been very nice and kind and all of that."

Samantha nodded, obviously pleased. Then she started telling Beth about everyone in the cafeteria, pointing them out, telling her stories about the groups and individuals. Samantha had them both laughing very hard in just a few minutes. Beth realized this was what having a friend would be like.

As Samantha was pointing around the room, Beth stopped her suddenly. "Who's that?" she asked, grabbing her arm to keep it pointing where it was. "The boy in the black T-shirt?"

"Oh, that's Tony Grimes. Stay away from him. He's bad news, not that he isn't a hottie as far as looks are concerned, but he *is* bad news."

"I think I met him once, on a dark road late at night. He and some other boys stopped my car. They really scared me."

Samantha sat up straighter. "What happened?"

"I was lucky, Holt came along just then. I had gotten really lost trying to get back to his house. His mother had him out looking for me—he got rid of them."

"The damsel-in-distress and hero-rescue thing? That must have made Holt feel pretty good about himself." Samantha's voice suddenly didn't sound so pleasant.

"I wouldn't have put it like that, but I guess it's true. He was just doing what his mother told him to do." Beth tried to reassure Samantha quickly.

A girl came up to their table, a pretty girl with long, dark hair and blue eyes and very long, dark eyelashes.

"What are you doing over here?" she asked Samantha.

"Getting too good for us?"

"Hi, Lindsey. I'm showing Beth here around the school today. She's new." There was a strange tone in Samantha's voice, a bit diffident.

Lindsey gave Samantha a look of disapproval. "We need to talk to you. She'll be back later, Beth." Samantha gave Beth a quick apologetic glance, got up, and left.

Beth felt exposed sitting there by herself, aware of the people looking at her. It hadn't bothered her when Samantha was sitting there, too. She kept her eyes down, staring at what was left of her salad, which had all but disappeared, although she had been so engaged in the conversation with Samantha that she didn't remember eating. She knew this day would be hard, but it was even more difficult than she had imagined. Everyone else was so at ease, so normal. Other than the conversations she had had with Holt and Samantha, and knowing Jack, she had never even spoken to anyone close to her own age. How was she supposed to know how to act? She was exhausted from trying to pick up the cues. She didn't know how to have a friend. Jack had been the only one she could have called a friend. And she didn't want to think about that.

This was new territory. A girl like herself. Yet one

minute Samantha was friendly and nice, and the next she seemed angry. Okay, Beth now understood that she was interfering in Samantha's territory with Holt. Her whole fantasy of how wonderful it would be to have another girl to talk to was evaporating fast.

She didn't notice anyone coming to sit at her table, not until she spoke.

"You're Beth Waterman?" asked the girl, plunking her tray down opposite Beth. The girl was short and fat, with most of her hair hanging in her face, a turned-down mouth, and hunched-over shoulders.

"Yes," answered Beth.

"I'm Denise Packard. I was supposed to be your guide." There was an accusation in her tone.

"Oh, yes. I hear Samantha traded with you."

"Traded what? And where is she? A guide is supposed to stay with a new student, especially at lunch."

"She was here. Someone just came and got her. I suppose it's hard, on the first day, not to be catching up with your friends."

Denise's tray was loaded with food: French fries, a sandwich, ice cream, a brownie, and a piece of pie. She started with the brownie. "You're not supposed to leave your new student," she declared. "And she's over there with the popular bunch. I doubt she'll be back. So who are you? Where are you from?" The questions were tossed out of her mouth between bites.

"I'm from Pennsylvania. My mother is sick. I came to be with my cousin, Dee Carter." The lie was getting easier. She should have known it would. That's how it had been before, too.

There were going to be more questions, Beth could tell. Denise's mouth was open and ready, but just then, Samantha came back.

"I'm so sorry to leave you in the lurch like that. Command from the Queens. I'll explain later, but now we'd better go," she said. "I sure don't want to be late for my next class. I have the wicked witch. Hi, there, Denise. Thanks again for letting me have Beth today."

Denise only grunted.

Beth got up and said goodbye to Denise and followed Samantha, mimicking her as they dumped their garbage, stacked their trays, and hurried out of the lunchroom.

They were going up to the third floor this time, and

there was the usual confusion of people trying to go up in the down lane or vice versa, bumping and pushing.

Just as Samantha showed Beth to her next classroom door, she stopped her.

"Be careful of people like Denise," she advised. "I know I sound like the greatest snob in the world, but you are judged by who you associate with. No point in not aiming for the top, is there? I mean, I'm not so totally in with the group I want to be in. But they semi-accept me and that's enough. Actually, there are a couple of them I can't stand, like Lindsey back there. There isn't a bone in her body that's not fake. And one of the reasons they accept me is because I dated Holt Floyd last year. It's all very complicated. I'm sure your old school had some sort of social hierarchy too, but here it's like life and death." She touched Beth on the shoulder. "Anyway, I have to run. Literally—run." She turned and raced down the hall.

During seventh period there was an assembly. Samantha hustled Beth through the crowds, into the auditorium, and found them some good seats. Beth couldn't imagine herself doing this on her own. The sheer volume of people was getting to her.

It was here she got her first glimpse of the principal, a

very tall, thin man named Mr. Jordan. It only took him a minute to silence the raucous crowd, and all he did was stand there with his arms folded. There had been so many things that Beth didn't get that day that she didn't even question this latest mystery.

When the room was pin-drop silent, Mr. Jordan introduced the guest speaker. It was the mayor, Maxwell Cummings, who took the podium.

He gave them a welcome to the new school year speech, talking about opportunities and the importance of education and other nebulous things. Beth looked around her, expecting everyone else to be as tuned out as she was. But they weren't. They were listening and smiling back at the man and laughing at the little jokes he threw in. She didn't understand, but it gave her a chance to study him. What was there about this guy that bothered her so? He was very good looking in an older, distinguished way. He *looked* like a mayor. More than that, he looked like the *idea* of a mayor. The white streaks running through his hair just at the temples, his tall stance, and his wide smile all made him seem perfect for the part. He exuded confidence. And his smile was contagious.

But Beth didn't believe that smile, not for a minute. It

177

reminded her of someone. Someone else who wasn't real and it made cold prickles run down her neck. Were there other C.J.s in the world? There couldn't be. Why bother to escape if there were? The world was suddenly not holding out the promise she had expected.

Two more classes and the day was over—at last. The afternoon went by as quickly as the morning had, and when the final bell rang, Beth felt worn out and limp, like she had been put through the spin cycle in a washing machine.

She waited for a few minutes by the door of her last class, but when Samantha didn't appear, she allowed herself to be pushed along with the exodus to the front door and into the bright sunshine of the August afternoon.

Beth stopped at the top of the steps, trying to orient herself. She had paid attention to where Holt parked his car, but that seemed like a half a century ago. The swarm of hurrying students billowed around her. The exhaust fumes of the yellow buses lined up in the circular driveway caught in her throat. Suddenly she felt someone grab her arm.

"So, you go to school here now?"

It was the boy in the black T-shirt, one of the boys who

had stopped her car on that dark night and dragged her onto the road, the boy she had seen in the lunchroom. Samantha had said his name was Tony something. Beth tried to wrench her arm away.

"Where're you going? Can't even be a little bit friendly?" He tightened his grip, and his tone was one she was all too familiar with.

"Leave me alone," Beth said, trying to sound forceful. "Let go of my arm."

"Aw, come on. You're new around here. What's your name? Consider me the welcoming committee." Tony's voice was threatening.

Beth looked across to the parking lot. Where had Holt parked? It was that lot off to the left, wasn't it? She could never get there.

"Actually, Beth Waterman, I already know your name," Tony said with a little laugh. "Leroy's been looking you up. Seems like you're the big mystery girl. He's getting pretty interested in where you came from and why you're here."

"The policeman?" asked Beth. "What does he care about me?" This was too much. Now Beth really was afraid.

"Just interested. Likes to check things out. Likes to do

his job." Tony still gripped her arm.

"Leave her alone." Samantha was running toward them. "I've already warned her about you, Tony Grimes. Just leave her alone."

"So? I'm supposed to fall down in fear because one of the princesses deigns to speak to me?" He laughed with obvious contempt. But he let go of Beth's arm and with a shrug turned to walk away.

"You'd better watch the company you keep, new girl," he said over his shoulder. And once again he laughed.

"Are you okay? He's such a jerk. You driving home with Holt?" Samantha asked when Tony had disappeared into the crowd.

"Yes. I'm trying to remember where he parked."

"It was this way," Samantha said and started leading Beth toward the parking lot to the left. "Remember, I saw you and him this morning."

Holt was waiting by his car, hanging onto the open door, looking around at the students now going off in every direction.

"There you are," Holt said. "I was beginning to worry about you." He hadn't, at first, seemed to notice Samantha.

When he did, he stopped abruptly.

They stood there for a moment in awkward silence.

"Hi, Sam," Holt finally said.

"I've been expecting you to call," said Samantha with a pretty pout.

"A lot of stuff has happened," he said.

"Yes. Sorry to hear about your dad," she replied quickly.

Beth felt like maybe she should walk away. But that, too, seemed awkward.

"Thought maybe you had lost my phone number or something," Samantha said with a coy smile. She was trying too hard. Even Beth could see that.

"No. I've got your number." Holt shifted his weight.

"There's a party Saturday night," said Samantha. "Lindsey's house."

"I'm not sure it's even appropriate for me to be going to parties just now," said Holt. "We've got to go. Beth here has a job, she doesn't want to be late."

"Oh," said Samantha, giving Beth a quick look. "Of course. I wasn't thinking. I am really sorry about your father... but... never mind."

"But I didn't get along with him. Is that what you were about to say?"

"I guess..."

"You're right. I didn't. But since your father seems to think I'm the best suspect, I'd better watch what I do."

"I'm sure he doesn't think that. He knows you, Holt."

"Yeah. Well. Gotta go. See you later." He got in the car.

"Thanks for showing me around, Samantha. I'd have been completely lost," Beth told her as she reached for the passenger door. "And thanks for getting rid of Tony."

"I'll be with you all week," said Samantha. She was looking at Holt, and she wasn't sounding as if she was looking forward to the rest of the week.

Beth and Holt left. Beth looked back at Samantha standing in the parking lot, looking very much alone. This wasn't the way she had intended this to go. Not at all. She wanted Samantha for a friend. But she wanted Holt for a friend, too. It appeared she couldn't have both.

Holt was not his usual self on the drive into town. For the first few minutes he didn't say a word. When he started talking, it was as though he couldn't get the words out fast enough.

"That might have been the worst day of my life," he began. "The rumor is all over the place that I killed my father and it's just a matter of time before I'm arrested."

"Nobody can believe that," said Beth. How could she, who knew him the least, know that he couldn't do such a thing? But she was absolutely certain.

"Even Mr. Jordan, he dragged me in, kicked me off the school paper. Said I had enough on my plate at the moment, but what he meant was that he didn't want a killer running the paper. What ever happened to innocent until proven guilty?" Holt banged his fist against the steering wheel.

Beth kept trying to reassure him, but he wasn't about to be reassured. And she couldn't blame him. She knew how it felt to be blamed for something. It was the most helpless feeling in the world.

She was flattered that he was talking to her like this and appalled that she couldn't say anything to make him feel better. Maybe he recognized some sort of kindred spirit in her. She felt that way about him. Not a boyfriend-girlfriend thing like he had with Samantha. Nothing like that. Just a meeting of two minds. Just a friendship, and that was fine with Beth. That was plenty. Because Holt didn't know she had secrets of her own.

18

Josh Winters had to get out of the office, even if only for a few minutes. Maybe a cup of coffee and a piece of pie at Dee's was in order. Leroy was driving him crazy. Yet how could he complain about an employee who was working hard at his job? Over-zealous, perhaps, but that wasn't such a bad thing. He probably just had a crush on the girl and thought that looking her up would give him some knowledge to help his case. But the guy was obsessed and a bit unstable as far as Josh was concerned, had a Napoleon complex, the small and twitchy kid trying to act tough. It should have been amusing, but somehow it wasn't. It was disturbing.

He left Leroy to his Internet searches and walked down the street to Dee's. It was four o'clock in the afternoon. The place wasn't crowded. He took a booth by the window.

Somehow, he was surprised when the girl herself came up to take his order, surprised just because he had been thinking about her and, suddenly, there she was. He had heard from Leroy that she was going to school. He hadn't expected her to still be working at Dee's. Probably after school and on weekends.

He said what he hoped was a friendly hello and ordered his coffee and a piece of apple pie. He'd have to run an extra mile tomorrow morning, if he got the chance. Lately, there kept being reasons not to run. Excuses that shouldn't be examined too closely.

"I hear you're going to the high school," he said casually.

"Yeah, first day today. It's a bit confusing. But your daughter helped. She showed me around."

"Sam?"

"Yes. She was really helpful."

Josh choked off another *Sam?* Then he said, "It must be hard—a new school and all. Is it bigger than your last school?"

"Yes, much," she said, thinking how ridiculously bigger it was than C.J.'s small, cramped, and dark classroom, where the door was always locked.

Josh couldn't help but study Beth. There was something about her that was disturbing. She was uncomfortable around him, for no reason at all. She didn't exhibit that same degree of unease around other people. It was the unease people with a guilty conscious showed. Why should she be wary of the law?

Maybe he was imagining things because of Leroy's poisoning suspicions. But there *was* something a bit off about her. She was pretty, she was nice and polite. Obviously, she was a hard worker, getting a job like this. She could certainly use a bit more self-confidence, although maybe he was just comparing her to Sam, who had an overload of that.

When she brought the coffee and pie, he couldn't help himself. "What was the name of the school you transferred from?" he asked.

"It was a charter school. It's closed now," she said hurriedly.

He was watching her eyes. She wasn't telling the truth. Maybe Leroy was onto something after all, as much as Josh hated to admit that.

The girl had already turned and hurried away. The chief had nothing else to do; he watched her as she filled water glasses and brought more coffee to the other tables and booths. She was very careful to never glance his way.

When he had finished, he dropped a generous tip on the table and walked to the register. She had to pay attention to him then. She had to come and give him the bill and take his money. But she didn't look at him, not directly, and the smile she gave him was weak at best. He was making her very nervous.

Back at the office, Josh didn't share his new suspicions with Leroy, who was still lamenting that he could not find out anything about her. Maybe he should start looking her up himself. But Leroy was better at the computer than he was. Computers made him impatient, so right now Leroy was actually useful.

That night, when Josh got home, he had a lot of questions for his daughter. Sam, of course, didn't saunter in until dinner was already cooked. He had become expert at pasta and sauces out of a jar. Sam always made the salad.

"We need to eat more fresh vegetables," she announced, as she did about every other day. But when he bought them, they usually ended up rotting in the refrigerator. Josh thought of Jenny, as he often thought of Jenny. She hadn't been a very good mother or a good cook, either. But she was beautiful. It wasn't easy being the wife of the only cop in town. It meant no vacations, no normal hours, no normal life. He hadn't been particularly surprised when she left. But he knew he wasn't a great substitute-mother himself. And it was ironic that now he wasn't the only cop in town. Now they could have taken a vacation, or presumably so when Leroy got his act together.

Sam had inherited her mother's looks, thank God. He hoped she hadn't inherited the lack of an ethical core or Jenny's inner meanness. Sam had been such a great little girl, kind and thoughtful. Everyone had warned him about the teen years—he hoped that this last summer of moodiness was just that. He had attributed it to Holt Floyd being gone all summer. And as far as he knew, Holt hadn't called her since he came back, but obviously that kid had a lot on his mind. He truly hoped that it wasn't a guilty conscience. He liked Holt, had loved watching him on the football field, had felt sorry for him having to deal with his father, and had always thought of him as a really good kid. He had a good mother. Josh hoped that was all it took, one good parent.

"I hear you did your good deed for today," he said to Sam as they sat down at the table. He insisted that at least a couple of times a week they eat at the table and not in front of the TV, although that was getting harder and harder to enforce, since microwave dinners made life so much easier and, frankly, he enjoyed it so much more himself.

Sam looked at him, questioningly.

"The new girl, Beth Waterman, she told me you took her around today. That isn't something you usually do, is it?"

"No. It's a loser thing. I only did it this one time."

"Why?"

She continued to push her pasta around her plate, but her voice grew noticeably louder. "Because she's living at Holt's house. Why? She says she's staying with Dee but she's living at Holt's house. Does that make any sense?"

"I guess Dee doesn't have enough room. She's living above her café. It's only one room."

"So why didn't they both move into an apartment for as long as Beth was going to be here?" Sam's voice was almost shrill.

"I don't really know, Sam. But I wouldn't worry about Holt. He's had quite a shock with his father dying."

"Holt hated his father. Everyone knows that. And Beth says you think he killed him." Now, Sam sounded angry.

"I haven't accused him of anything." Josh tried not to sound defensive.

"Well, he didn't. Holt could never do anything like that.

But he's acting really weird. He hardly spoke to me today."

"His life has taken a huge turn. He doesn't know what's going on right now. Give him a little break."

"So you're defending him?"

"I feel sorry for the kid. I always have." Josh changed the subject. "Beth Waterman—what do you know about her?"

"Nothing. She's nice enough if a bit... I don't know. It's like she doesn't get it half the time and like she knows more than she should the other half. I know it must be hard changing schools, but she acted like she had never even been in a school before. It was weird."

"Hmm." Josh was both enjoying the fact that he and his daughter were talking more than usual and disturbed by what he was hearing. He would definitely give Leroy all the encouragement he needed to find out more about Beth Waterman.

There was plenty more Josh wanted to talk about with Sam. But he got a call, and it was, as always, an emergency. He gobbled a few more bites and left the rest of his dinner untouched.

"The dishes—in the dishwasher, not in the sink," he said to Sam before he went out the door. He received the usual eye roll and gave it a fifty-fifty chance.

19

Stan Jones figured he had everything set up: a night-vision, motion-activated camera mounted in the hallway and aimed toward his office door, and his car parked in the parking lot in an obscure corner, but close to the entrance and facing in the right direction, ready to follow C.J. Watson out of the lot.

It was eight p.m. The building held a fitness center, so it was still busy, cars in and out of the lot, guys in grubby sweats, women in matching workout clothes, all coming and going.

Stan sat low in his seat in the darkened part of the lot. He wouldn't be noticed. He had his thermos of coffee, a bag of chips, and patience. He had plenty of patience. He had been a detective on the force long enough to have suffered through plenty of stake-outs. Boredom was the big word. He allowed his thoughts to wander, trying to imagine what C.J. Watson would look like. Not that there was any possibility of that being a real name. That had been another fruitless pursuit, as he had known it would be.

Harry was snoozing in the backseat. Stan had almost left him home; this could go on for a long time. But Harry hadn't liked that idea, and the dog would warn him if somebody was sneaking up on him.

At ten-thirty there was a mass exodus of the fitness people, calling out their goodbyes to each other. But even after they all left, there were still three cars in the parking lot. Stan figured that C.J. would probably wait until later, more toward the empty hours of the night. He poured more coffee, ate some chips, and waited. Harry raised his head to watch the gym people, but immediately went back to sleep.

A short while later the maintenance man came by and locked the door. So how would C.J. get in? But then, how had he ever gotten in before? Picked the lock, probably.

Finally, at twelve-thirty a man came out of the building. He walked toward one of the cars. Was this C.J.? Had he been in there the whole time? Just waiting? Stan had presumed that he'd come and go fast. He contemplated not following this guy; waiting some more, but what if this was C.J.? Already, the man had started the car and was pulling out of the lot. Stan tried to see the license plate, but it was too dark and the car was angled wrong. He'd follow, just for a few blocks, catch up right behind, and get his lights on the license.

Harry wasn't paying any attention, sound asleep on the backseat.

Stan waited a minute before pulling out of the lot, but in time to see which way the car turned. He followed, at first keeping a distance between them. When the car pulled onto a busier street, Stan caught up close enough to catch the plate. He wrote it down and turned a corner and retraced his drive. This wasn't the guy. He'd check out the license, but somehow he knew that this wasn't the guy.

There were still two cars in the lot, but they were the same ones he had seen earlier. Sometimes people parked there when they went away, vacation or business, especially if they only had street parking at home.

He waited some more, dozed off several times, not completely, but those little head catches as his chin reached his chest.

At about four a.m. he admitted to himself that he had played this whole thing wrong. He should have stayed in his office and put a sound-catching device out in the hall. Oh well, he could do that next time.

Stan's every instinct told him that he had missed C.J. Maybe C.J. had gone in and out with the fitness people; maybe he parked someplace else, walked a block or two, and went in the front door.

Stan got out of the car and used his key to get into the building. He'd see if there was an envelope and look at the video surveillance. At least he had that.

The hallway was dark. He opened his door and turned on a light. There was an envelope there, but it wasn't thick like before. He picked it up and opened it. There was a piece of paper on which was printed in bold letters: **DON'T EVER PLAY GAMES WITH ME AGAIN.**

Stan glanced out into the hallway. The camera—his very expensive camera—was gone.

20

Another body? This couldn't be happening. Years of no serious crime and suddenly three bodies in just a few days? Something very weird was going on around here.

Josh Winters looked down at what remained of Slim Carry, packed in ice in the outside freezer chest at Floyd's Marina, along with some bags of fish. This time, Josh felt sick.

Slim was just a kid, a nice kid; everyone liked him. All he ever wanted to do was join the Army, couldn't wait for his eighteenth birthday to join up. And for all the right reasons—service to his country, all that idealistic stuff. In the meantime, Slim had joined the militia. At first he had loved it, but not lately. Everybody knew that since Hank Crowell took over, Slim had been upset.

And what was Tico Zane going to say or do about this? He had taken Slim in and practically raised him. Slim's mother had slipped more and more into her world of drugs and depression since her husband left her. She'd spent more and more time in the state psychiatric hospital.

Josh looked around at the men standing next to him, Doc Purdy and Leroy, some curious onlookers, people he thought he knew. But one of these individuals could be the murderer; anyone in town could be the murderer. He didn't feel like he could trust anyone anymore. They were all suspects until proven otherwise. Maybe he needed some help here. The county sheriff wasn't interested, but maybe he should contact the state police.

Slim had been shot in the back and in the head, which seemed like overkill. Did that represent anger or just making sure? Making sure would make sense. You didn't fool around with Slim. He was a skinny little guy, but he was tough, best known for having beaten up a boy twice his size who Slim felt was disrespectful to a girl, a girl whom Slim had hardly known. Nobody had ever wanted to mess with Slim. Until now.

"He's what? Sixteen, seventeen? This has gone way too far," said Doc. "Bert Floyd, I could understand. But what's with the innocents? Lillian and Slim? What's that all about?"

Josh only shrugged.

Just then Mayor Cummings broke through the crowd. "What's this I hear? Slim Carry? What's happening around here?" He put an arm around Josh's shoulder, a comrade-in-arms sort of gesture. "First my wife, now this kid?"

"Wish I knew," Josh answered.

"Well, this is three murders in a week, Josh, including my wife. What are you going to do about it?"

Josh wasn't looking at him, but he could hear the strain in the mayor's voice. He wished he had some answers.

Max Cummings made him angry much of the time, like when he insisted that Josh hire Leroy. But he was just trying to do a good deed. Surprising how often one person's good deed imposed on another person. Not that Josh had given up on Leroy yet. The kid's big problem was that his opinion of himself was just running so far ahead of his skills. That didn't bother the mayor, though.

"Leroy needs some self-confidence," Max had said often enough. "That's what we're trying to do here. And it's working."

"Maybe too well," thought Josh, as he watched Leroy tell the mayor his opinion on what had happened.

"They can take him away," Doc Purdy said. "I'm finished here. How about a cup of coffee at Dee's, Josh?"

The doctor was looking at him in a way that made Josh accept quickly. Doc Purdy wanted to tell Josh something that he didn't want the others to hear.

Max Cummings seemed to get it too. He looked at both of them, back and forth. Josh was afraid he would invite himself along. And he might have, if Leroy hadn't been demanding his attention to such a high degree.

"I'll finish up here and follow you," Josh told the doctor.

It was another half hour before Josh walked into the diner. Doc was sitting in the last booth in the corner. It was after the main rush of dinner; there were only a few stragglers.

As Josh sat down, Doc waved over the waitress.

Once again, it was Beth. She had the coffee pot in her hand, as well as a cup for Josh.

"Anything else?" she asked.

Josh was hungry. He ordered a piece of pie.

"Apple, again?" Beth asked.

"You know it. Nothing like Dee's apple pie," Josh said. The doctor gave him another one of his looks, over his glasses.

"I didn't have time to finish dinner," Josh protested.

"Pie is not dinner. You had your cholesterol checked lately?"

"Don't doctor me. Tell me what's on your mind."

"This was just a kid, Josh. A kid, still in school, wasn't he?"

"Yeah, he was a senior," said Josh. "He'll never join the Army now."

"This can't go on. These killings can't go on. If it's the militia, you've got to close them down. It *is* the militia, don't you think?" asked Doc.

"That wouldn't explain Lillian Cummings," said Josh. "And the mayor is pretty upset about that."

"Well, everything doesn't have to be related, does it?"

Beth delivered the pie and then started clearing the next table. They looked at her and waited until she had finished, which only made her more curious. She moved several tables away. She could still hear.

"Any idea of when Slim was killed?" asked Josh.

"It's going to be hard to tell, with him being put on ice like that. But the state lab may give us some answers."

Beth was now picking up dirty plates, trying to do it quietly so she wouldn't be noticed. She remembered Slim from the motel. He was the reason she was here. He had suggested she go back into town to breakfast, to Dee's diner. He had been nice that first morning, when she was feeling so scared and alone. She wondered how Tico was going to take this. She would hate to have *that* big guy mad at her.

Would they blame Holt for this too? Why did the body

have to be found at the marina? Maybe Slim had been killed before Holt even got back in town. No, that didn't work. She had seen Slim in the morning. She had met Holt that night. But if Slim had been a senior, that meant Holt knew him, too. Another connection. More dots for Leroy Conner to join together to blame Holt.

Her tub of dirty dishes was full. She should take it back into the kitchen. But she hesitated, fiddling, rearranging the plates for more balance. She hated to miss anything.

"Think we've got a serial killer in our midst?" Doc asked the chief.

"I can't even imagine that here in Beaumont," said Josh. "I know, I know," he held up his hand to stop an interruption. "These things can happen anywhere."

"Bound to be that militia, except for Lillian," Doc said. "Those guys are fighting among themselves. Real fundamental disagreements." Doc stopped, sighed, then said, "You know, I had a crush on Lillian when we were kids. She was a nice girl. Way too rich and prominent for me, but I could still be smitten, even from my other side of the tracks." The doctor had a dreamy look in his eyes.

"That's why you never married?" Josh asked with a teasing smile. "You carried a torch all these years?"

"Life is never simple. Complexities my boy, complexities," said the doctor. "And you can't be such an advocate for marriage. Yours didn't turn out very well."

"I got Samantha. I'd call that a plus."

"Even now she's a teenager?"

"Well, things have been a bit hairy lately. She missed Holt this summer and now she's really mad at me because Leroy has zoned in on the kid as a suspect. And time-wise, he's got no alibi, and he made no secret of not getting along with his father."

"Shows the boy has good sense. How could he get along with his father with what Bert was doing to his mother?" Doc said with a sigh of disgust. "And Holt wouldn't have had anything to do with Lillian or Slim."

"I don't think the kid had anything to do with any of it," said Josh. "I've always liked the boy. He was good for Sam when she was dating him. I trusted him a lot more than I did some of those other kids."

This was very interesting to Beth. She came and poured them more coffee, hoping to hear more. But they stopped talking and waited for her to leave. Once again, she didn't go far.

"Thought any about Harvey, the guy at the marina?

He'd have more access to the freezer than Holt," said Doc. "And Bert didn't treat him very well."

"Anyone would have access to that outside freezer," said Josh. "I don't think it was ever locked—there was never anything in it except leftover fish. And it's open all night when nobody's around. And Harvey's a good guy. Patient. Put up with Bert. Didn't let Bert bother him. I could take some lessons from Harvey. You, too. And he was really shook-up when he found the body. Really."

"I take lessons from no man," said the doctor with a smile. "Well, I guess I'll leave you to work it all out." He started getting up, feeling in his pocket for his wallet.

"I'll take care of this. Your sage advice is worth the price of a cup of coffee. Not more than that, understand. And any ideas you might have, feel free. I sure could use some help here."

Beth hurriedly carried her dirty dishes into the kitchen. She didn't want them to see how close she had been standing. She hurried again to get behind the register.

She was in plenty of time. They were still standing and shaking hands. The doctor left and the chief came to pay the bill.

"So," Josh said, making conversation as he took out his

money. "Does my daughter show you around again tomorrow?"

"For a week, I'm told," Beth answered.

"I have to tell you I'm surprised. That sort of thing, it doesn't sound like Sam."

"I think it's because she thought there was something going on with Holt and me. There isn't."

The chief looked at her, studying her. A very different kind of pretty, but pretty just the same. As pretty as his daughter? He was a father and prejudiced. But there was sure something about her that he would imagine would appeal to a young boy, would appeal to any male. She was no—what did Sam call it—*fashionista?* She wasn't trendy. She was natural, unadorned. There was something both very old and very young about her. She was... different, and that made her interesting, more interesting than the average teenager, because she wasn't like the average teenager. He could see what Leroy found so fascinating about her. He would definitely not discourage Leroy's searches.

21

The next morning, when Beth approached Holt's car for their drive to school, he stopped her.

"Is it okay if you drive yourself to school?" he asked.

Her stomach gave a lurch. He probably wanted to be with Samantha, but that was the way it was supposed to be, she reminded herself.

"Sure," she answered.

"I'm going out for football again. The coach called me last night. Coach Scully is such a great guy. I mean, he could lose his job over this, with the principal's attitude. But he actually believes in the innocent-until-proven-guilty thing. And he knows I didn't do anything like that. He said it would be okay, even if I didn't do any practices yet." He looked like he was trying to underplay his excitement. It wasn't working. "So I wouldn't be able to drive you home."

"That's great. I would really love to see you play," said Beth, feeling better about the ride. It wasn't about Samantha, it was about football.

"Several of my friends called last night, too. They're not buying it anymore, especially after they heard what the coach said. Oh, and another thing, I was going to mention it before. I noticed you don't have a computer. You can use mine anytime. Feel free."

Beth didn't answer immediately. She had never used a computer in her life. Why would she need to use his?

"For your school papers and research and stuff," he said, when she didn't answer.

"Oh. Yes. That's very nice of you." She didn't even know how to turn on a computer. But would that mean she could spend more time with him? No, she wasn't supposed to be thinking like that.

"I'm sorry about going off so much on the way home yesterday. But I was really low."

"I'm just glad things are working out like they should," said Beth. She loved the fact that his whole posture had changed from yesterday. He was standing tall again.

She followed behind him to school, although she didn't really need to; she was getting to know her way around. She was determined that she would never become lost again.

Samantha was waiting for her outside of Miss Jensen's office.

"I'm really going to pay attention today," Beth told her. "Yesterday was so confusing that I didn't get any directional sense at all."

"It's easy, but it does take a while. I remember my first few crazy days as a freshman," Samantha told her.

Today, Beth was also going to make an effort to act like a normal teenager going to a normal school. She had paid a lot of attention yesterday to what people around her were saying and doing, studying their gestures, their facial expressions, the words they used. *Conversation. Constant conversation.* That's what went on.

"Holt says he's going out for football again. He can't drive me to school anymore," Beth said to Samantha, making conversation.

"He is? He can't?" This information was obviously pleasing to Samantha.

"I guess he was pretty good, when he played before," Beth ventured.

"He was spectacular," said Samantha. Then she paused. "So how did you get to school? Take the bus?" This was said with obvious disapproval.

"I have a car," said Beth.

"You do? *Your own car?*" She looked at Beth again, a quick up-and-down reassessment.

"Yeah, I have to have it. I'm pretty much on my own."

"Wow, would I ever like that," said Samantha. "My dad sees way too many traffic accidents with kids. I hardly ever get to drive our car. You have no idea of how difficult it is to be the daughter of the police chief. I'm supposed to follow all the rules. I mean, according to my father, everything I do reflects on him. So I'm supposed to be Saint Sam. That sounds like fun, doesn't it?"

Beth gave the necessary laugh. They had reached homeroom and this time found seats in the back.

"Mr. Glazier will have a seating chart all too soon," said Samantha. "He never learns our names. You can sit in the wrong seat forever and he will never notice the difference, unless you try to sit in a boy's seat. He can recognize the difference between the sexes. Of course, that means you get handed the wrong papers all the time, which can be embarrassing. But everybody does it anyway."

"Why?"

"Because we can," said Samantha, as though that was perfectly obvious. "Because seating charts are ridiculous."

Several things were starting to sink in for Beth. There was an us-against-them attitude between some of the kids and their teachers. What Beth couldn't figure out was why. It was like it wasn't cool to listen or appear interested, even if it was interesting. The kids hovered a notch above outright rudeness. It made Beth fear for them, shrink back in her seat, expecting instant repercussions. But they seemed to get away with it.

Samantha sat with her at lunch again. And when Holt came over and joined them halfway through, Samantha lit up like a Christmas tree.

Again, Beth could sense that Samantha was trying too hard. But what did Beth know? She understood what dating was, knew about going to movies and having a hamburger. But the little she had gleaned from sparse moments of TV viewing didn't really tell her anything. C.J. hadn't approved of teen entertainment; The TV was quickly turned off. She had only been allowed to watch educational programs under supervision. Not that she hadn't turned on the TV when she was left alone. But she never knew when C.J. would be back and, often, C.J. would feel the TV to see if it was warm. If caught, that meant that C.J. would lock her in the closet when she was left alone. It could be months before she was given another chance.

So when Beth cheated and watched something, it was a nerve-wracking experience with waiting-for-the-door-to-open apprehension. She was going to enjoy watching TV in her own room with nothing to fear. She smiled just thinking about it.

Samantha was gushing about seeing Holt play football again. Beth could see it made him uncomfortable. The guy just wanted to play. He didn't want his father making a fool of himself on the stands, and he didn't want a girl going all to pieces about it. Couldn't Samantha see that? He didn't want the hero worship; he just wanted to play.

But Beth couldn't say what she thought, not to Holt and not to Samantha She tried to back out of any conversation and leave it to them. But Holt kept including her.

"You liking your classes?" he asked her.

"I guess. They're all assigning a lot of homework today."

"They do that," said Samantha with authority. "Second-day scare tactics."

"You think?" asked Holt.

This was a good time to leave. Beth got up, saying she

was going to get a soda.

"You mean a pop?" asked Samantha, with a little laugh and a look at Holt.

Okay, she got it. That's what they called soda around here. What difference did it make? They knew what she meant.

Holt didn't look at Samantha; he was watching Beth.

When she got back, Holt was gone and Samantha was looking at her like it was her fault.

This whole thing, trying not to interfere between Holt and Samantha and having Samantha mad at her anyway—it was getting very tiring.

"What did your father tell you about Slim Carry getting killed?" Beth asked Samantha after she sat back down. Change the subject. Make conversation.

"Slim Carry? Yeah, I heard that he was killed. He's that skinny guy who wears fatigues, one of that militia bunch. But I didn't hear it from my dad, he never tells me anything. Besides, he thought I was asleep when he got home. What happened?"

"It was another murder."

"Come on, another one? We're becoming murder city around here. And how would you know who Slim Carry was, anyway?"

"I was staying out at that motel that the big man, Tico Zane, owns."

"You've got to be kidding." Samantha looked at her like she had suddenly grown a second head. "That dump? Why would you stay out there?" Her lip curled up with distaste. "Don't you have any sense at all?"

"I was tired. I needed to stop." Then Beth remembered her story—the lie. "I was totally lost," she added. "I didn't realize I was so close to Beaumont and stopped for the night. The next morning Slim directed me into town."

The bell rang before Samantha could ask any more questions, and they both got up, got rid of their trays, and Beth didn't have to say any more about her night at Tico's motel. But she knew that she had fallen yet another step down in Samantha's estimation. She wished she actually understood the criteria on which she was being judged.

When the day was over and Beth walked to the parking lot to get her car, she glanced over to the field where the football team was practicing. She stopped and watched for a minute. It looked like a crazy jumble to her, everyone knocking into each other, some boys practicing kicking, some throwing a ball.

She'd better learn something about it before she saw a game, or she'd make a fool of herself. Dee would know. She'd ask Dee.

The day had exhausted Beth; she was already tired when she showed up for work, and she had all that homework to do after they closed for the night. This wasn't going to be easy. How was she possibly going to manage everything? Maybe school wasn't an option after all. But if she quit now, would she have to leave town? Didn't you have to go to school until a certain age? She had her name in the system. Was it illegal for her to quit? She'd ask Dee about that, too.

She pulled up into the rear parking space behind the café and got out of the car. Leroy Conner was standing by the back door, standing so that he was blocking it.

"Hello, Beth Waterman," he said, making his voice unnaturally deep.

"Hello, Officer. What can I do for you?" She didn't like him or have much respect for him after Holt told her he had been friends with those terrible boys who had stopped her car.

"You're a busy little girl these days," Leroy said, "working and going to school. Did you do that before? Where you came from? What kind of a restaurant did you work in there?"

"I've never been a waitress before," Beth told him. She made a motion toward the door, but he reasserted himself in the middle of the doorway, making it impossible for her to go around him.

"Exactly where was that—where you came from?" he asked.

"Philadelphia," She answered.

"What part of Philadelphia? It's a big city. It has all sorts of sections, doesn't it?"

"Look, I'd love to talk to you, but I'm late for work here."

"I'm afraid you have to answer my questions. I am a police officer, you know."

The pompous way he said it almost made her laugh. Except he was still the police and she was still running away and couldn't afford to be caught.

"Let me go in. I'll answer your questions while I get started. I need to get some set-ups ready." She was thinking that she could use some help from Dee right about now.

He reluctantly opened the door for her and followed her through the kitchen.

"Hi, Dee," she called.

Dee was standing at the chopping block, slicing tomatoes. She turned and looked, said a quick hello to Beth, then watched Leroy as he followed her through the kitchen.

"What do you want, Leroy? That door is for employees only," said Dee.

"I'm just conducting my business here. I have a few questions for Ms. Waterman."

It was Dee who burst out laughing. "Oh, Leroy, you're priceless," she said.

His pale skin showed an instant blush. He was obviously aware of it, and it made him angry.

"I thought you had to get busy right away," he said to Beth.

She grabbed some silverware out of the dishwasher and started filling the bins that she would use later.

"What is it you want to know?" Beth asked, making sure Dee was still standing and listening.

"Where did you live? What was your address? What are the names of your parents? What is your birth date?"

"Whoa, there," Dee interrupted. "Just what's going on here?"

"I have a job to do," Leroy insisted.

215

Dee came to stand beside Beth. She put her substantial arm around Beth's shoulders. "This is my cousin, and you are harassing her. She's a citizen. This isn't some dictatorship. You have no reason to be asking her these questions. And she's underage and shouldn't be questioned without me there. What on earth are you thinking?"

"I'm conducting a murder investigation," he said.

"What's Beth got to do with that?"

Now Leroy looked uncomfortable. He shifted his weight and hitched up his belt.

"There's a customer out there who probably wants a coffee refill. Would you see to him, Beth?" Dee said. "Now, Leroy, let me tell you a couple of things..."

That was all that Beth heard as she went out into the restaurant.

When she had taken care of the customer and returned to the kitchen, Leroy was gone.

"Thanks, Dee. He is really annoying," said Beth. She loved that word, *annoying*. Everyone at school used it often. She liked the way it sounded. Her plan was to add one new slang word a day. She'd be sounding like the rest of them in no time. *Normal.*

"Don't worry about Leroy," Dee said. "I'm going to talk to Josh and get him off your back."

"Holt is going out for the football team again. How can I learn about it? I don't know anything about football and I'm going to make a fool of myself at the first game."

"No, you won't, you cheer when everyone on your side of the field cheers. I'll tell you a bit about it, but you certainly don't need to know the ins and outs. You've never seen a game, not even on TV?"

"No, never."

Dee gave her that look again, the one that was equal parts sympathy and wonder.

"How old do you have to be to quit school?" Beth asked.

"Sixteen. You thinking of quitting after two days?"

"I love it. But I'm not sure there are enough hours in the day to get all the homework done."

"I've been worried about that myself. I'm looking for some more help so you won't have to put in so many hours. And there's down time between now and dinner. You get the tables ready and then take your books over in the corner and do your homework. You'll be able to get a hunk of it done before the supper crowd comes in. And you can work between customers, too."

"That wouldn't look very professional, would it?"

"That's the best part of being my own boss. I decide what's professional," Dee said, smiling.

It had seemed overwhelming when the teachers were assigning the work, but Beth managed, before the diner got too busy, to get most of it done.

It was at the height of the supper crowd when the café door opened with a crash. Everyone looked up. Tico stood there, glaring around the room as though he wanted to kill someone. His fists were clenched; his face wore a fearsome scowl.

Beth could see people shrink back in their seats.

"Dee," he shouted. All conversation stopped. His voice echoed around the room.

Dee came running out of the kitchen as if the room were on fire.

"What the..." she exclaimed.

"Who did it?" he shouted. "Who killed Slim?"

"Well, it wasn't me," Dee shouted back. She walked up

to him, took his arm, and led him to a booth in the back corner.

"Get this man some coffee," Dee told Beth.

When Beth brought the coffee, Tico had calmed down. And maybe that was worse. He looked like he was about to cry. Beth set the cup gently on the table before him and walked away, but not so far away that she couldn't hear. The room was still relatively silent. It wasn't that everyone was still staring— only those who faced the booth he was in. The others were listening, just as Beth was. But Dee kept her voice low, and the customers weren't going to be able to hear very much.

"How could anyone do that to Slim?" Tico asked.

"Don't you worry. Josh will find out. He'll get to the bottom of things."

Tico didn't look convinced.

"What's he know about anything, anyway? He's a small-town cop. He doesn't know how to deal with something like this."

"He's got good sense," Dee answered.

"It's that militia. It's Hank Crowell. He's crazy and he's making the rest of them crazy. Slim didn't like him. Kept going up against him. Nobody else had the nerve."

"Did Bert Floyd go up against him too?" asked Dee.

"Don't know about that. They were two of a kind. Both of them were surly mean. Both of them disagreed with everyone about everything. But what am I going to do without Slim around? He was such a good kid. He never had much of a life. It isn't fair."

Dee reached over and patted his arm. "I know," she said. "I know."

"I gotta get out of here." Tico pushed his coffee away.

"You can go upstairs to my apartment and lie down and rest," Dee told him.

"No. I gotta find Chief Winters. I tried before, but he was out. I'll try again."

"He's doing all he can, Tico. He doesn't have anything to tell you at this point."

"No. It's what I'm going to tell him. Whoever did this... I want him. Just for a little while, I want him."

"You know that's not going to happen," said Dee.

"It is, Dee. It's going to happen." He got up and left.

There were only a couple of people still dawdling over their coffee when Chief Winters came in around closing time.

He ordered his usual coffee and apple pie. Beth

wondered if Tico had found him, and then she wondered why he wasn't home with Samantha. What did Samantha do by herself, alone so much of the time? Or was she with Holt?

Because the place was so empty, Beth had time to pay attention when Dee came marching out of the kitchen to sit down opposite the chief. Beth was back at her corner table, with her books, and couldn't really be seen. But she could hear them.

"Tico find you?" Dee asked.

"No. Haven't seen him. I can imagine how upset he must be."

"Threatening to do in whoever did it," said Dee. "And he will if he gets ahold of him. But I've got another bone to pick with you. Get that pesky cop of yours out of Beth's hair." Dee's arms were folded on the table, and her face was thrust toward Josh.

He jerked backward from her, except his head was already resting on the seat back.

"He's just trying to do his job," Josh said defensively.

"His job is not harassing a young girl, especially one I'm responsible for. You mess with her, you're messing with me."

221

Beth smiled to herself. To be defended like that, to have someone on her side to that degree—it was amazing. Meeting up with Dee Carter was the best thing that had ever happened to her.

"I admit to being puzzled by the girl, myself," said Josh. "She comes out of nowhere? You suddenly have relatives nobody ever heard of?"

"You think you know all my business? I told you before, there is a lot about me that you don't know, and neither does anyone else in this town," said Dee. "I have always kept myself to myself." She could fill her voice with a great deal of authority without raising the volume even a notch. "And how on God's green earth are you trying to lump her in with these murders?"

"Oh, I don't think that for a minute," said Josh. "I don't think Leroy does either. Actually, I think he's interested in her in a much more ordinary way. She's a pretty little thing."

That statement made Dee pause for a minute.

"Well, then, he can't come on like Joe Law. He can't use his position to intimidate the girl. You can't allow that," said Dee.

"I'm still curious," said Josh.

"Don't be. And what about these murders, anyway? You still harassing Holt Floyd? You know he couldn't kill anyone."

"We're not harassing anyone—we're investigating."

"What do you even know about investigating?" She had taken her arms off the table and now leaned back in her seat.

"I'm trying here, Dee. Give me a break. If it's your aim to make me feel inadequate in this current situation, don't bother, I'm doing a good job of that myself." He took a last sip of coffee. He had already finished his pie.

"You want more of that?" Dee pointed to his cup.

"No, I'm good. I need to get back. Sam went out with some friends, but she's due back about now—school night and all."

"You're a good man, Josh. I shouldn't be picking on you. But both Beth and Holt are good kids. They both need to be let alone. And I'm worried about Holt. That boy had every reason to hate his father. But he's got a conscience, and I bet you anything he's feeling some guilt about that right about now. They're both kids, just like Sam. Just remember that."

Josh looked at her thoughtfully. He nodded. "Yes, I know." He laid down some bills and walked out.

22

It had been a busy day and a busy night at the café. Beth couldn't wait to climb up the stairs and get her head on her pillow. She was too tired to watch TV, just as she had been the previous night. Was she ever going to get a chance to just veg in front of it? *Veg*, wasn't that a great word? She so loved using these new words, even silently to herself. Especially since C.J. would have hated them so much. She was becoming someone else. She could feel it. There was a transformation taking place, and it delighted her. Not that the morsel of fear wasn't still down there—it was ingrained. But she wasn't buying into it anymore; she wasn't paying attention to it. She felt herself relaxing like she never had before. Some chains had been cast off. She wasn't peering at the door, dreading it opening.

So it was, perhaps, ironic for her to hear the slight noise in the bushes. She was halfway up the stairs. She looked down and couldn't see anything. Molly still hadn't changed the dead light bulb in the back yard. It was very dark.

Beth stopped, listened. She didn't hear it again. Some animal, probably. She wasn't used to living in the country with raccoons, skunks, and other small animals.

But when she got up to the apartment, she made sure to put the latch on the door; before she got undressed and into her nightshirt, she made sure the curtains were tightly closed. Maybe she wasn't as relaxed as she thought, if a little animal could give her the creeps like this.

She got into bed and turned out the light. She hadn't heard anything else. It wasn't that. She didn't know why she got back up and pulled the curtain back open just a sliver. She stood watching the dark woods, although she couldn't see anything.

And then there was something. It was slight, but there was movement of some kind. More, she thought, than a small animal would make. She stood still, barely breathing.

It was moving around toward the back of the garage, the leaves of the bushes swaying just enough to show the path.

It could be a dog or something; certainly something bigger than a raccoon.

Beth dropped the curtain and moved to the other side of the apartment, where the bathroom window was. It was high, and she had to turn over the metal wastebasket and stand on it to see out. The wastebasket wasn't very strong or very steady. She hoped she wouldn't break it.

At first she didn't see any more movement. The night was still, except for the crickets.

Suddenly, a figure stood straight up. Beth jerked and fell off the wastebasket. It clattered on the floor, a loud din of metal against tile.

By the time she had picked up the basket and climbed back on it, there was no one in sight. The night was dark, and with the trees so close to the garage, she wouldn't have been able to see more than just a few feet.

But someone had been there. She had seen something. *Someone.*

Why would anyone be sneaking around like that? The first thing Beth thought was that C.J. had found her. But C.J. would come straight for her. C.J. wouldn't be messing around in the woods. She was sure of that.

Beth tried to picture what she had seen. How tall a person? How broad? But it had only been an instant. She couldn't recall any details.

She wished she had a phone and could call over to

Molly's house. Maybe she should save up for that next. There was a phone jack on the wall, but if she got a phone, it would have to be a cell phone. Everyone at school had them. It would be another thing to make her look normal. Even if she had no one to call—yet.

Her exhaustion had left her. She closed the curtain, turned on the light, and watched TV. Just the sound of voices helped. It wasn't long before she became sleepy again. Three times that night, she got up and looked out the window. C.J. always said she couldn't hide, that she would always be found, that everyone left footprints. Had it happened already? Her car was parked in the driveway. That, in itself, was like an announcement.

The night seemed endless.

At school the next day, Beth made a new friend. Her name was Sidney Lee, and it turned out that she was in all of Beth's AP classes. She was small and slight, with the beautiful straight, black hair bequeathed to her by her Asian ancestry.

"You are good friends with Samantha Winters?" Sidney asked her in history. She had a soft voice and shyly bent her head down when she asked the question.

227

"She's about the only person I know in this school. And I can't say I know her very well," Beth told her. The teacher was late coming into the room, and they had a few minutes to talk.

"I see you walking from class to class with her. She's very pretty and popular, too."

"She's showing me around school. They do that for new kids."

Sidney nodded. "I like Mrs. Herman, don't you?" And they talked about their history assignment.

The teacher came in and class started, but since they were sitting in the back, they were able to have whispered bits of conversation throughout the period.

When the bell rang, it became a little awkward. Beth and Sidney walked out of class together. Their next class was together, too. So Beth felt it was rude not to walk with her. But she was supposed to wait for Samantha.

"Stay here with me, so I can tell Samantha I can get to my next class," Beth told Sidney.

"That's all right, I can see you later."

Just then Samantha came running down the hall, sliding to a stop.

Kids, Beth had noticed, didn't seem to do introductions to other kids. So how was she supposed to handle this?

"Hi," Sidney said shyly. "Beth and I have the next class together, so I can show her the way."

"Great," said Samantha.

"And the one after that, too," offered Sidney.

"Okay," said Samantha. She seemed relieved, if anything. "I'll see you at lunch, then," she said to Beth. "I've been thinking you pretty much know your way around now." She dashed off as quickly as she had come.

It was nice to have somebody to talk to before and after class started. And Beth did pretty much know her way around now.

At lunch time, Sidney and Beth walked to the cafeteria together. Beth grabbed her usual salad, and Sidney got a sandwich. When Beth rejoined her and headed for her customary table, Sidney stopped.

"Why don't you join us?" Beth asked. "Unless you planned to have lunch with somebody else."

"It's not that," said Sidney. "It's... well... you really need to be invited."

"I'm inviting you," said Beth and started to walk again.

229

"Well," said Sidney. "You're not the one to do the inviting."

Beth stopped and turned.

"What do you mean?" She was truly puzzled.

"I can't even explain it, but I know if I sat down at that table, it could be embarrassing."

"Oh, this is silly. Wait here, I'll be right back." Beth went over to the table and put her tray down and looked over the room, trying to spot Samantha.

She saw Samantha coming in the door and walked over to her. "I asked Sidney to eat with us. That's all right, isn't it?"

Samantha looked over at Sidney standing in the middle of the room, holding her tray and looking very conspicuous.

"Sure," she said. "Actually, you eat with her. This would be a good time to re-establish myself with the Queens." And she walked over to the crowded table where she had gone with Lindsey that first day.

Beth and Sidney had the table to themselves. It turned out that Sidney had only been in Beaumont for a couple of years.

"It's not an easy place to get accepted," Sidney said. "These kids have known each other forever. I mean, they're friendly enough, but only up to a point."

Just then, Holt approached the table and plunked his tray down.

"I know you," he said to Sidney. "You played the violin at the show last year. You were awesome." He turned to Beth. "She had the whole audience standing up after she finished."

Sidney looked down with a shy smile.

Beth couldn't help herself. She looked across the room to the crowded table and, sure enough, Samantha was looking right back at her. Samantha wasn't happy.

Beth gave an exaggerated shrug to her shoulders. It wasn't her fault Holt had joined them.

Holt had Sidney talking, asking her how long she had played the violin and how many hours she practiced.

Denise stopped at the table just then, balancing another full tray. "Your guide left you alone at lunch again, I see. It's was supposed to be for a week." She apparently blamed Beth for this and walked away in disgust.

Ten minutes later, Samantha sat down at the table. She must have finished her lunch; she only held a cup in her hand. She barely looked at Beth.

"How's the football coming, Holt?" she asked. She

smiled her bright smile. She did have the whitest teeth Beth had ever seen.

He mumbled something that was hard to understand, then said, "You know Sidney, don't you, Sam? She's the one who played that amazing violin last year."

Samantha briefly turned her smile to Sidney. "Yes, I remember. Amazing."

"Your dad and his mini-cop haven't called me in for a couple of days. Did they finally decide I'm not a mass murderer?"

"Is that what you're upset with me about?" Samantha asked. "I have no control over what my dad does. And I certainly don't pull the strings with that stupid Leroy. But I know perfectly well that my dad doesn't think you had anything to do with any of that. How could he?" She flung her hair back in a practiced gesture.

Holt just looked at her. The little flare-up of anger was over quickly. She smiled again. "Is that why you didn't call me when you got back in town?"

Holt didn't answer immediately, and Beth felt very awkward sitting there, listening to this. Sidney must have felt the same way.

"I think I'll go refill my cup," Sidney said and got up.

"Me, too," said Beth, although she barely touched her drink.

"They were quite an item last year," said Sidney when they were out of earshot. "They made a great-looking couple."

Beth turned and looked back at them.

"They still do," she said sadly.

23

That afternoon, when Beth approached her car, Tony Grimes was leaning against the driver's door. *How did he find her car? Why was he bothering her again?* She looked around for help.

"Excuse me," Beth said. "This is my car, and I need to get going."

"Why?" he asked, not moving.

"I'll be late for work. Please move." She was tired of people barring her way. First Leroy the other day, and now this jerk. Both were dangerous, too.

"So where do you work?" he asked. His voice was gentle, he had a half-smile on his face. Nothing threatening, but Beth wanted no dealings with him. He had threatened her before, had grabbed her arm. Had pulled her out of her car on a dark road.

"Move, or I'll call a teacher."

"I'm quaking. But I'm not here to upset you." He moved a foot away from the door. "My name's Tony Grimes.

You're Beth Waterman. Now we're introduced. Isn't that nice?" he said, with that same half-smile that Beth didn't trust. "You know, nothing bad was going to happen the other night. I wouldn't have let it. But I do apologize for my friends. They can be a bit stupid when they've had a couple of beers. I'm sorry if they frightened you."

"Okay, you're sorry. Now I've got to go."

Tony put up his hands, as if in defeat, and backed away. He watched her pull out of the parking lot.

On her drive into town, Beth couldn't help but go over the brief conversation. There wasn't any menace in it. On this bright and sunny afternoon, it seemed harmless. But that night he had scared her—so had the other boys. She didn't like being scared.

Beth thought again about the figure she had seen outside her window the night before. Could it have been Tony Grimes? What did he want with her?

But she wanted to forget about that. It was probably just someone walking in the woods. Maybe someone who had tripped or something and then got up. She wasn't going to keep thinking that bad things could be happening to her.

When she got to work, Dee told her that the diner was

going to be closed on Mondays from now through the winter.

"We'll see a definite slowdown from here on in," she told Beth.

More time for homework and TV, but not as much money. Was everything always such a juggling act? Beth didn't know if she felt relief or not. She had found that she liked being in the diner, liked talking to all the people, listening to their conversations. She was learning so much about people, both the good and the bad. Sometimes the gossip disturbed her, the willingness to believe anything that was said and to pass it on. But there were wonderful conversations, too. People concerned about each other, willing to help and not take credit for that help.

And, of course, Beth loved picking up more expressions. The adults had as many odd sayings as the kids. At least to her they were odd, and the café was a good place to try them out. When she didn't get a puzzled reaction, it was like she had just passed some sort of test, that normalcy she kept striving for.

Beth tried very hard to put the figure she had seen last night out of her mind. But still, she made sure she locked herself in that night when she went back to her apartment. And twice that evening, she turned out the lights and stood at the window, looking out. There was nothing. The previous night had just been something normal, non-threatening. She had been acting silly.

She didn't know what made her look one last time. She had turned out the light for good, had already pulled up the covers ready for sleep. Then she got back up and looked out the window.

Immediately, she saw movement. This time she was sure it was just an animal. She tried to think of all the nocturnal animals there were: mice, opossums, moles, badgers, raccoons, wolves. It was probably a raccoon.

She kept watching that one spot. Now it was perfectly still. She wasn't going to stand here watching all night. This was ridiculous.

But she had such an overwhelming feeling that C.J. would eventually find her. There was a part of her brain that told her it was inevitable. She knew where that came from: brainwashing. C.J. had been a master at it. Beth had never had a word for it before. But she had heard about brainwashing at school. Used casually, overheard briefly, and added to her mounting vocabulary as one more thing that filled in the gaps. The things she heard around her each and every day were putting words to what had only been sensations before. And she had to keep reminding herself that so much of what C.J. had told her simply wasn't true. C.J. had said she could never leave. *Well, she had, hadn't she?*

She had been staring at that one spot when, out of the corner of her eye, she saw something off to the right. The night was dark and cloudy; only occasionally would the moon peek out from behind the clouds. The trees were a shadowed mass, except for a brief second, a lightening. That's when she saw it: definitely a figure, dressed in dark clothes, almost camouflaged. She saw it only for an instant, and then the night became dark again. But she had been staring out the window for several minutes, and her eyes had adjusted to the dark. The figure was standing still. This was no harmless animal. This was someone watching her apartment.

Why? What were they waiting for?

Her heart began to pound. Maybe she had stayed here too long. What should she do? Tell Molly and Holt? She could run over to the house. But whoever was watching would hear her footsteps going down the stairs. Even without shoes, it would be impossible to be silent—the stairs creaked.

Beth looked around the apartment for some sort of protection, a weapon. But there was nothing. There were some knives in one of the drawers in the tiny kitchen, but she didn't want to get close enough to anyone to use anything like that. What she wanted was something like a baseball bat. But nobody had conveniently left anything like that around.

Even though she couldn't see him, not really, she somehow knew he was still there. She stared so long and so hard that her eyes stung.

If it were C.J., there wouldn't be this waiting, would there? C.J. was not known for patience. But C.J. could send someone—hire someone.

Since the stairs were so creaky, she would be able to hear anyone climbing up them. So that was an advantage. There wouldn't suddenly be the sound of tampering at the door.

The person had been here last night and had made no attempt to get in. Perhaps she was only being watched, observed, stalked. That was another word she had picked up. *Stalked.* She hadn't intended to experience it personally, only add the word to her list.

She saw movement again. Nobody could stay perfectly

still for an extended period of time. That made her aware that she probably wasn't staying perfectly still either. Did slight movement make her visible?

An hour later, exhaustion overtook her. She hadn't seen any more movement, or she was too tired to notice it. If whoever it was wanted to stay out there on the cold, damp ground and look up at her window, there wasn't anything she could do about it. She wasn't going to make the first move by running over to the house and giving him an opportunity to grab her. She went back to bed and once again pulled the covers up. She had to get some sleep. But she could probably never get to sleep, not with all this fear. That was the last thought she had before she drifted off.

When she awoke the next morning to the sound of the alarm clock, she realized the sun was up and she was still alive.

But wasn't that even more strange? Who was just watching her?

She had to talk to Holt. She didn't want to alarm Dee or Molly, but Holt wouldn't overreact. Maybe he'd even have a sensible explanation, although that was doubtful. There wasn't anything sensible about this whole thing. She was just hoping, again. But if she talked to Holt, how much could she explain?

She didn't want to mention C.J. She must never mention anything about where she came from.

Maybe it was Tony Grimes, and it was just because he was some kind of a nut-case. Another new word. There was so much about her life right now that she loved. Nothing bad could happen to spoil all this. She couldn't go back to how things were before.

When Beth got to school, Sidney was waiting for her, and they went into the building together. It made Beth feel like she belonged, joining the crowd, walking and talking, part of the flow through the big doors and down the halls.

Samantha still took her to homeroom and to her first class, and then basically turned Beth over to Sidney. Beth was convinced she actually didn't need a guide anymore. She knew her way to her classes, even if she hadn't figured out the rest of the building yet.

At lunch she and Sidney sat together, and Samantha didn't seem to be anywhere around. She wasn't sitting at the crowded table with the popular girls. Beth kept looking around for Holt. Not that she would have talked to him about the stalker in front of Sidney, but she could tell him she needed to talk later.

It never happened. She went to work and went back home. But this time she didn't go up to the apartment. She knocked at Molly's back door.

Molly answered the door. Her face lit up when she saw Beth.

"Come in, come in. I baked some cookies today. I was going to bring you over some. Now you can take them with you."

"Thank you," Beth said and watched her put some oatmeal-raisin cookies into a plastic bag. "You know, Mrs. Floyd, we've never discussed rent. I'm sure I owe you some money."

Molly gestured Beth into a chair at the table. She put her finger on her lip for silence.

"It's Molly, remember?" she said in a soft voice. "Now, you are one of the few people who know that I don't need the rent money. So just don't tell anyone. I still haven't told Holt. It's going to make him so angry that his father played poor and had all that stashed away. I don't know how to approach the subject with him. So forget about rent. I would feel guilty taking money from you."

"But that doesn't seem fair."

"Dee was going to pay it for you anyway. So what difference does it make?"

"I wouldn't have let her do that."

"Yeah? I would have loved to see you stop Dee Carter from doing something she wanted to do." Molly laughed. "Now, I have something else to talk about. I'm thinking of taking the boat out and spreading Bert's ashes on the lake. I don't think it's quite legal, but I don't want any fuss. I'm not sure Holt will go with me. Would you?"

"Of course, if you want me to," said Beth, but inwardly she shuddered. She didn't want to be on the lake again or with a dead person, even if he was already cremated.

"We could do it late at night, when there's nobody around," mused Molly. "I haven't figured out the details yet. Maybe Dee would go with us, too."

"I'm sure she would."

"Good, that's a plan then. But I'm thinking you didn't come here to chat with me. Holt's up in his room, studying, I hope. Go on up."

Beth climbed the stairs and knocked on the door. Loud music vibrated from the room. She still didn't know anything about the music everyone listened to and talked about. New things were coming at her so fast and furious that she couldn't deal with everything at once.

She knocked again, louder, and called out, "Holt?"

"Come on in," he shouted.

When she opened the door and he saw who it was, he turned down the music. Now it was only a small pulsation in the background, no longer bouncing off the walls. Another new expression—she really loved them. They were like a layer of richness added to her life, the black and white turning more and more into color.

Holt got up from his computer and offered her the chair he had been sitting on. He sat down on the bed, his long legs spread out in front of him, and he gave her one of his wonderful smiles.

"Good to see you," he said. "Sorry we aren't riding together anymore. How are things going for you?"

"School is good. I'm meeting people. I really like it. But that's not what I came about. Something is kind of worrying me, and I didn't want to upset your mother with it."

She told him about the person she had seen outside her window.

"Hmm," he said. He didn't seem too concerned. "I bet it's just the militia guys practicing maneuvers. They've used those woods back there before. I think it was my dad's idea, a way to check up on my mother and me. He was always so full of suspicion." Beth wanted to grab at that idea. It could be, couldn't it?

"But he was standing so still," she said.

"When they play soldier they do it up right—post guards, send scouts, all that stuff." Holt laughed. "I guess it's not really funny. They take it so seriously. And some of them are really good guys. But there are some real nut-cases, too."

She still wanted to ask him if she could use his phone that night, but he had dismissed her fears so quickly that she didn't quite know how. She looked at his computer behind her. "Can you show me how to use this?" she said instead.

"It's pretty much like all the others," he said.

"I've never used one."

His eyebrows went up. "Never?"

"No. I know that sounds strange..."

"That's okay," he quickly reassured her. He got up and stood over her shoulder. "I can show you the basics." He was patient, not just explaining but insisting she try everything herself. She caught on quickly.

"Use it when I'm here for the first few times, I can explain things better you need them."

Beth felt she had taken up enough of his time, but the explanation he had given for the figure outside her window wasn't reassuring her.

"I'm still worried," she said as she went to the door to leave. "Could I possibly use your cell phone so that I could call the house tonight if I see anything? I hate to wake your mother, though."

"It's okay." He took the phone out of his pocket and handed it to her.

"You'll have to show me how to use this, too," she said.

Now Holt really looked perplexed, but he didn't say anything. He put his home phone number in the display and showed her how to send a call.

"I feel better already," she said. "I can't thank you enough. I'm being absolutely ridiculous, I know."

"Oh, no. That's all right. I don't want you all scared up there. I bet it is a little creepy, being alone like that." He was standing up, looking down at her, again with that contagious smile.

"I don't mind being alone. I just don't like people outside my window in the middle of the night."

"Yeah, well, don't worry. You call and I'll be right there." He reassured her and offered to walk her downstairs.

She told him it wasn't necessary. But he did anyway.

24

Leroy Conner ran into the chief's office. He was excitedly waving a paper in his hand.

"I've got it, sir, I've got everything figured out. And it's enough evidence to make an arrest."

Josh had a headache, and this wasn't going to help. Once again, he mentally cursed the mayor for insisting on Josh hiring Leroy.

"Sit down," he told him. "And stop waving that paper in my face."

But sitting didn't help. Leroy fidgeted like a kid who had to go to the bathroom.

"I've got a list. Just listen to this," Leroy waved the paper once more before he started to read. "Suspect: Holt Floyd. Motive: he hated his father. Couldn't play football while Bert was around, but is playing again now. No alibi for the time of the crime. Access to his father's guns. And, a *new* motive, his father was sitting on a pile of dough. Holt and his mother are going to inherit big money."

"Hold it right there," said the chief. "What money?"

"Check it out," said Leroy, with a smug smile. "Bert Floyd owned a bunch of property, most of it lakefront. And he had already sold a bunch more and had a whole pile of investments. The guy was a millionaire."

"What? That doesn't make any sense at all. Molly worked as a waitress, for God's sake."

"Yeah, which makes me think she didn't know anything about it, at least not for most of those years. But maybe she and her son found out about it recently. We've got evidence up the wazoo. Checked it out with a D.A.—not the D.A. from here, but an A.D.A. from Lansing. He said it sounded like plenty of evidence to him. Motive and means."

"Where did you get this money information?" Josh demanded.

"I can't reveal my sources," said Leroy self-righteously.

"Leroy. We're on the same team here, aren't we?"

"Still..."

"If you're off going half-cocked on some rumor..." Josh started.

"It's not a rumor. It will be public record. Check it out

for yourself." Leroy couldn't sit anymore. He got up and started pacing back and forth.

"But I've got more," Leroy continued. "What about the fact that Holt went to see Mrs. Cummings because he thought she had seen something the morning Bert's body was discovered? What about that, huh? Who would be more interested in that than the murderer? It's all over town now that Mrs. Cummings had something to tell, that she saw the person who put the body into the water. Holt would have to get rid of her before she told anyone who it was. And he did."

"You're jumping to a lot of conclusions here," said Josh. "And what about the girl? She just got into town that morning. She couldn't have had anything to do with it—why would she be involved in murdering Mrs. Cummings? Why was she there?"

"We don't know how long she'd had been in town. She just suddenly appeared out of nowhere. Holt could have met her this summer, and they planned the whole thing together." Leroy sat back down, folded his arms, and waited. His smile was very self-satisfied.

It was now Josh who got up and began to pace. "Ridiculous," he said, as much to himself as to Leroy.

"Nothing ridiculous about it. All the evidence points to Holt Floyd. It's usually someone in the family, isn't it?"

"So explain Slim Carry," said Josh.

"That I haven't figured that out yet. If it's related, I'll find out how. But I've been thinking that maybe it's a copycat crime of convenience. Somebody wanted Slim dead, and they chose to do it now and make it look like it was connected to the other murders."

Again Leroy smiled that self-satisfied smile. Josh had a great urge to wipe it off Leroy's face with his fist. He had to remind himself that the kid was young and he had a lot to learn, at least about how he presented himself. As far as legal footwork was concerned, he had lined up his facts in pretty good order. He had come up with a lot more than Josh had managed to do. But no way could Josh get his head around the thought that Holt Floyd had anything to do with the murders.

"Murderers don't look like murderers," said Leroy, as if he were reading Josh's mind. "There have been a lot of big athletes in big trouble in recent years. Football is a *violent* sport."

"You know, kid," said Josh, purposely trying to put him down a bit. "Once you get hold of a theory, it's very tempting to arrange the facts to justify it."

"You got any ideas to dispute my theory?" asked Leroy.

"We're going to keep looking into the militia. Two out of the three victims were in the militia."

"And the third wouldn't fit at all."

"Yes, it would. Your scenario, Lillian Cummings saw who put Bert's body in the water, and the militia murderer got rid of her. Later, Holt and Beth came on the scene."

"Remember, they didn't call you right away," insisted Leroy.

"There is that," Josh admitted. His headache was much worse. "But what about the girl? You really see her standing by and watching a woman be killed?"

Now it was Leroy who looked out of sorts. "I'm having trouble with that, I admit. But, like I said, murderers don't look like murderers. And she and Holt seem pretty tight."

That was not good news to Josh on a couple of levels. Sam wasn't acting like she and Holt had broken up. Or, at least she wasn't accepting it. What was going on with the boy? Josh didn't think Holt was a killer, but he would be very angry with the boy if he hurt his daughter. *Mustn't let that get in the way of anything,* he thought. For the first time, he was questioning his career choice. Maybe he needed to go fishing.

Then he had a thought.

"Leroy, you said that it's all over town now that Mrs. Cummings had seen something and was going to tell."

"That's right."

"So, if it isn't Holt, and it isn't, then the real perpetrator is hearing this rumor. He thinks Holt and Beth talked to Mrs. Cummings and know what she knew. That's dangerous."

"Ah ha," said Leroy, jumping up again. "See. That proves it. Holt and Beth are just fine. Nobody's threatened them or done anything to them. That proves my point exactly. It's them."

"Boy, I was really wrong about this," said Josh.

"You agree with me? You admit I'm right?" Leroy asked, hitching up his belt.

Josh laughed. "I was wrong in that I thought you had the hots for Beth Waterman."

Leroy's face turned instantly red. "I don't like the idea of her being involved, if that's what you mean. And I don't like the idea of anything happening to her in case I'm wrong. But I'm not wrong."

"You have the makings of a good law enforcement

officer, Leroy. What you did here, it's good, it's logical. I just happen to think it's incorrect. Now, you should go out and do the same thing with the militia in mind. Then compare. Keep an open mind—that's important at this stage of the game."

Leroy slumped back in his seat. "Is that an order?" he asked.

"Yes," said the chief. "It's an order."

25

Beth very much resented the fact that something out her window—be it militia maneuvers or whatever—was spoiling her enjoyment of her little apartment. She did not eagerly run up the stairs, but walked slowly, dreading another night of watching.

But this time she had a phone. This time she could call for help. Except that Holt had dismissed her fears so readily. Would he just think it was silly, her calling? But then, she shouldn't care about what he thought of her. He belonged to Samantha. Except he wasn't acting like he belonged to Samantha—only Samantha was acting like that. There was so much Beth didn't know. It was too bad that she couldn't spend a year as a fly on the wall at Beaumont High, just observing and learning, before she was thrown into the melee. She didn't understand the interaction between people, the subtle little messages passed back and forth, so much unsaid. Her black-and-white world had been so much simpler—but so very horrible. She'd take this world and she would learn all she had to learn.

She put the little phone right by her bedside. She didn't look out the window; instead, she watched television. She wasn't enjoying it as much as she had thought she would. There was just too much else going on. When she was finally ready for bed and had turned out the light, only then did she move the curtain slightly aside and look out.

Everything was still. She could see no movement. The thought of another night spent watching was just too much. She closed the curtain and went to bed.

It was the middle of the night that she woke, listening. The clock radio read 3:43 a.m. She had heard something. She listened intently for several seconds. Then she heard it again, barely audible, but someone was slowly turning the door knob outside.

She groped for the phone, then turned on the light to help figure out how to call. The number was preset, all she had to do was push the green button. Her fingers fumbled, the button seemed so small.

It rang a good three times. She listened for any further noise outside her door and held her breath as she waited for the phone to be answered.

"Beth? Is that you?" Holt's voice sounded heavy with sleep.

"Someone is outside my door," she said, trying to speak quietly. But instantly she heard footsteps hurrying down the stairs.

"He's leaving. I hear him going back down the stairs," she told Holt.

There was a crash of a phone being dropped down hard. Almost immediately she heard someone running on the gravel driveway toward her apartment. But she heard no movement up the stairs. Instead, she heard the footsteps going around toward the woods.

She leaped out of bed and pulled open the curtain. Holt had a flashlight. She could see the light waving all around in every direction, crazy arches up, down, and sideways because he was running fast.

She stumbled across the room and ran out and down the stairs, the steps rough against her bare feet. She should have stayed where she was; she could see what was happening from above better than down here. Now, she only caught glimpses of the flashlight as Holt ran through the woods.

"Do you see anyone?" she called out.

His answer seemed far away. "Not yet."

She didn't have a flashlight and she couldn't see anything. Holt was getting farther and farther away. She didn't dare go into the woods. She would only stumble and fall, and she was barefoot. The night was so dark, without any moon.

Standing there, shivering, she realized that she was very vulnerable. If someone were watching, he would have seen her come down the stairs and would be aware that she was standing in the open.

She walked tentatively toward the woods. Her feet felt every rock, twig, and root as she stepped on them.

Now she heard more crashing; the flashlight beam was coming back toward her.

"Holt?" she called out. But what if it wasn't him? Was she signaling her position to the wrong person?

More crashing, then Holt was suddenly in front of her.

Beth had to keep herself from reaching out to him, she was so glad to see him.

"I heard something," Holt told her. "But I couldn't see anyone. Maybe it was just an animal."

"An animal doesn't wiggle door knobs," said Beth.

"Yeah, I forgot," said Holt. But maybe it was that he didn't believe her. Maybe he was thinking that she had just imagined it.

"It woke me up," Beth said. "It was the noise of someone fiddling with the door that woke me up."

Holt put his arm around her, turning her back toward the garage. "I believe you," he said. They started walking. Her feet were cold on the damp earth, but his arm felt so good and reassuring. He knew she was scared. It was just a friendly gesture. He belonged to Samantha. But it still felt good. Holt didn't have any shoes on either, they were both dressed for bed, Beth in her night shirt and Holt in just his shorts, no undershirt. Beth could see the muscles rippling in his stomach as the flashlight swung back and forth. She tried to think about something negative about the boy walking beside her. She couldn't.

When they reached the bottom of the stairs they stopped.

"Do you want to come and sleep in the house tonight?" Holt asked. "Are you afraid to go back up there?"

"No," said Beth. No more fear. She was through with that. No one was going to have that kind of influence in her life, not ever again. To be afraid was to give up control. She couldn't think of anything worse than that. Whoever was out there, whatever he was going to do, it still couldn't be worse than the fear itself.

"I think the militia has been doing maneuvers out there. Weeds were trampled down and twigs broken, that sort of thing," said Holt.

Beth shook her head. "It wasn't the militia," she said with certainty. "It was one person, standing and watching." Holt was probably trying to be reassuring, but he only convinced her further that she was very much on her own. She'd have to help herself. She really couldn't depend on Holt or anyone else—wasn't that always the way? She had become too comfortable here. The people were too nice, too helpful. That didn't mean that evil didn't exist, even here, even in beautiful Beaumont by the lake. Perhaps she had brought it with her. Perhaps it was C.J. out there. But whatever it was, she was on her own and she was in danger, and she would have to handle it.

Having taken on the responsibility, Beth felt better. She had erased any false hope. She did better without hope. *Action.* She did better with action. It was clean and neat, like the feeling she had when she finally left C.J. Scary, yes. But satisfying.

26

The next day was Saturday. Beth worked at the diner until four o'clock. The diner was then closed until six-thirty.

"There won't be hardly anyone coming in," Dee said. "Everyone will be at Lillian's funeral and at the reception after. And Sally's coming in to handle the few people who do show up."

Even though the church had an ample parking lot, it wasn't enough for the crowd. Folks had to park three and four blocks away. The church filled up early, with people were standing in the back and even in the vestibule, where they wouldn't be able to see anything.

Dee, Molly, Holt, and Beth had seats in the middle of the church. Dee had insisted that they all attend—they were involved whether they wanted to be or not. And they got stares. Everyone knew who had found the body, who had been questioned by the police. Everyone knew everything except, of course, who really did the killing. In lieu of that, they had no one else to stare at but the four of them.

Lillian Cummings may have been a recluse in recent years, but that wasn't always the case. She had been a dearly loved native of the town. Her family had done a lot for the town and its people. In her own quiet and unobtrusive way, she had continued to do good deeds, giving money where money was needed. She tried to give anonymously, but in Beaumont, people knew everything.

And then she had married the man who had become the well-liked and diligent mayor.

There were many eulogies. People came forward who knew her when she was a young girl and told of how kind she had been. Others told of her helping them out when they really needed it. Everyone mentioned her solitary early mornings on the lake. They would miss seeing her out there, they said. It had become a Squall Lake tradition.

When the last hymn had been sung, the mayor invited everyone to the cemetery and then back to his house for refreshments. There was a general exodus to the cars.

"I can't go back in that house," Beth announced as they left the church.

"Me, neither," said Dee. "And I have no desire to go to

the cemetery. We've done what we had to do."

"I have another plan anyway," said Molly. "This would be as good a time as any."

"What?" Holt asked.

"Just get in the car. No questions," said Molly. There was a new grim and determined set to her lips, one that none of them had seen before. They didn't argue.

As they drove, there were sporadic bits of conversation, especially from Molly and Dee about Lillian Cummings. It seemed to Molly that she had led a sad and lonely life.

"There are some people too gentle for this world, and Lillian Cummings was one of them," Dee said.

Molly drove them to the marina.

"What are we doing here?" Holt asked impatiently.

"Tell Harvey to get the boat ready," said Molly.

"The boat? Now? We're not dressed for that." Holt had been forced into a sports jacket and a tie by his mother, which he had taken off immediately after leaving the church. But they were all dressed up, even Beth, who was wearing a skirt loaned to her by Molly. It was too big and too long, appropriate for a mother, not a kid, but she had cinched it together with a belt.

"Do it," Molly insisted. Holt gave his mother a look.

She was not the mother he had always known. She was developing a whole new personality. He didn't recognize her anymore. A backbone, that was what she had suddenly acquired. Where was it all those years when her husband had pushed her around? It irritated him, and yet he couldn't help but admire her for it.

"We're not going out until it gets dark," announced Molly. "There's sandwich makings in the refrigerator inside. That will help us kill some time."

"But why...?" Holt started.

"No questions, remember?" said Molly.

Beth had been quiet all day. She didn't quite understand why she was being included in all of this. But these people included her in everything. They had adopted her. In one sense, it made her feel wonderful, having even such a disjointed family, but in another sense it made her constantly afraid that she was interfering, like she should leave the room during most of the discussions. Again, she wondered if it was all too much, if she shouldn't keep apart, keep her independence and her secrets. They shared everything. She shared nothing.

By eight o'clock, the sun was setting. Harvey had left for the day. He lived in a little house at the edge of the marina property, so he didn't have far to go. It was a house that Bert had charged Harvey an exorbitant rent for, but Molly had changed that. Now it came with the job.

Molly sent them down to the boat. She went back to her car and got something out of the trunk. When she joined the others, she was carrying a shopping bag.

"What's that?" Holt asked.

"You'll see," said Molly.

Once out on the water, they heard the noise even before they passed the Cummings' house. There were candles and little lights, tables and chairs scattered over the lawn. People were milling about, being served food and drinks. Their voices drifted over the water. Molly told Holt to steer around the bend. When they were far enough away that they could no longer hear the noise from the Cummings' gathering, she told him to stop.

The boat drifted for a few minutes, and no one spoke. Then Molly reached into her shopping bag and pulled out a cardboard box.

"What's that?" Holt asked.

"Your father's ashes," she said calmly.

"Oh no, oh no. Why didn't you tell me?" he asked,

angrily.

"Because you wouldn't have come."

"You've got that right," he said, looking around as if to escape.

"I couldn't allow you to miss this," Molly said. "You don't know it now, but someday, you might be very sorry."

"In my wildest imagination, I can't see that happening. I'm so sick of this, of you pretending he was a nice guy just because he's dead now. What's with that?"

"After today, I don't intend to mention his name again. But in a civilized world we take care of the dead. We will do our duty and then we will move forward," said Molly. Her voice no longer contained even a hint of the apologetic tone it had always had before.

Holt shrugged. "It's illegal to do this. In the lake I mean. I think you have to have a permit or something."

"That's why we're doing it at night," Molly told him.

She stood up and opened the box and held it out over the water. There was a slight breeze, but most of it sank out of sight; only a little wafted in the air or floated for a few minutes.

There was no eulogy, no prayer—only silence. The boat drifted on the current. The last of the ashes sank.

It was dark and difficult to see each other's faces, but Beth had the distinct impression that Holt was no longer frowning.

They started the motor and headed back toward the marina. Once again they passed the Cummings' house. The gathering was going strong, a little louder, if anything. Bits of conversation and a little laughter could be heard across the water.

"That doesn't seem appropriate. The laughing, I mean," said Beth.

"No, that's what's good. That's the part where life goes on," said Dee. "It's not quite the Irish wake thing. But the getting together, that's what's important. The sun comes up the next day, no matter what."

Molly looked over at Holt. He was listening. She would have loved to know what he was thinking.

They weren't speeding back, which was unusual for Holt, who either went full throttle or drifted, but nothing in between. Molly wondered if this was some kind of acknowledgment for his father. She hoped it was.

Suddenly, not far past the Cummings' place, there was a loud crack of sound. Something tore up the water right next to the boat.

"Was that a shot?" Dee asked, stunned.

"It sure sounded like one," said Molly.

Then it happened again. This time there was no doubt. A bullet hit the motor, which died instantly.

"Duck," shouted Holt.

They all tried to lower themselves below the gunwale, which was impossible. Two more shots rang out.

"Ohhhhh. Oh my God, I'm hit," Holt cried out.

"Where? Where are you hit?" Molly wailed.

Holt didn't answer her. "Overboard!" he shouted. "Now!"

"I can't swim," cried Beth.

They had all put on life jackets, Molly had insisted, and even Holt wore one. He grabbed Beth and held her while he jumped into the cold water, taking her with him. Her head went under and she gulped in some water, but he was holding her tightly and she came up fast, choking.

At first they all clung to the side of the boat, away from the shooter. But more bullets hit the boat.

"Make for the other shore," Holt yelled. There was something in his voice—pain or fear?

The night was so dark, the water seemed like a pool of ink. Only the outline of the shore gave any indication of which way they were going.

More shots rang out.

Dee was a surprisingly good swimmer. Even with the cumbersome jacket, she managed an even, quick stroke, rhythmic in sound as her arms broke the water. Molly kept trying to talk, but she managed to keep up. Holt was obviously struggling, trying to swim and carry Beth along at the same time.

He's been shot, she kept telling herself. *He can't do this, he's been shot.*

"I'm okay," Beth finally managed to say. "I'm bobbing up like a cork, just like you said I would. I can make it on my own." When his arm left her, she felt an acute sense of panic. But that's what Holt said was the reason people drowned. She wasn't going to drown. The life jacket wouldn't let her. She thrashed ahead, one arm and then the other, wiggling her legs at the same time. And she sensed a slow forward motion.

Holt hadn't left her side.

The others had reached the shore, and called encouragement in soft voices.

"You can touch bottom here," Holt finally said. And sure enough, Beth put her feet down and felt the security of the earth once again.

One more shot rang out. It was too far away to reach them now.

There was silence and darkness all around them. They were shivering in their wet clothes. They sat down on the rocky beach and for a few minutes didn't speak. No noise, except for their breathing.

"Where were you shot?" Molly repeated her question, once she had caught her breath.

"My arm," said Holt, holding it tightly.

"Is it bleeding badly?" Dee asked.

"Not so much, I think. Maybe the water helped."

They sat there, the darkness of the woods behind them, the darkness of the empty expanse of water in front of them. They could see the lights from the cottages across the water. There didn't seem to be any lights near them on this side.

"I could go see if I can get some help," Holt offered.

"Not you. I'll go," said Dee. "You rest. We don't know how much blood you've lost. I'd try to see if I could help your wound, but I'm afraid that in the dark I'd do more harm than good."

"They were aiming at us," said Beth. "Weren't they?"

"It sure seemed like that," said Dee.

"But why?" Molly was crying. "Why would anyone try to shoot us?"

"It's the man. The man who's been watching me," said Beth.

"We don't know that," Holt argued. "Not with all the strange things that have been happening around here."

"What man?" demanded Dee.

"Who?" Molly said, at the same time.

Suddenly, there was the sound of boats, more than one starting up.

"The Cummings' thing. It's breaking up. Some people must have come by boat. Get ready to start yelling," said Dee.

They stood up. As soon as they saw the lights of the first boat heading their way they started shouting and waving their arms, as if anyone could see them in the dark.

"Hey, hey, over here."

Finally, a boat, not the first one, slowed down and a spotlight was aimed at the shoreline.

"Over here," they shouted again.

The light caught them and stopped. The boat turned toward them.

It came in as close to shore as it could. The four, still wet and bedraggled, waded out and climbed aboard.

"Could I use that light?" Molly asked.

A man was piloting the boat and a woman, dressed in a fussy navy-blue dress and heels, sat in the back. She handed over the spotlight.

Molly shone it on Holt, who was holding onto his left arm tight above the elbow. Blood was oozing from the wound. His shirt sleeve was saturated.

"What did you mean, there wasn't much blood?" demanded Molly, sounding angry.

"It was better when I couldn't see it," said Holt.

"What happened here?" asked the woman. The spotlight, although still aimed at Holt, lit up the boat enough for her to look at the new passengers.

"Dee Carter," she exclaimed "What are you doing out here in the dark all wet and cold? And Molly Floyd. And Holt Floyd. You're hurt, son. What happened here?" she repeated.

"Somebody shot at us. From the eastern shore," said Dee. "That looks bad, Holt. We need to get you to the hospital.

I'm sure glad you saw us. Beth, this is Mr. and Mrs. Norman Bell. This is Beth Waterman, new in town."

"More of that militia nonsense?" exclaimed Mrs. Bell. "It's time we put a stop to it. That's what you always say, don't you, Norman?"

"Right now I say we get a line on your boat so we can tow it to the marina," he said. Holt got up to help but was quickly pushed back down by Molly. It was only a few minutes before Molly and Dee and even Mrs. Bell had the line secure between the two boats.

Once underway, Mr. Bell looked up from his intense scrutiny of the dark waters as he steered his boat. "To answer your question," he said to his wife, "yes, I, for one, am getting pretty tired of the militia stunts. And this time they've gone way too far. Shootin' kids, for God's sake."

"I'm sure it was an accident. But there've been way too many accidents around here," said Mrs. Bell, still indignant. "And poor Lillian…"

"This was no accident," said Dee. "They kept shooting. After Holt was hit, we jumped into the water, or we'd all be bleeding."

"Hank Crowell's place is right across there," said Mr.

Bell. "They've been known to put a target on a raft in the water and shoot at it for practice sometimes. Maybe that's what was happening."

"We had our lights on," complained Holt. "They couldn't see that?"

"Who knows?" said Mr. Bell. with disgust.

"Well, we'll call the police the minute we get to shore," said Mrs. Bell.

"Just take us to the marina. Our car's there. We need to get Holt to the hospital."

"I'm all right," he protested. But he was still holding his arm tightly.

"That's not your throwing arm, is it?" Mr. Bell asked. "There's quite an article about you in the paper coming out tomorrow. How you're back on the team and we're expecting a winning season."

"No, it's not my throwing arm," said Holt. For the first time, he didn't try to keep his voice up. "Who wrote it, Mr. Bell? I didn't want anything like that."

"My editor. Gave half credit to the school news runner, but it was my editor who suggested the article. Don't be shy about your abilities, kid. You give this town something to be proud about. I miss you not giving me the school news anymore."

"Yeah. Me, too. Our principal doesn't want an accused murderer anywhere near the school paper," said Holt.

"Nonsense. Everyone knows that's nonsense," said Mr. Bell. "You can come write for me anytime you want. But right now we need to get you get to the hospital. They'll fix you up. Can't keep a good guy down," said Mr. Bell cheerfully.

The boat was now heading toward shore. The marina's lights were on, big flood lights that lit up the docks, so it was easy for Mr. Bell to zone in on his target.

"Do those lights go on automatically?" asked Dee. "I don't remember you turning anything on."

"No, they don't, and I didn't," said Molly. "But maybe Harvey turned them on."

As they approached the dock, they saw Harvey standing there, looking worried.

They pulled up. Harvey leaned down and, with great care, helped Molly onto the dock. Then he noticed Holt.

"My God, what happened to you?"

It was like daylight under the floodlights. Holt was covered in more blood than anyone had realized. Blood coated his orange life vest where he had held his arm against it, and it had dripped down onto his khaki pants.

"Somebody shot at us," said Molly.

"I heard it. I heard the shots," said Harvey. "I was worried about you."

"Why would anyone purposely shoot at you?" Mr. Bell asked. Now that he wasn't piloting the boat anymore, he seemed more interested in what was going on. It wasn't so much commiseration as an eager newsman's interest.

Holt was immediately wary.

"Probably what Mrs. Bell said before, probably the militia showing off. Probably just meant to scare us. Not all of them are good shots."

Mr. Bell didn't look like he was buying that.

"We need to get Holt to the hospital," insisted Molly. "Now."

Harvey had helped the others out of the boat.

"Thanks again," said Dee. To the Bells "We sure needed a rescue."

"Anytime," said Mrs. Bell cheerfully, as though thanking someone for coming to a tea party.

Harvey helped Holt walk down the dock. Holt didn't

refuse the help. That surprised Beth. He had seemed so determined not to show his injury until now. He was definitely feeling worse.

"I just can't understand why anyone would shoot at us," Molly said as they made their way toward the car.

"Oh?" said Harvey. "I can." For some reason, Beth thought that Harvey appeared taller than when she had first seen him. He stood up straighter, his shoulders were back.

"What do you mean?" Beth asked him.

"It's all over town. Everyone is talking about it. They think you and Holt know something. That Mrs. Cummings told you something she had seen. That she told you who she saw dumping the body." Harvey realized how that sounded. "Saw Mr. Floyd being put in the water that morning. Saw who did that."

"Oh my God," said Dee, turning to Beth and Holt. "You are in serious danger."

"Maybe that's the man..." Beth looked toward Holt, who turned and looked back at her.

"I wonder if Josh knows about this," said Dee.

"Leroy does," Harvey told them. "He's the one doing most of the talking. Can't keep his mouth shut lately. Feeling a bit of his oats since people are suddenly listening to him."

They got Holt into the car. He sat in the back seat with Molly. Harvey waved them off, and they drove as rapidly as they could to Keene. When they pulled into the hospital emergency entrance, Holt didn't resist the gurney they brought out. He was very pale.

27

Molly, Dee, and Beth spent a lot of time on the hard plastic chairs in the ER waiting room. Molly was periodically allowed into the cubicle where they were tending to Holt, but nobody told her much more than that the bullet was still in his arm, they were going to take him up for surgery in the morning as soon as the surgeon arrived, that he had been given medication for the pain, and was sleeping on and off. He had been admitted him, but there wasn't a room yet. That was all they knew.

One nurse was at least trying to keep them informed and came by every half hour or so.

"The authorities have to be informed," she said several times. "Always in the case of a bullet wound, the authorities have to be informed." She made it sound as if they were somehow to blame and were going to resist the police.

Beth had never been in a hospital before. She found everything about it fascinating. There were strange smells, and the doorways up and down the halls were open, you could see people lying there asleep. It was such an invasion of privacy, yet she always looked. There were moans and groans and the clatter of things being dropped.

The reason Beth saw all that was because she had started pacing the halls. A person was only capable of sitting so long. It was now almost midnight. She couldn't doze off like Dee had done several times, sitting upright. She wasn't allowed into Holt's cubicle, like Molly was. So she walked up and down, back and forth.

She wasn't in the waiting room when Chief Winters came. She saw him on one of her return trips and didn't approach. Instead, she stood down the hall and listened. It was another occasion when she felt like she didn't belong, like somebody was going to ask her just what she thought she was doing.

Besides, Josh Winters had a deep, booming voice. It carried well.

Molly parroted the same reassuring words about Holt's condition that the doctor had spoken to her. Beth liked hearing them repeated. It made her feel better. She really wasn't worried about Holt. It was not a life-or-death situation. But Holt had lost a lot of blood. He had been very brave about carrying on through the swim, and he hadn't even complained. Still, Beth was trying to ease off her admiration for Holt. She needed to pull back from all these people.

Dee was telling the chief the whole story, about the shots coming from the shore, that there was no doubt they were aimed right at them.

The chief listened and nodded, with an occasional grunt.

"I think I know what this is all about," he said finally. "Leroy tells me it's all over town that Mrs. Cummings told Holt and Beth who she saw the morning Bert was found. Where is she, anyway? The girl? I was told she was with you."

Beth eased back around the corner. She didn't want to be caught listening.

Dee explained that Beth was restless, that she had taken to walking up and down the corridors just for something to do.

"Did Holt or Beth tell you anything?" the chief asked Dee and Molly.

"No," they answered in unison.

"They don't know anything. That's why they went back to Lillian's place—when they found her... like that," said Dee.

"So why did they think she knew anything?" the chief asked, overly patient.

"What *had* she said?" Dee asked Molly, who only shrugged. "Some words that didn't make much sense," Dee continued. "Beth will be back here any minute, ask her. She told you all that after Lillian was killed. It didn't make sense then, and it won't make sense now."

Beth had to make her reappearance casual. Why hadn't she just walked up in the first place? She was over-thinking everything. She was always putting herself in an awkward situation. These people included her. She needed to accept that. Stop backing away. And yet—she was still so unsure of everything. They discussed such personal things, and she was used to secrets, to never discussing, to always pretending, to always listening, unobserved, if possible.

She walked around the corner, feeling like every step looked fake.

"Just in time," said Dee.

Beth sat down. They were a line of three women. The chief had pulled up a chair and turned it to face them.

"Beth," he began in a calm, kind voice. "I need you to tell me anything that Mrs. Cummings told you, even if she asked you not to. I think you're in a lot of danger unless you do."

"She didn't tell us anything," Beth insisted. "We went

back to ask her what she meant, but she was..."

"What did she say the first time?"

"It was all scrambled. Something about seeing something she shouldn't and that she should tell, but that something terrible would happen if she did."

"No hint as to who she had seen?"

"None. And she looked upset, so it didn't seem like we should ask, you know?"

The chief muttered something under his breath. "Well, we've got to squash this talk around town that you know something. We've got to let people in on the fact that you don't."

"Just tell Leroy," Dee said. "I hear he's the one spreading the rumor in the first place."

"What?" The chief seemed genuinely surprised. Every time he started giving Leroy the benefit of the doubt, something like this seemed to happen. Life had almost been easier when he was the only cop in town.

For some reason that Beth couldn't understand at first, this conversation was making her relax in her chair. Someone wanted to kill her. That shouldn't make her relax. But it did. And then she realized something that her unconscious mind had already keyed into. It wasn't C.J. It wasn't C.J. who had found her and had been watching her, waiting for a chance to—what? Shoot? From a distance? No way would C.J. handle it like that. No satisfaction there. C.J. would want to see her face before any final blow was struck. C.J. would never give up that sort of twisted pleasure. And C.J. might have no intention of killing her. C.J. might just want to take her back. She shuddered. That wasn't happening.

But *this* shooter, *this* watcher, wasn't C.J. She was still free. The idea of a shooter didn't frighten her half as much, no matter who he was.

"Is something amusing you?" the chief asked Beth.

She hadn't realized she was smiling. And there was no way to explain what was going on in her mind. Beth simply shook her head. "I'm just really tired, I guess," she said.

"This is silly, us all waiting here," said Dee. "I'll stay with Molly. Josh, could you take Beth on home?"

Josh thought that was a very good idea, a time to talk to the girl alone, to find out a little something about her. He immediately agreed.

Beth didn't think it was a good idea at all. But what could she do?

Tonight, the chief wasn't in his squad car. He drove a Honda, several years old. Beth suspected that he usually kept it neat, because the litter that was now scattered around the car was definitely Samantha's: lipstick-smeared tissues, a couple of textbooks, wadded-up papers, and a half-eaten apple. So, Beth thought to herself, Samantha *did* get the car occasionally.

They had hardly left the parking lot before the chief started.

"Had you seen much of your cousin, Dee, before you came here?" he asked.

"Not much," she answered. She figured not much could include never. Why not? Stick as close to the truth as you can, she told herself.

"Just birthday presents, stuff like that?" he asked.

"In my house, we didn't do much about birthdays," she said. That was certainly true.

"Dee goes out of town every now and again. She never says where. I just wondered if it was to visit your family, your mutual family. Are you pretty spread out, or are they all in Philadelphia?"

"I don't know much about our family, not extended family," Beth said. That too was true. C.J. had never ever mentioned any family. Now, for a brief moment, she wondered about that. Did she have family somewhere? Family she would like? Family who would be like Dee, Molly and Holt?

As far as Beth was concerned, it was time to change the subject. "I really appreciate how Samantha showed me around and everything. I'm doing pretty well on my own now, but that school was really confusing the first few days."

The chief looked over at her. She had tried to make it sound like idle conversation, but from his look, he knew exactly what she was doing.

"It's unusual, a relative showing up out of the blue. I was sorry to hear about your mother. What exactly is her illness?"

"They tell me that sometimes things are really hard to diagnose," said Beth.

"Is she in the hospital?"

"Yes," Her first out-and-out lie.

"What hospital?"

Beth could not think of the name of one hospital in Philadelphia, try as she might. They never talked about hospitals. She had never had anything to do with hospitals, but she knew there were several really big ones. *Think, think,* she told herself. But if she named one, would he check?

They had reached the dirt road part of her trip home. The chief's old Honda took the ruts in the road just as hard as her car. She was bouncing around in her seat. That was her excuse for not answering immediately.

"Your shocks are in the same condition as mine," she said. She had never heard of a shock absorber until Holt had mentioned her problem to her. But she felt good saying that. That sounded normal.

"Yeah, they're pretty bad," he agreed. "About the hospital?"

"They were going to transfer her. And nobody tells me anything. Everyone's afraid to upset me, so nobody tells me anything. Don't they know that's the most upsetting thing of all?"

He gave her another quick glance. It was dark, and she couldn't see him, not really. But there were so many things that betrayed what somebody was thinking. Almost invisible things, such as a quick shift in posture, a turn of the head, or a slight change in voice. It was true of almost everyone. Not C.J. Beth had never been able to tell anything about what C.J. was thinking. That was one thing that had made life so terrifying. But the chief was an open, honest man. She knew she had gained his sympathy, even if just for a minute.

The chief slammed on his brakes.

"Saturday night. I should have expected something like

this," he said.

There were cars parked helter-skelter on the narrow road. A big fire was burning in a field and kids were sitting around it; some were dancing. There was music playing loudly.

"I need to check this out," the chief said.

He got out of the car and several people started running away in various directions.

"Stay here," he told Beth. "It's kids and beer, that's all."

The few kids who hadn't run away tried to explain themselves. Beth heard snatches of their protests of innocence. It seemed that none of them had actually done any of the drinking.

The more they protested, the guiltier they sounded. Beth wouldn't have believed them for a minute. She was sure the chief didn't either. He was calling them all by name—they weren't getting away with anything. That had to be another disadvantage of a small town.

But the distraction had ended the questions. Silently, Beth thanked the kids. She was going to have to make up a story, a good one that she could pull out when she needed it. Having no past wasn't working for her. She should have thought of all of this before she exposed herself to people. But there wouldn't be all these questions if she hadn't stumbled into the one town where murders were being committed, would there? If the murders ended, would the questions stop?

28

Holt spent day in the hospital after the bullet was removed. It hadn't damaged any muscle or tendons. But he had to stay home from school for the rest of the week.

Holt didn't just rest, as instructed. When Beth got home from school and work the next night, he was waiting for her at the bottom of the steps.

"Got a surprise for you," he said smiling.

His arm was in a sling. And he didn't jump up from the steps as agilely as he usually did.

"Are you feeling okay?" Beth asked.

"Fine. Just grateful it's not my throwing arm. But come on—open up your door. I really need to show you this."

Beth climbed the stairs. What could he show her in her own apartment?

As soon as they got in, he walked over to the window, opened it, and pulled an extension cord over the ledge. Beth moved to stand beside him.

"What is this?" she asked.

"Just watch," Holt said, sounding pleased with himself. He plugged the cord into the socket below the window.

The yard below them and the woods beyond lit up with tiny white lights.

"If you think somebody is watching you, just plug that in," he said.

It seemed like magic. Beth had to restrain herself—she felt like hugging him. This was so perfect. She really didn't have to be afraid anymore. And what was even better was that he hadn't dismissed her fears, as she thought he had. Of course, the bullet in his arm probably helped focus him.

"This is... wonderful," said Beth. How could she let him know how wonderful and still not...? She had to keep thinking about Samantha. "Thank you so much. How did you ever do all this?"

"Easy really. Just some strings of Christmas lights. We had them in our basement." He had that shy look that Beth liked so much. But it was his back-off look, too. The one that Samantha failed to recognize.

"I am actually going to sleep tonight," Beth said. "After I give everything a good look."

"Don't turn the lights on too often. We'd like to catch the guy. See who it is."

"Then what?" Beth asked.

"We tell Chief Winters," said Holt.

"And then you're off the hook," agreed Beth.

"Hopefully." He gave her one last smile and left.

But it was as if the watcher knew. Beth had no sense of anyone out in the woods again.

When Holt returned to school, it was as though having been shot in the arm gave him some sort of reprieve. Most of those who had been suspicious of him were back to being best buddies again, a fact about which he was much more wary. But football was out, at least for a while. He went to practices anyway, sitting and watching, and he was developing a permanent scowl. He expected to return before the second game.

Beth's world became better. She was feeling comfortable at school. There were now four of them who sat together at lunch: Beth, Sidney, Heather, and Amanda. Heather was in Beth and Sidney's English class, and Amanda was a friend of Heather's. Both Heather and Amanda were small and both wore their brown hair short and spiky, making them look alike. Samantha joined the group occasionally, but not for the whole meal, only long enough to ask Beth how she was doing. And sometimes Holt and one or more of his friends would sit down with them. That, of course, guaranteed Samantha's appearance.

More students said hi to Beth as she walked down the halls. The kids with lockers next to hers were now friendly. Several boys had stopped to talk to her. One of them, Andrew Miller, started walking with her to several of her classes. Since he made a point to not include Sidney, Beth tried to hurry away from each class before he found her.

Beth had also been invited to a couple of parties. But her work schedule interfered, or she knew she'd be too tired after work. That wasn't, of course, the whole reason. She didn't think she was ready for parties. Not yet. Soon. But a whole evening of making *normal* conversation? That thought was exhausting. She liked the little snatches between classes or at lunch. Limited time, limited mistakes.

The kids were great, though. She didn't always understand them, but she was getting away with it. Sometimes, when she said something that made them give her a second glance, they would pause, she would hold her breath, and then they would decide she was being ultra-cool, or at least they told her that. Part of it was the fact that she didn't get upset about the things that others got upset about. To her, their concerns were petty. Not that she ever said that. She was not going to go to pieces about the wrong shade of lipstick or not being invited to a party. What possible difference did it make? You can't come out of survivor mode directly into petty nonsense. She was living in between those two worlds. She often looked at the kids around her and felt totally remote from them. But that was happening less and less.

It was on a Wednesday, after school, as she was heading for her car, that she saw a commotion out of the corner of her eye. She stopped, trying to figure out what was happening. A bunch of girls were behind a group of cars. They were surrounding someone who was trying to back up, trying to get away. At first, Beth didn't sense anything unusual about the situation.

But then she heard a shout.

"Leave me alone," the girl in the middle protested. She tried to push her way through the crowd.

That was when Beth recognized Denise Packard, the

girl that had been supposed to show her around the first week. Denise looked as if she were about to cry.

Beth didn't think about what she was doing. She might not get upset about the things the other kids got upset about, might not have a fit about a boy ignoring her or a bad hair day, but this was a whole different thing. This wasn't fair. So many against one? She identified so much more with the girl in the middle than with any of the others. This had to be stopped. How often had she wished for somebody or something to stop her from being hurt or humiliated?

"What do you think you are doing?" Beth demanded, coming right up to the group.

They turned and looked at her, shocked by her interference. There were other people watching, from a safe distance, standing and looking, but not saying anything.

Others came up close and watched.

Beth didn't know the names of any of the girls. She had seen some of them in the halls, knew that at least a couple of them were seniors. Shouldn't they know better?

"Who do you think you are?" one of the girls turned to her and demanded. Nothing physical had happened. Beth didn't think there was any danger of that. It had just been taunting, name calling, laughing at Denise's distress.

"Who are you, anyway?" asked another. This wasn't good. Beth hadn't meant to call such attention to herself. But she didn't answer the girls, either of them.

"Want a ride home, Denise?" she asked.

Denise nodded and started walking toward her. The circle had become even more disorganized.

Suddenly, Sidney was at Beth's side, and the three of them started walking away. Nobody stopped them. But there were shouts at their backs.

"If it isn't Miss Super Girl and her squint-eyed sidekick," said one of the girls.

"They always have a squint-eyed sidekick," said another.

Now it was Sidney's face that was turning red. Her head was down and she was walking fast.

Beth stopped and turned back.

"Seriously?" she said with disgust. "Did you really say that?" One of the girls who had spoken took a step backward. And the people watching laughed.

At that moment, Beth wasn't sure who they were laughing at. She didn't care. The circle had disintegrated.

"Good going, Beth," said a voice from the crowd. It was Andrew Miller. So why had he been just standing there?

"The show is over," Beth said. She turned again and walked with Sidney and Denise to her car.

"You are so lucky to have your own car," said Sidney.

"This is yours?" Denise asked, her voice ringing with disapproval.

"My father doesn't believe in me driving. Ever," said Sidney. "He says that's just asking for trouble."

"It's old, isn't it" said Denise, getting in the back seat. "It even smells old, musty-like."

Beth didn't bother to answer. It was obvious. Yes, the car was old. Now that the altercation was over, Beth felt a little bit shaky. Everyone had been looking at her. She hated that.

She started the car and drove out of the parking lot. There was still a group of people standing where it had all happened, talking excitedly.

"I can't believe how brave you were," Sidney said. "How can you get up enough nerve to go against all those people?"

"I don't care what they think of me," said Beth. "What difference does it make to me?"

"But..."

"They weren't actually going to do anything," said Denise. "Sticks and stones and all of that."

Sidney turned and looked at Denise in the back seat. "So, you're not happy that she saved your sorry butt?"

"I probably could have handled it," said Denise. She was looking out the window, not at the people in the front seat.

"Where do you live, Denise?" Beth asked.

"Out by the lake," she said.

"Direct me." And Denise did, taking her on a roundabout way that was probably going to make her late for work.

Beth must have glanced at the car clock once too often. Sidney spoke up.

"After we take Denise, you can drop me off at the diner, I only live a couple of blocks away."

"We'll see how late we are," said Beth.

They drove onto Lake Road, the one that would have eventually taken them to Keene. Denise finally told Beth to where to turn.

She hadn't given them any warning. Beth slammed on the brakes and made a turn onto a driveway that went up a steep hill. The house at the top was beautiful, modern in the extreme, different from the other houses around the lake. It had sharp angles, several sets of stairs, and lots of glass. It must have had a beautiful view of the lake.

"Thanks for the ride," said Denise. "It's nice not to have to take the bus." She hopped out of the car and approached the house without looking back.

There was a narrow turn-around that Beth found extremely hard to negotiate. Sidney kept quiet while she made the turn. As soon as they were driving back down the driveway, Sidney spoke. Her tone was furious.

"*Thanks for the ride*? That was it? I can't believe her. She didn't even say one word of thank you for stepping in like you did."

"I didn't do it for a thank you," said Beth. "I did it because it made me mad—them picking on her like that."

"You have to admit, she's difficult. It's like she asks for it," argued Sidney.

"Maybe she can't help it. We don't know what she's going through," Beth said.

"She's always been like that. Everyone says so," said Sidney.

Beth shrugged. It didn't matter how long you knew somebody. You still might not know what they're going through at home. But she didn't say that.

"You know Andrew Miller likes you," said Sidney.

Beth shrugged. "I don't have time for any of that," she said.

"What about if his name was Holt?" asked Sidney, a teasing lilt to her voice.

"He belongs to Samantha."

"I guess. I did hear they went to a party together."

"Oh... that's nice." Beth could control her voice, her posture, her facial expression. But she couldn't control the lurch in her stomach.

She didn't want to talk about Holt anymore.

"I am really late," Beth said as they were pulling into town. "I hope you don't mind if I take you up on your offer to walk from the diner."

"Of course not, or I wouldn't have offered. Better that way. My father doesn't even want me riding in other kid's cars, not without previous permission and lots of talking about it."

Beth knew she didn't have to worry about being late. This was a slow time and it wasn't like she punched a time clock. Dee wouldn't say a word. And that was the trouble. Because Dee wouldn't say anything, it made Beth twice as determined not to take advantage. What she had said was true, that she didn't care what people thought about her. Most people. Not Dee. She cared very much what Dee thought about her. Beth wouldn't want to disappoint Dee for the world.

29

Everyone was talking about what Beth had done, stepping in when Denise was being "taunted"—that's what some kids were calling it. Beth wished she could rewind the whole thing. She hated the attention. It was the last thing in the world she needed. At least her little lunch group had enough sense not to mention it. Beth thought that Sidney had probably warned them.

They were halfway through eating. Heather was telling them about her embarrassing moment of falling up the stairs when she was all dressed up with stiletto heels, trying to look very sophisticated with a really hot boy who she had met in the summer.

"*Up* the stairs," she repeated. "Not *down*, which could be excused, but *up*. Sprawled like a rag doll with everyone watching. Right in front of half the town at that new fancy restaurant in Keene."

Her image was effective, and they were all laughing so

hard that they didn't notice Denise Packard until she sat down at their table. Her tray was as full as it had been the last time she had sat with Beth.

"What are you all laughing at?" she demanded.

The laughter stopped as if a switch had been pulled. There was silence. Everyone looked at Denise, whose eyes were on her tray. She was already spooning her macaroni and cheese into her mouth.

Beth felt sorry for her. She tried to explain what they had been laughing at. The others just kept looking at Denise.

"That's not funny," said Denise, when Beth had finished.

"Probably I didn't tell it right," said Beth. She looked at the others for some help. She wasn't going to get any. Amanda got up from the table and left.

Heather and Sidney looked like they wanted to follow.

Beth saw Holt coming toward the table. He wasn't wearing the sling today, but he was carrying his tray in one hand. He stopped, did an about-face, and sat down with a group of boys in the corner.

Beth felt even sorrier for Denise.

This silence at the table was unusual. And awkward.

Beth tried again.

"Are you a junior or a senior, Denise?"

"Senior."

"That must feel good. What are you going to do, after you graduate?"

Denise looked up, looked at Beth as if she had just asked the most stupid question known to mankind.

"Go to college, what else?"

"Do you know where?" Beth tried again. These were questions she had overheard people asking. She figured they were normal. So why was Denise looking at her like that?

"I don't have to know yet. I'll decide later." Denise's tone was argumentative. Maybe she was just being defensive, maybe all that teasing she received made her strike out first, before being struck. Beth was thinking of all sorts of excuses for her, but she certainly was hard to talk to.

"I'll see you all later," Heather said. She must have crammed the rest of her lunch down while Beth wasn't looking. She was already up from the table and walking away.

"Wait for me," said Sidney. "I'm through."

Even Sidney? Beth felt totally deserted. What had she started here? She had so enjoyed having lunch-time friends.

Had she just ruined that?

After trying a couple of more conversation attempts, Beth gave up and remained silent. Maybe if she waited long enough, Denise would actually begin a conversation on her own, talk about what she wanted to talk about and not be so determined to shoot everything down.

But Denise didn't say a word. She just sat and shoveled food into her mouth and occasionally looked around the room and frowned.

Beth finished her lunch. She continued to sit there, not wanting to leave Denise alone.

"You can go," said Denise. "I don't need you to babysit me."

"That's all right," said Beth. "I hate to sit alone in here, myself."

"I'm used to it," said Denise. Again, she sounded angry.

After a few more minutes of silence Denise spoke again.

"You know that guy, Tony Grimes?"

"I'm afraid I do," said Beth.

"He keeps asking people about you. What's with that? You two got something going?"

"Absolutely not," said Beth. "I think he's creepy." She still didn't like to think about the night the boys stopped her car.

"You're crazy. He's hot," declared Denise, ready to argue again.

Beth wondered if she should tell Denise about that dark night, if she should warn her.

"He and that Slim guy, they were friends, kind of," Denise said.

That made Beth prick up her ears. "Did you know Slim?"

"He talked to me. Our lockers were right next to each other. He was a nice guy."

"He *was* a nice guy. Any ideas of who could have killed him?" Beth had to ask.

Denise pushed her tray away and leaned toward Beth. "There's a lot that goes on in this town that I know about. I listen. Most people don't listen." She nodded her head in agreement with herself.

"Like what?"

"Like why would I tell you?" Denise pushed her chair out, ready to leave.

It was so bald-faced rude. Beth's sympathy dissolved into anger. But did Denise actually know something that would help get suspicion off of Holt?

Beth held her breath. She no longer had to literally count to ten. She had done it often enough to know when ten would arrive.

Denise stood up, holding her tray in one hand and clinging onto the back of her chair with the other.

"You think you're so special, don't you?" Denise asked, her face suddenly red and furious. "You swagger into this school and take over, like you're some sort of Lady Gaga or something. You play it so cool that everyone talks about you and wants to get to know you. Well, I don't think you're special. Too good to even have me take you around. Got Samantha Winters to do it. Got all those girls talking about you like you're extraordinary. Got all the boys wondering about you. Got the big football hero all interested."

Beth couldn't say a word. She was aware that her mouth was open, and she closed it. But Denise was just getting started. Where had all this come from?

"You made me look ridiculous yesterday. You had to come by like some superhero and put your nose in the middle of something I could handle perfectly well by myself. You think that just because you come from the East, from a big city, that you're somehow better than anyone else here. You walk around with your nose stuck up in the air and think we're all a bunch of hicks."

"Excuse me?" Beth managed. Another new phrase, but could anything be further from the truth than what was spewing out of Denise's mouth? The lunchroom was as quiet as Beth had ever heard it. Everyone was listening. Once again, Beth was the entertainment of the moment. There were people who reveled in attention and didn't get any. Beth wondered why she attracted it like a magnet, and she would like nothing more than to crawl under this very table.

"You know who my uncle is, don't you?" Denise demanded.

"I have no idea," said Beth.

"Well, he's Hank Crowell. And he runs things around here. Even the mayor sucks up to him. So don't think you're so special. He was asking me about you the other day, and not in a way that you should be flattered about."

"Why? What was he asking?" Beth wanted to know. Was this more danger? Or just Denise spouting off?

"Just things," said Denise mysteriously.

Beth really wondered what had set Denise off. And why were they off on this tangent, just when Denise had said something about Slim and was, perhaps, going to talk about the murders?

Denise once again had her mouth open. She probably had a lot more to say. But she didn't get the chance. Holt came up to the table and took Beth by the arm.

"Denise, your diarrhea of the mouth has gone way too far this time," he said, as he led Beth away.

When they got into the hall, he stopped.

"Do not have anything to do with her," he said. "She's like poison. I'm surprised Sam didn't tell you."

"I felt sorry for her," Beth said, holding back the pesky tears that seemed to have suddenly become part of her.

"That's like feeling sorry for an animal that has every intention of eating you. The animal can't help it, that's its nature. Denise's nature is to hate. She hates everyone. The teachers feel sorry for her and even they end up regretting it. She keeps reporting them. Her family threatens lawsuits. I hear the guidance counselor just got reprimanded for calling Denise into her office too often. A suggestion of harassment or something. Leave her alone—way, way alone."

Beth looked through the open cafeteria door. Denise was again sitting, again eating her lunch. She looked totally forsaken. How could you not feel sorry for her?

The rest of the afternoon, Beth kept thinking about Denise. What made her act like that? And did she know something about who was doing the killing in Beaumont, something that would get Leroy off Holt's back? If so, then Beth had to find out. She owed that much to Holt, didn't she?

Beth had a paper due in English. On Nathaniel Hawthorne's short story "The Birthmark." She had already written the paper, but now she needed Holt's computer. She found him after school, before he went to football practice.

"Can I use your computer tonight?" she asked.

"Sure, just come on over when you need it. You don't have to ask. You're ready to use it on your own. Have been for a while, but I liked you being there." He smiled.

He kept saying things like that. She was trying so hard to tell herself that Holt belonged to Samantha. And he kept saying things like that. She didn't know how to play this game at all.

There was a group of boys who hung around the north side of the high school parking lot. As Beth walked toward her car, she made a point to go as far around them as she could. Tony Grimes was often there, and she thought she recognized one of the other boys from that night. They leaned against the fence, smoking and looking menacing. Beth thought they looked stupid, but she couldn't forget that dark night alone on the road.

Suddenly, Beth distinctly heard one of them mention the name Slim Carry. She stopped, bent down, and fiddled with her shoe lace. They didn't try to keep their voices low. They talked above each other, each vying for attention.

"He was asking for it," said a deep voice. Beth managed a quick look. Two of the boys were in fatigues. The taller of the two was speaking. "He had no respect for the colonel. None at all. He should have known he wouldn't get away with that."

"Colonel Crowell would never do anything like that," insisted the other boy in fatigues.

"Not himself, maybe, but a lot of people do his bidding. You'd better be one of them."

"You dinks are so full of yourselves," said another boy, this one in torn jeans, not fatigues. And the others laughed and went back to slouching against the wall.

Beth walked to her car.

She kept hearing that name, Colonel Hank Crowell: Denise's uncle, leader of the militia, big influence in town. She realized that she had seen him the first day she came to town. He was one of the men who had left her such a lousy tip. He was the one the others listened to so intently. He had been in since then, sometimes in his fatigues, sometimes in a business suit. People always seemed nervous around him. He never tipped well. Was the chief considering him as a suspect? And if not, why not? Because he was influential? There were some things Beth was learning about the world that were not good at all. She had wanted to think of this world as in color—lush and good. But it wasn't, not all of it. Sometimes it was more than black and white, it was dark, bad, and as unjust and dangerous as the one she had come from.

30

The next weekend, Holt was playing football again. He was going to start for this, the second game. Everyone understood that he wasn't one hundred percent yet, that he probably wouldn't play the whole game. But he would be there, giving a hint of what he would be able to do later in the season. They were playing against Tremont High, which wasn't considered a difficult school to beat. Their big game, their natural rival, was Keene High. And that was only three games away.

Dee insisted that Beth not work that afternoon. Molly, Dee, and everyone else in town was going to the game. Dee left Sally to handle the café. It would be lucky if anyone came in.

Beth picked up her friends, first Sidney, then Amanda, Heather, and Samantha, who had called her at the last minute for a ride.

Sidney, as soon as she heard about Samantha, wanted to bet Beth five dollars that Samantha wouldn't sit with them on the bleachers, not for the whole game, anyway.

"I don't bet," said Beth. Five dollars was way too big a risk and besides, what difference did it make?

The parking lot was packed. Beth had learned a lot about driving since she left Philadelphia, but parking, especially parallel street parking, still eluded her.

So they parked several blocks away.

"Where did you get your driver's license, anyway?" asked Heather in a not altogether teasing voice.

"You could have parked between those two cars in the first block," agreed Amanda.

"I could have almost walked from home," said Samantha.

"If you don't like my driving, next time, you drive," said Beth. She used to be so careful of what she said, trying it out in her mind before allowing it past her lips. Now, she was often quite surprised at what came out of her own mouth.

"I didn't say a word," said Sidney.

They joined the mass of people all heading toward the field. It cost five dollars to get into the game, even with a student pass. Beth wasn't expecting that. Every time she built up a little cash reserve, it seemed to dwindle away.

The others stopped to get drinks and snacks.

"You make me sick," said Amanda to Beth. "No

wonder you stay so thin. You never cheat even just a little bit."

Heather bought a hot dog. It smelled delicious to Beth. She was hungry, and watching Heather bite into that roll, wiping up the mustard and relish from her mouth, made Beth hungrier. She had never had a hot dog, hadn't wanted one until right this minute. She didn't bother to answer Amanda. What could she say? That she wasn't thin by choice? That if she didn't work at Dee's and get an occasional breakfast from Molly, she probably wouldn't eat? Food was not a priority to her. Going to the grocery store and spending money on food just didn't enter into the picture. Money was her getaway, her security that she could leave at any time.

There were two sets of bleachers, one on each side of the field. Beth didn't have any trouble spotting which one she should sit in. Almost everyone had on green and white, the Beaumont High colors. She hadn't known about that.

The band was on the field. Suddenly, they stopped playing. The cheerleaders came bounding around the end of the field house. They formed a double line and yelled at the top of their lungs as the football players followed them and dashed through the tunnel they had formed.

Everyone stood up. Beth stood up, too. She thought the players looked silly. Those huge helmets and shoulder-pads made them look top-heavy. They reminded her of little kids packed into padded snowsuits. The ball was tossed and the game began. Everyone sat down. Beth sat down. Dee had been right. All she had to do was follow.

Beth liked the feeling of being part of a crowd that all concentrated on the same thing, of being part of the whole—liked disappearing into it. It was a cozy feeling of belonging. It reminded her of something C.J. had once told her. Beth had been very sick with a sore throat and a high fever and had asked C.J. if she was going to die. For once, C.J. wasn't angry and had told her that dying wasn't all bad. You just merged back into the whole, became part of what you were always meant to be. C.J. wasn't religious, didn't approve of religions. Perhaps that's why Beth remembered that particular incident. Or, perhaps, it was because C.J. hadn't been angry. That was unusual enough on its own.

But the game itself totally confused Beth. She didn't know what a down was, or why people got called back, or why the two teams stood and suddenly banged into each other. On the very first play, Holt was knocked down. Beth couldn't help herself. She yelled out, thinking he was hurt.

Samantha yelled, too. "Get up. Get up," she shouted. And he did.

317

The next time, Holt threw the ball. Someone ran out and caught it and started running for all he was worth down the field. Everyone stood up, and the cheering was deafening. People were stomping on the bleachers, making Beth fear they would break apart. Then someone kicked the ball between the poles at the end of the field, and everyone went crazy with the cheering all over again. Fifteen minutes later, she happened to notice the scoreboard. The Hornets were ahead by seven points.

It went on like that, back and forth. She couldn't figure out why they called it football. There was much more running and carrying and throwing than there was kicking.

There was an intermission, called halftime. The band came onto the field and marched themselves into formations, spelling out HORNETS, and then rearranging themselves into some pictures Beth couldn't make out. When they left the field, the players came back and the whole thing started all over again.

Holt stayed in the game. Toward the end of the game the Hornets were only a few yards from the goal post when everyone started yelling.

"Quarterback Sneak," yelled the people sitting behind Beth.

"No. A roll out," yelled someone else.

Suddenly, Holt charged right through the players in front of him and the crowd went wild again, cheering, stomping, dancing on the bleachers. By this time, Beth knew he had made a touchdown. She too cheered.

When it was over, and the Hornets had won by twelve points, everyone gave Holt a special cheer and yelled his name, and Beth shouted as loud as the rest.

Samantha had sat with them for the whole game. Beth wondered if it was because she got too excited to move around and find her other friends, or if she had planned to stay with them all along. And what difference did it make?

They didn't leave right after the game. Everyone stopped and talked to everyone else. It seemed like they all felt the same sense of accomplishment the players had the right to feel. She wondered what they would do if they had lost. Then she saw the Tremont team, getting forlornly into their bus. That said it all.

"Beth," Dee called to her from a distance away. "Don't come in tonight." She yelled loud enough for everyone to hear. "Celebrate instead. I've got Missy coming in." Missy was another new addition, another older woman with kids, like Sally, who wanted a few hours of work.

Once again, Beth was torn. She knew Dee was being kind. Dee wanted her to have the "high school experience." But each time she took off work, it was less money.

They ran into the Queens as they passed the parking lot. But they, too, were so pleased with the day, that they went out of their way to say hello to everyone.

"We missed you," said Lindsey to Samantha.

"Yeah, missed you, too," Sam replied airily.

"Coming to the party tonight?" Lindsey asked. Then she turned to the others. "You, too. You coming?"

Beth caught the look Amanda and Heather gave each other. "Maybe," said Heather.

It was obvious to Beth that her friends had not known anything about a party. But it wasn't until they were all in Beth's car that Sidney asked the question Beth had wondered about.

"What party? Where?"

"It's at Lindsey Morrissey's house," said Samantha. "Are you really going to go?"

"Are you going?" Sidney asked.

"Yes, of course," said Samantha.

"Then why shouldn't we? That was an invitation, wasn't it?" Heather asked.

"I guess," said Samantha. She didn't sound at all convinced. "It might turn out to be kind of wild."

"I do wild," said Heather.

"How wild?" asked Sidney.

"Well, her parents are out of town. It's bound to get wild," said Sam.

"Where is her house?" asked Amanda.

"Way out on the point. There's nothing else around there. It's a perfect party place," said Sam.

"Can you drive, Beth?" Sidney asked.

Beth hadn't even considered going. She would have used the work excuse, except everyone for miles around had heard Dee tell her not to come in to work that night. But the thought of the party terrified her. She wasn't ready for that yet, not a whole evening of just talking. Lunch worked for her because Sidney and Heather talked so much that Beth wasn't required to contribute a great deal. But a party? With all those people she didn't know? That was terrifying. There would be questions. These people talked in questions. And the ones she didn't know, like most of the seniors, seemed eager to pounce on any little mistake she made. It was like they were setting traps for her.

"I don't know..." Beth said, trying to come up with

some sort of excuse.

"You've got to come. You've got to drive," said Heather. "My mother hardly ever lets me have the car."

"I don't even have a license yet," said Amanda.

Beth thought about that one. She didn't have a license either, not really, only the Tico kind. Amanda should go to Tico. She could just picture that. That would be a laugh and a half. Had she just made that one up, or had she heard it someplace? She was getting better with the slang thing. And why was she thinking about that, instead of her excuse for not going tonight?

"I, of course, will never drive, according to my father," said Sidney.

"What about you, Samantha?" Heather asked.

"I can probably get a ride. Maybe Holt already plans to take me."

Beth was getting used to the stomach lurch that any mention of Holt by Samantha caused.

"I heard a rumor a while ago that you two had broken up," said Heather.

"When? From whom?" Samantha demanded.

"Let it go, Heather," said Sidney.

"Like a week ago. Everyone was talking about it,"

Heather said, ignoring Sidney.

"Well. It's not true," said Samantha, sharply. She turned to Beth. "I don't think you should go to this party."

"Why not?" asked Amanda.

"You can go if you want to," Samantha said to Amanda. "But I don't think Beth should go."

"So it is true, the rumors," said Amanda. "That it's Beth that Holt's interested in now."

Beth couldn't see the expression on Samantha's face— Samantha was sitting directly behind the driver's seat. But she could imagine it.

"That wasn't what I meant at all," Samantha said, her words clipped, coming through tight lips. "I don't trust Lindsey and the others. I think they're setting you up. I think you're walking into something you might not like."

"Don't be ridiculous," said Heather.

"You don't know them," Samantha noted.

"You just don't want the competition," said Amanda.

Beth could feel the fury radiating off of Samantha, even from the front seat.

"I'm not sure I want to go anyway," said Sidney. "I think it is a little strange, them inviting us after ignoring us forever."

"Well, I'm going, and nobody's going to stop me," said Heather.

"Me, too," agreed Amanda.

"Fine," said Samantha. "Just remember, I warned you."

They had arrived at Samantha's house, the first on the route. She got out of the car quickly.

31

Beth let Sidney off last. She liked being with her more than the others.

"They shouldn't go to that party," said Sidney.

"I know," agreed Beth.

"I think Samantha was sincere, warning them."

Beth wasn't sure about that. Maybe Samantha really did just want Holt to herself.

Neither Sidney nor Beth felt the need for constant conversation. Their silences were comfortable.

"We could go watch," Sidney said, finally.

"What?"

"Take a boat. Ride by. See what's going on. You know? Then we could stop in if we felt like it. People around here arrive by boat all the time."

Beth was getting used to boats, but nighttime boating wasn't her favorite thing, especially not after being shot at.

"What kind of boat?" she asked.

"We should take the canoe. It's quiet."

A canoe. Beth had seen them gliding across the lake. They didn't go very fast and looked serene and graceful as they glided along. She thought she would prefer that mode of transportation.

"But it will be dark out there," she said. None of the canoes she had seen had lights.

"We'll stay close to shore," said Sidney. "And we'd be there for Heather and Amanda if they should need us."

A mission of mercy. That made it hard to refuse. But the last time Beth tried to help someone, it had only meant trouble.

"Come on. I can't go alone," said Sidney.

Beth finally agreed. She'd be at Sidney's house at nine-thirty. The party would just be getting started around then. Sidney's house was on the water, but in town, near the park beach. Beth thought it was the perfect place to live—town and lake all together.

As Beth climbed the stairs to her apartment, she saw a big bag on the top step. She paused a minute. Anything different spelled danger to Beth. Not that she was thinking of bombs or

IEDs, but it was out of the ordinary. And now that her whole world spelled "out of the ordinary," it was suspicious. She approached it slowly. Not touching it, she leaned over and peered inside.

All she could see was white tissue paper. Before she had dared move a finger toward it, Molly shouted at her from the back door of her house.

"Wait a minute. Wait," she said and hurried across the yard and up the stairs, an immense smile widening across her face.

"Open it, open it," she told Beth, with the excitement of a child.

Beth picked up the bag and opened her door. "Come on in," she said.

"Oh," said Molly, looking around. "You're keeping this so neat and nice. It's a cute place, don't you think?"

"I love it," said Beth, the words totally inadequate for how she really felt.

"Well, open it. Quick now, open it," said Molly.

Beth sat down on the sofa and pulled away the tissue paper.

"Oh," she exclaimed. One after another, she drew out a

skirt, two T-shirts, a pair of jeans, a shirt, and a sweater.

She just looked at Molly. She didn't understand.

Molly was watching her hopefully, and that made Beth more confused than ever.

"You know about the money," Molly said. "Nobody else is supposed to know about it. Can you realize how frustrating that is? I mean, I'm rich and I can't buy myself anything new. I was thinking I could buy something and just never wear it, but I know everyone around here, including the clerks in the stores, so that wouldn't work. Josh Winters knows about it, and he says for me to keep quiet about it. He's afraid for me until they know who killed Bert. He thinks there may be a money angle.

"And this was such fun. I've always wanted a daughter as well as a son. You can't believe how much I loved picking these things out. There's a gift receipt in there, you can choose different sizes or colors. But I had to get it out of my system. I had to buy something. And the idea of nobody criticizing me for what I bought—I just can't tell you how much I enjoyed that. Josh said getting these things for you was all right. Like maybe I was given money from your mother or something. The people in the store wouldn't know that wasn't true."

Beth was about to say she couldn't accept these beautiful things. She had her own policy about accepting charity, but a refusal would remove the smile on Molly's face.

Molly wasn't quite through. She pulled out one more tiny bag from her purse and handed it to Beth.

"Open it," she said, the look of excitement still on her face.

Beth pulled out a cell phone. She looked at Molly with wonder. Was all this real? It felt like dreaming.

"Oh, God," said Beth.

"It's the pre-paid kind, limited minutes, but it's good for you to have it," said Molly. "I'll feel better if you have it. It's a safety thing. You drive home at night in the dark and you should have one."

If only she knew, thought Beth. And then she burst into tears.

"Oh, my dear girl," said Molly, rushing over to sit beside her on the sofa. "I didn't mean to upset you."

Beth couldn't speak. *Would she ever get used to kindness?*

"If you don't like what I picked out, you can exchange everything, if you want. I was so hoping that maybe next time we could go together. I saw some really cute shoes, but you'd have to try them on. We could have ourselves a shopping day, stop for lunch, all that, you know? Things I never get to do with Holt." Again Molly looked at her with those hopeful eyes.

It made Beth's tears turn into sobs.

"I've gone too far, haven't I?" said Molly. "Bert always told me I go too far. I've infringed on your privacy or something." She sounded sad, again.

Beth had to force the words out. "No. No," she said.

"No, you don't want them?" Molly asked.

"No. I love them. Everything is perfect."

"Then, what's the matter?"

More tears came, making the words harder. "It was so nice of you," Beth blurted out.

Molly didn't understand. But she knew when to give a kid a hug.

"I'm going to go back to work at the café. I don't know how to play Mrs. Rich-bitch. When people do find out about the money, I won't be able to do that anymore, will I?" Molly looked at her, as though Beth would have an answer.

"Why not? You can do whatever you want to do," Beth said.

"Not in this town," said Molly. "We all have our roles here. I hope it's a long time before anyone finds out about the money. I like things just as they are."

When it was time to leave for Sidney's, Beth scrutinized herself in the small mirror. She thought her blotchy face had gone back to normal. She hoped so. Anyway, it would be dark.

She had met Mr. and Mrs. Lee. They were polite and very proper, and Beth was nervous around them. She over-thought her every word, trying not to make a mistake. But this time, Sidney met her at the door and they walked around the house to the lake front. A canoe was tied up to the dock. Sidney handed her a flashlight and a life jacket. Beth was grateful for both.

Sidney had to give Beth a paddling lesson. Beth wasn't as smooth and silent as Sidney, and when she changed the paddle from one side of the boat to the other, she got everything wet, including herself.

Sidney gave her instructions in a very soft voice. "Remember, sound carries over the water," she told Beth more than once.

There was moonlight tonight. The beam it cast across

the water looked like a roadway. The lake was still and glass-like.

Their trip took them past the Cummings' house, around a point, and across the far arm of the lake.

Everything was so quiet. Sidney kept her promise to hug the shoreline. They saw the lights of some houses and cottages, less so as they paddled away from town. Many places were dark, the summer people gone until the next season.

They heard the noise long before they spotted Jenna's house; music played full blast. The big bonfire in the middle of the yard provided enough light to show shadowy figures vibrating around the fire and moving over the lawn.

Beth knew enough to be quiet, now. Sidney's last command was for Beth to take her paddle out of the water. Sidney would handle it from here. So Beth was paying close attention to the people on the lawn. It was, she thought, the opposite of what she had seen at the Cummings' house after the funeral. No linen tablecloths or little lights here, only darkness and loud music, and figures that seemed unable to stay still.

Voices shouted above the music, so they could be heard from the water. But only occasionally could Beth understand actual words, only when one person dominated the conversation and others actually stopped talking to listen.

If Holt and Samantha hadn't been standing on the end of the dock, their voices would have blended into the crowd.

"Get them out of here," Samantha was pleading.

"What do you expect me to do?" Holt answered. He turned to walk away. But she grabbed him.

Sidney eased the canoe into the tall reeds beyond a birch tree. They would be difficult to spot.

"The Queens are planning something, I know they are," said Sam. Her distressed voice carried well over the water.

"Well, they're your friends," Holt argued.

"Not so much anymore," Samantha said. "I'm not being loyal enough. I'm probably next on their list to be set up."

"I never thought you fit in with them, anyhow," he said.

"Just let's get Amanda and Heather out of here," Samantha insisted.

Sidney scooted up to the bow of the canoe on her hands and knees. She whispered in Beth's ear, "What should we do?"

"Let me out," said Beth. They were halfway beached on the shore. "Wait here. I'll go get them."

Beth got out of the boat as quietly as she could. She took off her life jacket so she could move more quickly, but grabbed the flashlight.

They weren't beached enough to keep Beth's feet dry. She should have taken off her sneakers. She continued to get wet as she walked through the swampy reeds. Then, when she made it to dry ground, she had to climb over fallen branches. It wasn't easy to stay quiet as she headed down the shoreline.

Now Beth could see that the fire blazed from a fire pit with benches around it. A boy was telling a story and everyone was listening and laughing.

Beth made for the dock, stooping low.

"Holt, Samantha?" she whispered, standing below where the dock rose out into the water. They didn't hear her at first. She ventured farther out into the water, still keeping her voice low, still stooping under the dock.

She whispered their names again.

Holt turned and peered over the dock. "Beth?" he asked, with surprise.

"Shhh," Beth cautioned.

Neither Holt nor Samantha had on shoes. They jumped off the dock to join her. Holding her finger to her lips, Beth led them under the dock and a foot toward shore, where it was shallow.

"What's happening with Heather and Amanda?" Beth asked.

"Nothing yet," Samantha assured her. "But I just know the Queens are planning something."

"Where are they?" Beth asked.

"In the house. They just don't get it," said Samantha. "I tried and tried to tell them. I know Lindsey, and especially Laura, have something planned. And Jenna giggles every time she looks at them. Something's up."

"Show me where they are," said Beth. And Samantha led the way up the lawn toward the house.

Lights blazed from every window, none of which could be seen from the lake because of all the trees. It was a perfect party place. There was different music playing here, vying with the outdoor music.

Nobody paid any attention as the three of them walked through the rooms. The fact that Beth squished in her sneakers went unobserved.

"They really won't listen to you," repeated Samantha. "But I know there's something planned and I know it isn't good."

They reached the small library off the main room of the

house. There *was* something planned, and Samantha was right—it wasn't good.

Seven people sat at a table, five boys and two girls. They had cards in their hands and bottles of beer in front of them. In the middle of the table was a pile of clothes: five shoes, a couple of socks, a sweatshirt, a nylon jacket, a fleece jacket, a T-shirt, and a pair of jeans. Everyone was decently dressed except Heather, who was down to her bra and panties. She was trying to hold up her head with her hands, but it hovered just above the table. Her laughter held a sharp edge of hysteria.

When she saw Beth, Holt, and Samantha, she suddenly stopped laughing.

"Wha you… here?" she asked, her words slurred.

Amanda was at the table, too, but she was fully dressed. "She doesn't really know how to play poker," Amanda explained. And she laughed when the boys laughed. Her words were only slightly slurred.

"Now everything's ruined," said a voice. Beth and the others turned around. The voice seemed to come from nowhere.

Then a curtain opened, revealing a balcony above

where people clustered together, peering over the railing. They burst into laughter, like many breaths released at the same moment. At the front of the group a boy was holding up his phone, still recording the scene below.

"All ready for YouTube," the boy said, laughing hysterically.

Heather looked up and burst into tears. She tried to grab her T-shirt, but one of the boys yanked it away from her.

"You lost it fair and square," he said.

Heather got up and, holding her arms in front of herself, ran in a staggering path toward the door.

Beth ran after her.

Holt headed up the stairs to the loft, grabbed the phone out of the boy's hand, and erased the video. He flung the phone back at the boy and tried to catch up to Beth.

As drunk as Heather was, Beth wondered how she could run so quickly through the room. But everyone stopped, getting out of her way in order to stare, and she easily ran past them. But Beth kept running into people as they rearranged themselves back into their groups. They were all laughing.

Heather dashed out a side door. It hadn't completely closed when Beth reached it, but she could see no sign of

Heather. It took a few seconds for Beth's eyes to adjust to the dark night. She looked around frantically, but Heather had disappeared.

Holt was right behind her. "Which way did she go?" he asked.

"I don't know," said Beth.

"I'll go that way," he pointed up the hill. "You go the other way."

They both took off as fast as they could.

Beth was heading toward the lake. She could make out a span of blackness through the trees. The foliage was thick and she kept stumbling. How was Heather possibly managing to stay ahead of her in such condition?

Then she heard a splash. She arrived at the beach in time to see Heather waist deep in the water, heading outward as fast as she could. She was in that highway of moonlight, her body disappearing by degrees as she waded out farther.

"Come back," yelled Beth, knowing Heather wasn't in any condition to swim.

"I'm never coming back," Heather called. The cold water had given some definition to her words.

Heather was now only a bobbing head, going farther

and farther toward the middle of the lake.

The Point, for which this piece of land was named, was a peninsula jutting out into the water. Beth ran along the shore continuing to call out to Heather, keeping abreast of her, and Heather was slowing down, but Beth was coming to the end of the strip of land.

There was more thrashing in the water. Then suddenly—nothing: no sound, no girl.

Beth was at the end of the point. She stopped shouting and listened intently. Sounds could be heard from back at the house—music, voices—but there was no sound from the water. It was still.

Beth didn't even think. She plunged into the lake.

Move your arms and legs and you're swimming, she remembered Holt telling her. She was frantically moving every part of herself, and she was accomplishing a weak dog paddle. She wasn't sinking and she was gaining distance, but at a very slow pace. She was afraid to stop moving to listen for Heather. If Beth stopped, surely she'd sink right down.

She thought she heard something and aimed toward it.

The moonlight had disappeared. Only blackness surrounded them. Beth's foot touched something and instinctively she jerked it away. Was it some kind of creature? But she was looking for Heather—had she found something? She put her foot back down. It didn't feel like fish scales, it felt like fabric.

It took every bit of courage she could muster to force her face into the water. Of course, she could see nothing, but she was heading downward, going deeper, reaching out, feeling her way. And she touched something with her hand.

Was it an arm? She pulled at it and had a moment of total confusion as to which way was up. Would she drown because she had lost what little sense of direction she ever had?

Suddenly, she burst to the surface, gasping for breath.

Kicking her feet as hard as she could to stay afloat, she hauled with all her might on the arm, and then Heather's head and shoulders surfaced above water. But there was no gasp of breath.

Beth screamed. Was Heather dead? Beth couldn't stand the thought of touching someone who was dead. A terrible memory flashed briefly, a memory she couldn't bear, of looking down at the rough grave, of seeing the whiteness of the body, of not being able to make a sound. Once again, she pictured Jack's dead face. This scream encompassed that horror, as well as the one she was facing now.

Still, she was holding onto Heather. She was making almost imperceptible progress toward the shore. It was taking forever.

Then, just as her last bit of energy played out, just when she was ready to let go, when the idea of just sinking seemed more of a relief than anything else, she felt a hand take over her hold on Heather.

"I'll take her." Holt said, and the burden was gone. "You can touch bottom here," he told her, just as he had the last time.

Beth put her feet down and, sure enough, her feet sank into the slimy ooze. It held her and it felt safe. *So safe.*

It took Beth longer to reach the beach than it did Holt, even with his burden. He was already holding Heather up, his hands under her stomach, her head and feet dangling limply. Water was pouring out of her mouth, a great deal of water.

He then laid her down on the sand and was breathing into her mouth.

Beth could only watch for the first few minutes while she tried to catch her own breath. Finally, she crawled toward them.

"What can I do?" she asked, still panting.

"Call 911," he said.

She struggled to get up onto her feet, then struggled more to get going up the hill. As she got close to the group around the fire, she managed to give a shout.

"Call 911," she said.

"You've got to be kidding," said a voice and there was instant laughter.

"Yeah, sure," said another. "Come, Officer, put me in jail. I really want to do that."

"Are you insane?" asked a voice. "Have another beer."

"She's drowned," Beth tried to shout. She was still panting and it was a half-hearted sound at best. "She's not breathing."

Instant quiet, and then a swarm of questions. "Who? Who is it? Where?"

"Get the beer out of here."

A girl closest to Beth had her cell phone to her ear. She was calling.

Beth turned and went back down to the beach. Most of the crowd followed her. Some were scuttling around, picking up beer cans and bottles.

"Oh, my God," Beth heard one boy say when they had all gathered around Heather and Holt. He looked like one of the boys who had been playing poker. Was he having a moment of conscience?

Holt was now giving Heather chest compressions.

"Is she breathing?" Beth asked.

"I think so. A little gasp, anyway," he said.

Several of the bystanders were giving advice, calling for mouth-to-mouth, not knowing what had already been done. More had hurried away, and once they heard a siren, even more of the crowd disappeared.

"Somebody, go up to the house. Direct them down here," Holt said, and a couple of the girls ran toward the house.

It was only moments later that Chief Winters appeared.

He pushed through the remaining onlookers. "Make room here. Give her some air. The ambulance is on the way from Keene." He knelt down and felt for a pulse.

"She's got a beat, slight, but it's there," he told Holt.

By the time the ambulance and the EMT crew arrived, Heather had opened her eyes. Someone had brought a blanket from the house and covered her up. The party was down to about a dozen people. Cars could still be heard revving up and driving away.

"Who is she?" the chief asked when the EMTs had started pushing the gurney back up the hill.

"Heather Galvin," said Sidney. She had been so quiet that Beth hadn't realized she was there.

"What happened?" asked the chief.

Sidney looked at Beth and Holt, as interested as the rest of them for this answer.

"She ran into the water," said Beth. That was true.

"This is the Morrissey house, isn't it?" he asked.

Nobody wanted to answer that question.

"I saw Lindsey a little while ago," Amanda said in a broken voice. There were tears coming down her face. "But Heather is going to be all right, isn't she?"

"Let's hope so," said Chief Winters. He turned back to the others.

"No parents are home, I take it?" It wasn't really a question, and nobody answered.

"You." He pointed to Holt. "You are going to give me the whole story, including the part where my daughter was going to go to a movie with you this evening."

Holt gave Beth a quick look and a subtle shrug of his

shoulders when the chief wasn't looking.

Beth looked around. She didn't see Samantha. She had disappeared with the vanishing herd.

Sidney tapped her on the shoulder. "We're getting out of here," she said. "They might be taking names or something. My father would kill me." She started walking, very slowly, which made her look all the more conspicuous.

Beth caught up to her. "Just walk naturally," she told Sidney.

"They'll definitely be asking you questions," Sidney said. "I thought you told me you couldn't swim."

"I can't. I don't know what happened out there. But I didn't sink."

"You're some kind of a hero. Again."

"Why am I always in the wrong place at the wrong time?" Beth wondered, half-aloud.

"Depends on your viewpoint," said Sidney. "I'm thinking Heather will think you were in the right place at the right time. At least she will when she's thinking again."

They had reached the canoe. Sidney heaved it out into the water and they took off quickly. There would be questions, Beth knew that, but right now all she wanted to do was get home and into some dry clothes.

32

On Monday, the general school chatter turned into a single conversation. Everyone was talking about the party. It was a coup to have been there, and there were many more people claiming to have participated than actually had. The fact that a girl had almost drowned and was rescued by another girl who claimed she couldn't even swim—well, what could be more dramatic than that? And then the police had come, and the stories escalated about the danger of being underage at a suspicious party and about how clever each of them had been to escape or how adroit they had been in fast-talking their way out of trouble.

From the moment Beth got to school, everyone stared at her. But nobody approached her, not with questions, not with comments.

As Beth walked down the hall, the noisy groups grew silent. They separated to let Beth pass, then re-formed. Beth could not have felt more self-conscious. She was grateful when she got to her first class and could sink low into her seat.

It wasn't until after that class that she could walk with Sidney and not feel quite so exposed.

"You're a celebrity," Sidney told her.

"I don't want to be a celebrity," said Beth. "I want to be normal."

"Well, forget that. There's nothing normal about you, and I'd like to be just like you."

Beth thought that was the most ridiculous thing she had ever heard.

"They're kind of scared of you, I think," Sidney continued. "Like you're too cool or important to disturb, or something."

Beth couldn't even begin to fathom that.

Suddenly, there was a flash. It took her a few seconds to regain her eyesight. Andrew Miller was aiming a camera a foot from her face.

"Just one more," he said. "I always like to take a second shot, just in case."

"What are you doing?" Beth demanded.

"It's for the school paper. This is going to be a great article." Andrew was down the hall before she could say another word.

"He's editor this year," said Sidney. "This will be his biggest story ever."

"Story?" asked Beth. She didn't want any story. And she certainly didn't want her picture in a paper, even a school paper.

At lunch, after Sidney and Beth sat down, all kinds of people joined them: Amanda, of course, who was unusually quiet, Samantha, Holt and his friends, but also several girls from the Queen's table. In fact, the only ones left sitting at the Queens' table were Lindsey, Laura, and Jenna.

Lunch was awkward, as far as Beth was concerned. She allowed the talk to go all around her, but she still felt them all looking at her.

In her last class, Beth was staring at the clock, watching the minutes slowly click by, when the teacher tapped her on the shoulder.

"You're wanted in the office," she said.

The office? That set the alarm bells ringing.

As she walked out of the room, every eye was on her.

When she got to the office, the two women behind the big desk both smiled at her.

"Mr. Jordan is waiting for you," said one of the women.

"You are to go right in." She opened the principal's door for her.

"Beth Waterman is here," she announced.

Both Mr. Jordan and the mayor were standing by the big desk.

"It's so nice to see you," said Mr. Jordan, as if he had actually ever seen her before.

"Yes, it is so nice to see you again," said the mayor. He reached out his hand to shake hers. Beth hesitated. She remembered the last time she had shook his hand. He held on too long and gripped too tightly. It was creepy. And it was the same this time, including his holding her elbow like before. But that had been her first day in town. She was used to things now. A handshake was only a handshake. Still, she was glad when he let go.

"You are a little lady of extraordinary courage," said the mayor. "We are proud to have you as a citizen of Beaumont."

Beth had no idea how to respond to that.

"Very proud, very proud," said Mr. Jordan. "It's not just that you saved a fellow student, although that's highly commendable, but you stopped an act of bullying. Twice. And we're starting a campaign against bullying. Zero tolerance. That's going to be our policy."

"We've created a new award. You're to be the first honoree. There will be an award ceremony on Friday night. We've made all the plans. You are to be the first recipient of the Beaumont Good Citizen Award." The mayor beamed and looked at her with expectation.

"No, no," Beth exclaimed. It came out louder than she had intended.

"Oh, yes, you deserve it," said Mayor Cummings.

"I don't want anything like that," she said. "Please, I really don't want anything like that. I just did what anyone would have done." Beth felt panicked.

Mr. Jordan carefully patted her on the shoulder. "Now, now, your modesty is admirable, but you deserve the admiration you will receive. You'll enjoy it. Just you wait and see."

"It's going to be good for the town," agreed the mayor. "We're going to make you famous, young lady. There'll be an article in the weekly, and everything. We already have a picture for them, the same one that they will be using in the school paper. And the local TV station in Keene will do a segment on you at the awards ceremony. Won't that be exciting?" His smile expected gratitude. Beth could hardly look at the man.

She tried to tell them, but they wouldn't listen. And

finally, all she wanted was to get out of that office and away from them. *Why, oh why did she keep doing things that called attention to herself?* Why couldn't she sit on the sidelines and watch like everyone else? Yes, she was determined to not be afraid any longer, but wasn't there some middle ground? When had she cast herself as some sort of hero? *Never.* But there was a lot of ground between hero and victim, wasn't there?

And the day wasn't over yet. After school, on the way home, Sidney insisted they stop in and visit Heather.

"I called her mother. She's been released from the hospital. And her mother said she really needs visitors, she's feeling all alone and embarrassed and everything. We have to do it," Sidney said.

"But I really don't know her that well," Beth replied. She had no idea what reaction she would get from Heather, especially after how angry Denise had been with her intervention.

"Well I'm going and you're coming with me. That's what friends do."

Beth had to accept her word on that.

They drove up to a large, Victorian house on the edge of town. It was painted pale yellow and surrounded by yellow mums in the garden. There were big yellow pots with more mums on the porch.

"You'll understand when you see her mother," Sidney said, noticing Beth's focus on the flowers. "She really believes in color coordination."

They rang the doorbell. The woman who answered was dressed all in beige: slacks, blouse, and shoes. Even her hair seemed to match.

"Sidney," she said, holding open the door and ushering them in. "You've come to see Heather. That's so nice of you. She's bored to tears with me. She'll be delighted." She turned to Beth, "I don't believe I know you."

Sidney made the introductions.

"Oh, Beth Waterman," the woman gushed, grabbing Beth and hugging her. "You saved my daughter's life. How can we ever thank you? I had heard so much about you, even before. Such an extraordinary story. You really didn't know how to swim? And Heather is such a fine swimmer. But becoming ill in the water, that was so unusual. I've never heard of such a thing. There are no words to thank you enough. Please, let me show you up to Heather. She'll be so pleased to see you."

She led them to a pink-and-white room on the second floor: pink plaid wallpaper, a pink cover on a white canopy bed, a white carpet bordered in pink. Heather was not in bed, she was sitting cross-legged on the floor, ear buds on, an iPod by her side, completely surrounded by stuffed animals.

She jerked in surprise and tore off her ear buds. She hadn't heard them approach. Her face grew instantly red.

"What are you doing here?" she demanded.

"Heather, dear, that's hardly polite," scolded her mother. "Beth saved your life."

"I'm getting rid of all this stuff in my room," Heather said, quickly. "I haven't had the time until now." She looked at the pile of animals a bit desperately.

"That's lovely, dear," said her mother. "I'll bring you up some bags and take it to Goodwill when you're through."

Heather had been holding a tattered bear. She now tossed it onto the pile.

"How are you feeling?" Sidney asked, when Heather's mother had left the room.

"I'm fine. Just fine," said Heather. She sounded angry. "People keep asking me that."

"Are you coming back to school soon?" Sidney tried again.

"I don't know." She hadn't looked directly at Beth yet.

"Everyone is asking about you," said Sidney.

"I'm sure they are," Heather said. "I'm sure I'm the joke of the century." Now she did look at Beth.

"That's not the way it's playing," insisted Sidney. "Nobody sat with Lindsey, Laura, and Jenna today."

"They didn't?" Heather asked, surprised.

"They sat with us," said Sidney, as if that was a personal triumph. She walked over and sprawled on the bed, which left Beth the only one standing.

"I don't understand," said Heather. "And why hasn't Amanda even called me?"

"I don't know anything about that," Sidney said. "Maybe she's embarrassed or something."

"*She's* embarrassed? What's *she* got to be embarrassed about? I'm the one who's so mortified that I'm never going back to school."

"Oh, come on..." Sidney said.

"Come on, nothing. I absolutely can't picture myself walking down that hall. Not ever again." She turned to Beth. "You didn't do me any favors, you know. You may want to play hero all the time, but what about how I feel?"

Beth stayed silent. She thought about the mayor and his making a big deal out of this award ceremony. That was going to make Heather feel even worse. Even Sidney didn't know about that yet. Everyone was going to think Beth was seeking praise and attention. She was going to have to stop that ceremony, somehow.

"People think what Lindsey and the others did was terrible," Sidney said. "They're on your side. And I don't believe for a minute you were going to kill yourself."

Heather got up off the floor and sat down on the bed beside Sidney.

"I don't actually remember what I was thinking," Heather said. "It's all like a blank. But I was in the water and I was crying and then I threw up, I mean really threw up. And I went under the water and I was still throwing up, and I breathed in and was choking. Then it got all crazy. I didn't know up from down. I was so scared. And everyone in the world is going to see that video. I *should* have killed myself." She turned to Beth. "You should have let me kill myself."

"Holt got the phone. He erased the video. There won't be any pictures anywhere," Beth said simply.

Heather burst into deep, breath-catching sobs, bent over, her head in her hands. When she looked up, she nodded her head and tried to smile, all the time sobbing. Sidney put an awkward arm around her. It took many minutes before Heather could bring herself under control.

"Thank God," she finally managed.

"I don't think you meant to drown yourself," said Beth.

"I don't know. I really don't know," Heather said, her breath still catching. "I remember thinking of getting to the other side of the lake. I'm a good swimmer. I could have made it if I hadn't thrown up. I'm never drinking another beer as long as I live."

"Not a bad plan," said Beth. She couldn't imagine purposely losing control, like she had witnessed at the party. Control was the most precious thing in the world.

33

Beth no longer needed Holt's help with the computer. On Tuesday night, Beth took his laptop over to her apartment and slowly typed her report for history. Now she was up in Holt's room, printing it out. She loved the way the pages looked as they tumbled out of the printer, like something someone else had done. She was on her own; Holt wasn't home. But she was doing just fine.

She heard the doorbell ring, heard Molly greeting someone. The pages continued to tumble out. This report was longer than she had intended. But it was kind of interesting— about corruption during the Reconstruction.

It wasn't until she noticed the distress in Molly's voice that she started to listen to what was going on downstairs.

"It's due me. Your husband made me a promise," said a deep male voice.

"But I don't know what you're talking about," protested Molly.

"I paid him for that property. He promised me the deed," the voice continued. "Don't try that innocent act on me. I know how much Floyd was worth. Plenty. I even know you've already accessed one of the accounts. Even before probate. You've got my money and I want the deed to my property."

Beth quietly took a few steps into the hall and stopped and listened.

Molly continued her protests: she didn't know anything about anything.

When the man spoke again, his voice was angrier. That's when Beth thought she had heard it before. She took more steps down the hallway toward the stairs. Who was it?

The two of them were standing in the living room, close to the front door. Even leaning way over the banister, Beth couldn't see much.

She took a couple of steps down the stairs, just enough to peek around the corner.

All she had to see was the haircut and the erect military stance. Immediately, she recognized Hank Crowell. Of course, she recognized the voice. Who else sounded so gruff? He hovered over Molly, his mere presence threatening. He didn't have to raise his voice to sound menacing.

Beth saw Molly take a step backward and then stand up a little taller.

"Do you have something in writing?" Molly demanded. Her tone of voice became firmer. Beth could hardly reconcile it with the timid whine of the Molly she had met that first day in town.

"I don't need anything in writing," he told her, saying the words slowly, deliberately. "Floyd and I always dealt with a handshake. You will hand over that deed, or else."

"Or else, what?" said Molly

"Or else there will be consequences and you won't like them."

"I know nothing about any agreement between you and my husband. And I don't have 'your' money. I'll ask the lawyer about it, maybe he knows something, but that's all I can do." Beth could hear her anger.

That was good, Beth thought. She had been about ready to walk down the stairs. Although what she thought she could do, she didn't know. And she was through helping people, wasn't she?

"Forget the lawyer." Hank was even angrier now. "I already told you, it was a handshake deal. It's my property, and I want the deed. Nobody is going to set foot on it without my say so. *Nobody*. Do you get that?" He reached out and grabbed Molly's shoulder. Molly flinched, pulling back.

"Stop right there," Beth heard herself say. She was already rushing down the rest of the stairs.

He turned quickly and glared at her. "What the...?" he demanded.

Beth picked up the phone. "I'm dialing 911 as we speak," she said, surprised that her voice sounded so calm. Nobody was going to hurt Molly. Beth couldn't stand the thought of that. Yet here she was, once again, rushing in, just after she had promised herself that she wouldn't do this anymore.

"Who are you? What are you doing here?" Crowell's voice was one of command.

"You need to leave," said Molly. "Right now. You are not welcome in my home."

Crowell didn't move.

"Go ahead and call," Molly said to Beth.

"Save yourself the trouble," said the colonel. "I'm leaving. But you haven't heard the end of this. In all good faith I asked for something that is owed me. There is nothing illegal about that." His big boots made a stomping sound, and he slammed the door behind him.

"Do you think he's the one?" asked Beth, after the door stopped vibrating. "Could he be the one doing the killings?"

"But why? He said Bert was going to give him something. He was worth more to him alive."

"Maybe Bert changed his mind. Why hasn't anyone thought of him before? He's as mean as they come, and he's probably a good shot," said Beth.

"Josh mentioned his name. He's on the list," Molly answered.

"Above or below Holt?" asked Beth.

Molly sat down on the sofa, once more refusing to discuss Holt as a suspect. "Now that he's gone, I feel all shaky," she said.

"You were great," Beth told her with admiration. "I've never heard you speak like that."

"It's a funny thing. With Bert gone, and nobody criticizing my every word, I find myself saying all sorts of things. It feels good."

Beth smiled. She knew exactly what Molly was talking about. It *did* feel good.

"But he knew about Bert's money. Who told him?" Beth asked.

"I don't know, but he sure knew about it, all about it,

even the fact that one account was in both of our names. That's the one I have now. I will never know why Bert put my name on it. I don't remember signing anything. He probably signed it for me. I now know he did it on tax returns, forged my signature. I had no idea about our finances. But I'm learning. I'm learning a lot of things."

"Life is full of surprises, isn't it?" said Beth.

"Some of them are very nice surprises," said Molly. "Like the money. And like you."

Beth had to talk quickly. When would she ever be able to hear something nice without wanting to cry?

"Are you afraid?" she asked Molly, "about the consequences thing?"

"What can he do to me?" Molly asked. "I'll tell Josh about it. He'll know what to do."

"You really trust Chief Winters, even though he's got Holt on his suspect list?"

"I do trust him. He's been giving me some really good advice. He's a nice man. He doesn't believe Holt killed his father. He's working very hard to find out who did."

Beth looked at Molly. There was a slight smile on her face, an interesting smile. She had been spending a lot of time talking to Josh Winters. Was more going on there than figuring out a murder? Then she had a thought. If Molly Floyd and Josh Winters ever got together, that would make Holt and Samantha step-brother and sister. She didn't think they'd like that idea. Better that the older couple wait, and then they could all have a double wedding.

But she couldn't joke about it, even in her own mind. She kept trying to put Holt and Samantha together as a couple, to acknowledge it, but every time she did, she experienced that same little stomach lurch.

"Let's have a cup of tea," Molly suggested. "Are you almost finished with your report?"

"Just need to gather up the pages," said Beth.

"You go do that. I'll put the kettle on."

Beth loved the times she had tea with Molly. She was even beginning to tolerate the taste of tea, something she had never had before. It was such a cozy feeling, the two of them together. She'd drink mud mixed with road tar for those brief slices of time.

It was good getting to know Molly and Dee so well; they were better than anyone she had ever known. The more she knew them, the more she liked and admired them. In many ways, being with them was easier than being with people her own age. There were so many pitfalls with her peers.

After Molly poured the tea, they again went over the visit from Hank Crowell.

"I think it's better that we don't mention anything to Holt," Molly said.

"Why not?" Beth asked.

"Just until I talk to Josh. He always comes up with something I hadn't thought of. I just want to bounce it off of him first."

Bounce it off? Did Beth have that phrase on her list? She supposed that the teen sayings of each generation kept adding to the language everyone spoke. Except C.J., of course. Which was odd, wasn't it? Where had C.J. come from? She had never wondered about that before. Now that she had the opportunity to step back and look at the life she had led, she was asking questions about it that she had never asked before.

"More tea?" Molly asked.

Beth wanted the time here to continue, but the price of having to swallow another cup of tea was too much.

"I'd better get going," she said, looking at the clock. "It's getting late."

Molly glanced at the clock as well. "It is, isn't it? Holt should be home by now. I wonder where he is."

"He's not getting enough sleep," Molly said. "Not with

the football and all."

"Are you ever going to tell him about the money and the property?" Beth asked. "He won't need the scholarship now."

"Josh cautioned me about telling people. He says it's good that we know things most people don't know. He says it may draw somebody out. And it did, didn't it? I've got to call Josh right now and tell him about Hank." She got up and went to the phone. Beth rinsed out the cups.

Molly held the phone in her hand as she spoke. "Besides, what's Holt going to say? Will he refuse the money like he refused the pick-up? The idea that Bert was so stingy, never letting us have anything. That will just make Holt madder than ever."

"But it will all come out, won't it?" Beth asked. "You can't hide it forever. And won't Holt be angry that you didn't tell him?"

"I can't win, can I?" said Molly.

34

Beth wanted something to happen before Friday. Something disastrous. Perhaps she could become deathly ill. But that wouldn't work. Dee was already worried about her lack of health insurance. If she should be sick, should have to go to a hospital, her lack of real identity would catch up with her. Dee kept warning her to take care of herself.

Maybe it would rain. Maybe the whole thing would be canceled.

But Friday night was perfect. There was an autumn crispness in the air. The leaves had begun to fall and they swirled in a dance of gold and red in the light breeze.

It wasn't anything like the crowded end-of-summer evening Beth had experienced her first night in town. There weren't that many people at the little band park. Most of those who did attend were kids from the high school, which only embarrassed Beth. Here she was, once again calling attention to herself. If only they knew how much she didn't want any part of this. It exposed her to more than embarrassment, and publicity was the last thing in the world she needed. She kept telling herself that this was a small town in the middle of nowhere—it wasn't important, and there was no way somebody in Philadelphia would hear anything about it. But she was still frightened. C.J.'s warnings that she would be found, that she couldn't escape, were permanently etched in her brain. And she still didn't know who had been watching her.

The gazebo was set up with a few chairs behind a podium with a microphone. Beth sat next to the mayor. The kids in the audience sprawled on the grass; the adults, scattered here and there, had brought chairs. Dee and Molly were sitting front and center and kept smiling and waving at her. Beth figured she looked as miserable as she felt, and they were trying to give her encouragement.

The mayor kept talking to her. At first it was only small talk. Beth loved that expression, *small talk*. It rang so true. What he was saying was small. It didn't require any input on her part. He liked to talk about himself, about his plans for the town, and what he had already done for it. But she resented even being here and she resented the mayor because he hadn't listened to her, had totally ignored her when she told him she didn't want this. Beth was beginning to realize that this whole thing wasn't really about her, it was about the mayor. He was the one using her to get attention. And even if she wasn't worried about the publicity, being found out, and all the terrible thoughts that brought about, even then, it somehow cheapened what she had done. She hadn't rescued Heather for a reward or attention. And making it about all that took away any small bit of satisfaction she might have had, degraded it. She thought about Holt and his reaction to Samantha's constant admiration about his football prowess. Now she really did understand. Besides, the mayor continued to creep her out. His smile was so fake. He reminded Beth of C.J., during the few times that C.J. turned on the "nice." That's what she and Jack had called it. Not that it happened often; it didn't. But when it did, it was creepy, mainly because they knew it was going to disappear at any moment and waiting for that moment was agony.

So Beth didn't listen to the mayor. Instead, she scanned the audience, watching as people came in and sat down. In the very back, a little apart from the others, a man put down a camp chair. When he settled himself, he looked directly at Beth.

When the mayor paused in his one-sided conversation, Beth asked him, "That man back there, Colonel Crowell. Do you know him?"

"I pride myself in knowing everyone in Beaumont, little lady," he said. "Of course, I know Crowell. Highly suspicious, that man. Highly suspicious."

"Why?" Beth asked, instantly interested.

"He's caused dissension ever since he came to town. The militia used to be an organization we were proud of. Now they're fighting among themselves, and besides..." He stopped himself.

"Do you think he could have anything to do with the murders?" she asked, then felt bad, remembering Mrs. Cummings.

Cummings stopped scanning the audience. He sat up straight in his chair and turned to her. For once there was no phoniness in his face.

"That's what I was about to say. It's been my thought from the beginning. It would make sense, wouldn't it? More sense than the boy my nephew keeps talking about." Beth could hear eagerness in his voice. He wanted to catch his wife's killer.

"A lot more sense than that," agreed Beth.

"Not that kids don't do that sort of thing. It's usually family. And it's usually young males. So Leroy's thinking shouldn't be ignored. But I've brought up Crowell's name to

Chief Winters several times. Hard to know what Josh Winters is thinking sometimes. Time to mention it again, I believe." He paused and again looked at Beth. "You met my late wife, I believe…"

Beth knew that some expression of sympathy was in order here. But she had no idea what she should say. "She was a nice lady. It was awful, what happened."

"Yes, well. You had a conversation. What did she say to you? I'm told it was something important. That you came back to ask her some questions."

Now Beth really didn't know what to say. Mrs. Cummings said she saw something, something that would get her in trouble if she told. Was she talking about her husband? But that seemed impossible. He was the mayor. Everyone in town liked him.

"It's just that if she did tell you anything," the mayor continued when Beth didn't say anything, "it might be putting you in some danger. I would certainly be careful around Hank Crowell. You don't ever want to mention anything about that to him."

"I think he knows pretty much of everything that goes on around here," said Beth, "and I hear that the rumor is all over town that we know something. We don't, you know."

"I'm glad to hear that—for your sake." The mayor smiled his fake smile. But Beth was beginning to think that he meant well. He seemed concerned about her safety. He was just a politician; maybe they all acted that way.

Just then they were interrupted. The program was about to start. There were three speakers before the mayor; two were city councilmen, who both took a long time to say nothing. They both rhapsodized about the new award, saying that it would let the state know about the people in Beaumont, make them realize that this little town by the lake represented the best in people and place. The third was Mr. Jordan, the high school principal, who spoke at length about bullying, how the school had a zero-tolerance policy, and how one person could make a difference if they stood up against it, as Beth had proved beyond any doubt.

Then it was the mayor's turn to present the award. He spoke at considerable length, saying many of the same things he had just tried out on Beth. The actual handing over of the plaque, inscribed in calligraphy with Beth's name and the legend "Beaumont Good Citizen Award," took far less time and wasn't as bad as Beth had feared, except for the cameraman. She was very aware of him.

After the ceremony, a woman from the local TV

affiliate came up to interview her. She had more years and more weight on her than Beth would have expected; not exactly glamorous. As she asked Beth questions, the newswoman would rephrase Beth's answers into her own words and nod. After she told Beth that this was taped, not live, Beth figured that she had already written her little piece and that Beth's participation was hardly necessary.

Then it was over. Beth could forget about it and go on with her life. At least she hoped so. She had decided the mayor wasn't such a bad guy. She couldn't use her hatred of C.J. as a measuring stick for everyone she met in life. Just because there was some obscure sense of familiarity, she couldn't condemn people. There was only one C.J. And the mayor was on her side about Holt. That counted for a great deal.

Afterward, Molly and Dee insisted they have a snack at the café.

"It's a celebration," said Molly. "And we get to be with the celebrity."

"Enough with the celebrity nonsense," said Beth. "I'm really uncomfortable with all of that."

They had barely sat down at the center table when Holt and Samantha joined them. Beth saw Molly and Dee give each other a look. Molly shook her head in some kind of warning. Whatever was about to be said was put on hold. Once again, the two women had been about to confide in Beth, but not Holt, and not Samantha. Once again, she felt that feeling of belonging that left her a bit limp and the same time filled up a very empty place way deep down inside her.

Beth cut off any conversation about the award, good deeds, or herself, and the talk soon turned to other things.

"I have a big announcement," said Dee, her face beaming. "And it's not about Beth, so it's allowed." She looked at Beth.

"Yes," Beth answered, trying not to look embarrassed at her bossiness that evening, "allowed."

"Actually, two announcements," said Dee. "I'm taking on a business partner, and I'm buying a house. No more living upstairs in that one crummy room for this old gal."

"Where's the house?" asked Beth.

"Who's the partner?" asked Holt.

"The house is that white Victorian with the pink door on Pine Street just off of Main. And the partner will remain anonymous just for a little while."

"Oh, I love that house," said Samantha. "I didn't know it was for sale."

"Never came on the market, but I hear a lot of talk here in the diner," said Dee.

"The mayor won't be happy about that," said Samantha. "He hates it when he isn't involved in selling a house."

"One more another advantage," laughed Dee.

Beth was about to defend the mayor, but she didn't get the chance. The talk went on too fast around her. Beth was very aware of the glances between Molly and Dee. She now knew what they were going to tell her and she didn't have to stretch too far to guess who the business partner was. Molly was investing in the business, which enabled Dee to buy her house. It sounded like a good thing for both of them. But she didn't think that refusing to tell Holt about the money was a good idea at all. It fact, it was a very bad idea, and maybe she should just go talk to Chief Winters about it, get him to release Molly from her promise of silence, at least with her own son. What could be the harm in that?

Chief Winters came in just as Beth was thinking about him. It was almost like a sign that she should, indeed, talk to him. So, before she left, she approached his table and asked if she could speak to him.

"Sure, sit down," he said.

"Not here." She looked around. There were still a few

customers left.

"You want to come to my office? Like tomorrow, sometime?" He was trying to be accommodating.

"Couldn't we just go outside?" Beth asked.

"Sure." He got up, left some money on the table, and followed her out the door.

The police cruiser was parked right in front of the café. He leaned against it, folding his arms, ready to listen. He didn't rush her, but seemed content to stay there as long as she needed. He listened, nodding his head occasionally to show he was following her.

She told him about her fear that Holt would resent his mother for keeping the money a secret from him.

"I didn't ever tell her she couldn't tell her son," said Josh. "I just didn't want that particular information zooming around town. Not yet."

"I half suspected that," said Beth. "She doesn't want to tell him. It's going to make him angrier with his father than ever. But he has to know sometime."

"I'll talk to her. I agree with you. The kid has a right to know. And nobody blames him for feeling like he does about his father. There are just some bad apples in the world, and Bert Floyd was one of them. Holt has a better understanding of what his father was than Molly ever did. And the money is going to solve a lot of problems for the kid."

"I want to ask you something else." Beth paused. How could she put this without raising his suspicions?

"If someone is accused of a crime, and the evidence really points to that person, would the police even entertain the idea of looking somewhere else? Would they even listen to that person when he said he was innocent?"

"You talking about Holt?"

"Holt, maybe, but what if it was a different thing altogether and there was even more evidence against the person?"

Josh looked at the girl. She was not just making suppositions; she was trying to tell him something. Was there even more evidence against Holt that she knew about? She looked so distressed. But he got the feeling she was talking about something else, but he had no idea what it was. He felt sorry for her and wanted to reassure her, but he couldn't really. He knew that she was running from something. What had she done? What could she possibly have done?

Beth had been looking right at the chief as they talked. It wasn't until she turned to go back into the restaurant for her purse that she noticed the man standing halfway down the block. If he was trying to blend in with his camouflage, it was having the opposite effect. He was out of place standing in front of the gift shop and he had obviously been looking at the two of them, although Beth didn't think he could hear what they were saying.

The chief followed her glance. "I think I'll check that out," he said and walked down the block toward Hank Crowell.

The colonel continued to stare at Beth, even after she went back into the building.

35

Saturday was always a slow news night, which was why the national news had picked up a story from a little town in Michigan.

Stan Jones always watched the eleven o'clock news. It was a ritual that included a bottle of beer and a small dish of peanuts before bed.

The introduction was about bullying and listed several examples of past episodes that had very bad outcomes. Then the story switched to the small town in Michigan and showed a young, teenaged girl receiving an award for twice stepping in and preventing something more serious from happening. Stan hadn't been paying much attention. He was waiting for the weather, which he had no particular reason to care about and usually missed by the time it came on.

But the girl caught his attention. He shot out of his chair. It was her—just like her picture. A tall, distinguished man with too-white teeth was putting a small plaque into her hands. She smiled a shy, one-step-away-from-a-grimace smile that indicated she'd rather be anywhere in the world than up by that podium.

Stan sat back down in his chair. He was home, and the picture C.J. Watson had given him was at his office, but unless there was really such a thing as a doppelganger, that was Beth Watson standing up there. She hadn't even changed her first name. Sometimes people didn't, they responded so much more naturally to their own name. What made her so easy to recognize was that expression on her face—a sadness that looked so out of place on someone that age. It made her stand out from the crowd—way out. The newscaster was making a big deal out of how it was possible for this one girl to stop a very bad thing just because she had the courage to care. That she had stepped in before the real violence had started, and that one courageous girl could make a difference.

Beaumont, Michigan. He went to his laptop and started a search. It sounded like a nice little town, ideal middle America. Except there was bullying going on, but wasn't there everywhere? It had been the hot topic for several months now.

C.J. hadn't contacted him since the night he outsmarted Stan's surveillance. Stan didn't know whether he was still working for him or not. Stan felt like he shouldn't call about this, that he should keep the girl safe and away from C.J., but he had accepted all of C.J.'s money. It was long gone and he still owed something in service.

The TV report couldn't have happened at a better time. Cautious C.J. had made one mistake. That phone number he had given Stan, that throwaway phone—C.J. had used it several times. And such phones could be traced if they were used. Stan had called in some big favors from an old pal in the police department, and he now had an address. It was time for a visit.

So Stan and Harry got into the car after he finished watching the news. He still didn't know if he was going to reveal this latest information or not. But he'd talk to C.J. Watson, see him, feel him out. If the vibes were bad, he'd go find the girl and decide what to do about her before he let C.J. know. If the vibes were good, he'd let C.J. in on his plans.

The house was not in the best neighborhood. There were vacant lots, boarded up houses, and a lot of trash. Number 307 had a porch that was falling down, and the steps were treacherous. Stan left Harry in the car with the window open.

Even before he tried ringing the doorbell, he felt the emptiness of the place. There was no corresponding ring when he pushed the buzzer, so he knocked loudly.

Empty. Somehow you knew, felt it.

He tried the door, expecting it to be locked. He had his lock picks with him. But the door swung open. Stan hardly ever carried a gun anymore, although he had a carry permit. But he had brought it with him tonight, in a holster at his side. He had a hand on it when he entered the house.

He paused and listened before he felt for a light switch by the door. Of the three bulbs in the ceiling fixture, only one lit up. It was dim, but it was enough. He had entered into the living room. The furniture was sparse—a ratty sofa, a couple of chairs, a dirty rug, sagging curtains at the window, and a great many books, in bookshelves, on the tables, and piled up on the floor.

Stan walked through the house. Average small house: a living room, a dining area, a kitchen, and upstairs, three small bedrooms. There were clothes in the closets of two of the smaller bedrooms, boys' clothes in one, girls' clothes in the other; these looked to him to be for somebody sixteen or so— plain white T-shirts, a pair of jeans, and a couple of pairs of pajamas. The third bedroom closet, bigger than the other two, was empty, as were the drawers in the dresser.

Back downstairs, opening up more doors, he saw something he really didn't like. It was the closet by the front door. It was empty of anything like coats or the ubiquitous vacuum cleaner. Empty except for an invalid's potty chair and some duct tape. He had seen a closet like this once before in a case of bad child abuse. Someone had been locked up in there.

Just then he heard barking from the back yard. Harry was such a good dog, Stan could hardly believe he had jumped out the window, but he had. Harry was out in the yard, digging furiously. When Stan came out, Harry stopped and stood still. That was his signal—the dog had found something. And Stan didn't like that a bit. Harry, in his years with the police department, had been a cadaver dog.

Stan pulled out his cell phone and called the station.

36

It is possible, as Beth found out Saturday evening, to be tired but not sleepy. The diner had been busy. Everyone still congratulated her, which was embarrassing, but left especially good tips, which made her pleased.

When she got home, she wandered around the apartment, turned the TV on and off, picked up a book and put it back down. She was still pacing when the news came on and showed her story, complete with footage of her accepting the award.

Beth stopped and stared at the television. She felt totally exposed. So many times, she had told herself that Beaumont was a small town and nobody cared what happened here. The idea of packing up and leaving came into her mind, but she couldn't deal with it. She just couldn't. This was home now. Dee and Molly were family. She had friends. And there was Holt. He wasn't hers, not the way she would have liked, but he was still a friend, and she liked being with him.

She got ready for bed, but didn't even pull down the covers. She turned off the light and looked out the window. She wasn't looking for anyone. Whoever had been out there hadn't been seen since Holt had strung up the Christmas lights. She was just gazing out at the darkness.

But there was movement, off to the left. She stayed perfectly still and watched. Again, some bushes moved slightly in almost the same place. There was no wind; nothing else was moving.

She waited only a few seconds and then reached down and plugged the extension cord into the outlet below the window.

Suddenly it really was like Christmas, all the little lights spread among the bushes and trees were twinkling brightly—it looked like fairyland.

The lights also made the figure by the bushes visible. It was definitely a man. He was in camouflage gear, but he could be seen, especially as he turned and ran.

Immediately, Beth thought of Colonel Crowell. Yet she couldn't be sure—the man was gone so quickly.

She saw Holt running from the house and into the woods. Had he seen the man? Could he catch up with him? But what would happen then? If it was Crowell, he'd have a gun.

Beth ran out her door and down the stairs. The ground, when she reached it, felt cold to her bare feet. Once again, the twigs and stones hurt her feet as she headed toward the woods. But she continued to run, hearing only her own footsteps. Finally, she stopped and listened.

There was some thrashing ahead and to her right. She ran toward the sound. She passed the place where the lights ended. She was in a part of the woods she had never been in before. It was hilly.

When she stopped for a breath, she called out, "Holt? Are you all right?"

But no one answered.

Now she didn't even hear any thrashing. Still, she continued to run. The woods grew darker. She couldn't see where she was going. Her hands were out in front of her, protecting her from bumping headlong into a tree.

Suddenly, someone grabbed her. She felt something soft and confining come down over her head, then a jab in her arm, and then there was nothing.

She wasn't there to see the little Christmas lights suddenly go dark.

37

Beth didn't show up for work on Sunday. Dee thought it was a good idea for the girl to sleep in; this had been a big weekend for her. So she didn't call her cell phone until after eleven o'clock. The place never got busy until the churches let out, anyway. When nobody answered, Dee thought that Beth was probably on her way in.

Molly showed up to help at noon. Molly tried calling, and still nobody answered. So Molly phoned home to Holt, to ask him go and check on Beth. Holt wasn't home.

"I forgot," Molly said, "there's that away game in Lunn. He won't be back until way late this afternoon."

"Then you go," Dee told her. "Go back and check on her. I can't believe she could have slept through all those rings."

"I can't either. I'm sure she'll have a good reason for not calling. It's so not like her—she's so responsible. I've told her it's like she's sixteen going on forty. She acts older and wiser than I do most of the time."

"That's a good description of her," said Dee, her round face creased with worry. "This isn't like her at all."

Molly called Dee from Beth's apartment, her voice full of fear.

"She isn't here. But her car keys and everything else are here. I don't like the look of this."

"This doesn't sound good at all. I'm going to call Josh. Wait for him." Dee said.

"If anything's happened to her... please God. Let nothing have happened to her," said Molly. She was already crying.

"We need to stay calm, Molly, for her sake," said Dee.

Molly paced the little apartment. She kept the door open, looking for Josh's police cruiser. *Would he have the sirens on? Would he realize this was an emergency? Would he hurry?*

In her restlessness, Molly walked over to the window and looked out at the woods. That's when she noticed the plug on the floor. The wire led right out the window. She inserted the plug into the outlet and saw the little lights in the woods, hard to distinguish in the daylight, but she could see them.

They looked like the Christmas lights she used. It was all too odd. She hurried over to her own house and checked in the basement. Yes, the Christmas lights were missing.

That had to be Holt, Molly said to herself. Beth would not have known where to find the decorations in the crawl space in the basement. *But why didn't he say anything to her? What was it all about?*

"Hurry, Josh, hurry," she said to herself. "I don't like this at all."

38

Beth's eyes were open, but she couldn't see. Her head was covered with something that smelled musty—smelled of stale cigarettes and old sweat. And it was scratchy as it rubbed against her cheek.

Her arms were in a terrible position, clamped together and pushed up above her head. When she tried to move them, needles of pain shot through her nerve endings. Better to keep them still and numb. Her shoulders, however, radiated pain.

She was sitting in a chair, confined to it, not able to stand. Her feet were free, but with her arms the way they were, movement was impossible.

Her mouth was dry and she was more thirsty than she ever remembered being before. She also felt sick to her stomach, but she couldn't vomit, not with that bag over her head. She hated to think of the consequences if that were to happen.

All the little mantras she had repeated to herself about

not being afraid, all that time she had spent convincing herself that it was the fear that made things frightening, the fear that made her vulnerable—all that now accounted for nothing. She would be a fool not to be afraid now. *Why wasn't she dead?* The others had been killed instantly, and maybe that was better. This waiting in the dark for something terrible to happen—it was too reminiscent of that old closet—was worse. This ending would be final.

She thought of Hank Crowell listening to her half a block away when she had talked to the police chief. He had given her a stare that seemed to portend this. She should have heeded the warning. Yet she had gone running into the woods without a thought of the danger. She had only pictured Holt getting hurt. *Stupid, stupid, stupid.* Everything C.J. said about her was true. She was too stupid to live in the world. She deserved everything that had ever happened to her. *So let it come. Just make it be over quickly.*

39

When Holt got home that night, he was in a terrible mood. He burst into the house and started up the stairs to his room, without a hello to his mother.

"The team lost?" Molly called from the kitchen.

"No. We won," said Holt, as if that were a tragedy.

"You played badly?" she ventured again.

"No. I played great." His anger was palpable.

Molly was used to treading carefully with the mood of a man, something that had carried over from Bert to Holt for the last couple of years. It was a difficult habit to break. She had been watching the door, waiting for Holt to arrive, anxious to burst out with the fact that Beth was missing, ask what the Christmas lights were all about, and to tell him how worried she was.

She hesitated, than came to the bottom of the staircase. "I need to talk to you," she said.

"Not now, Mom."

"Now. It's important. Beth Waterman is missing and I'm worried out of my mind." She walked into the living room and sat down. She knew he'd follow.

"She's *what?*" He pounded back down the stairs.

Molly sat down on the sofa. "She's missing, has been since last night, I think. She didn't show up for work today, and her car keys and everything are still in her room. What could have happened to her?"

"Oh, my God," cried Holt. "I should have checked. I chased a guy away last night, except I guess I didn't. I never caught up with him. Why didn't I check on her to see that she was all right? When I saw the lights turned out I guessed she was tired of watching and had gone to sleep. I would have checked if those lights hadn't gone out." He flung himself down in the new chair Molly had purchased to replace Bert's recliner.

"What are you talking about?" Molly asked. "What man? What lights? Are you talking about our Christmas lights being hung all over the woods? What's that all about? What man?"

Holt tried to explain, but he kept rushing it, and he had to go over it several times. His worry and anxiety increased with every repeat. "We've got to do something," he said, frantically. He had jumped up and was pacing.

"Josh was here. He's out looking for her. But I'll call him back. He needs to know about the man," said Molly, hurrying to the phone. "He said he's been afraid of something like this. He's afraid for you, too. Everyone around town is talking about Mrs. Cummings telling you something and that you two know who did the killings. Josh says you're both in danger."

"We *don't* know anything," Holt answered.

"According to Josh, that doesn't matter. If people think you know, and if the killer hears them say that you know—then you're in danger."

Holt started pacing the room again while his mother made the call. "We should go out and look for her. We can't just sit here and do nothing."

"We don't know where to look," Molly pointed out, having left a message for Chief Winters. "Josh will know what to do."

"Josh. I'm getting sick of hearing about Josh," said Holt. "You think he's so great, and he practically had me in handcuffs."

"That's not true. That was Leroy. It was never Josh. He likes you, he always has. Do you think he'd let you go out with his daughter if he thought you are capable of murder?"

Holt's face turned an angry shade of red. "Well, that's not happening anymore," he said.

"What do you mean?" asked Molly.

"We broke up, that's all," said Holt. "Samantha Winters is so... so... What did I ever see in her, anyway?"

Molly had a million questions, but this was hardly the time, not with Beth missing. Just then, the doorbell rang.

The room shrank in size with both the chief and Holt in it. Holt turned quiet and seemed embarrassed by Josh's presence, at least until they started talking about Beth. Then Holt explained, in a much more succinct manner, about how someone had been watching Beth's window from the woods, about putting the lights out there, how she had turned them on last night, and he had chased someone but hadn't been able to get close.

"It wasn't her imagination," Holt finished. "I saw him."

"And why wouldn't you have told somebody about this?" asked Josh.

"I was the one under suspicion. You wouldn't have believed me anyway," said Holt.

"I'd have believed Beth. Why didn't she tell me?" the chief asked.

"She doesn't like the police," Holt answered simply.

"I've noticed that," said Josh. "Anyway, give me a description of who you were chasing. He must have been in good shape to out-run you. Who do you think it was?"

"Couldn't tell. He was darting all over the place. I was thinking he'd be a damn fine ball carrier."

"Or someone with military maneuvering training," mused Josh, half to himself.

"Or that," agreed Holt. "You honing in on Hank Crowell? Because I thought the man had on camouflage. He really vanished."

"Circled back and grabbed Beth?" Josh tried the scenario out loud.

"Could be. Why didn't I check on her?" Holt gave himself a disgusted hit to his own head. He looked miserable.

"You did the best you could," said Josh, in an absent-minded way.

"If I had done the best I could, Beth wouldn't be missing."

"You know anything about the girl?" Josh addressed his question to both of the Floyds.

They both shook their heads quickly.

"I think it's time we stopped pretending she's related to

Dee," said the chief. "She's running, maybe for a good reason, but right now anything we know about her might help us find her. And that's become the important thing. If she had taken her stuff, I'd think she was just moving on. But I have to consider the possibility that whoever she is running from found her. She's scared. And there's something else. She talked to me the other day, indicated she might have done something very bad. She tried to tell me she was framed, but maybe that's all a set-up."

"She's an extraordinary girl. She doesn't have a mean bone in her body. I don't believe for a minute that she would do anything terrible or criminal," said Molly.

"Mom's right," Holt insisted. "Beth isn't like that. Not at all. She's... she's the opposite of that. She's wonderful. I mean she's different than anyone you've ever met. She's better, somehow."

Josh raised his eyebrows at that. "Just keep remembering that none of us know anything about her. We have only her word about who she is. She came out of nowhere, and she refuses to tell us anything about herself. And I don't believe that Beth Waterman is her real name."

Holt stood up. He was exactly the same height as Josh Winters. "Get off her back." His voice was one degree from shouting. "First me, and now her? You are accusing everyone of everything. Throw out a bunch of buckshot and see where it lands?"

"That's not how I do business," said Josh, calmly.

"It sure looks that way from where I stand," said Holt.

"Stop it, both of you," Molly said, in her new, firm voice. "We need to find Beth, not fight among ourselves."

"The voice of good sense," said Josh, with a quick smile to Molly. Then he turned to Holt. "And just because you and Sam broke up tonight, don't take it out on me."

Once again Holt's face turned red and he turned away from Josh.

"Is she all right?" Holt's voice was reduced to a whisper.

"She will be. Don't worry about it. I think it's probably a good idea. You both need to expand your horizons."

"So where are you going to look for Beth?" asked Holt.

"Unless we know something about her, I don't have a clue," Josh said, with something like despair in his voice. "Let's begin by finally being honest. No relation to Dee. School records probably made up, and Dee's friend Tico Zane probably had a great deal to do with that. She had a Pennsylvania license plate on her car. For all I know, it was stolen and she's from someplace else altogether. Who can tell me something more?"

40

Beth had no concept of time. The darkness, the silence, and her lack of movement turned minutes into hours. She hated the hood that covered her head. It was difficult to take a deep breath.

She sat there dreading what would happen, and yet, when she finally heard a door wrench open, it was almost a relief.

Beth listened to the footsteps as they came closer. Heavy boots—military? Or C.J., who had always walked ponderously across a room? A sound that had become part of the dread which had been her life.

"It's time for a little talk," said a voice, obviously disguised, a hoarse whisper.

But that was a good thing, wasn't it? There would be no reason to disguise the voice if the plan was to kill her. And C.J. wouldn't bother with such a thing. Beth was definitely getting a mental picture of Hank Crowell bending over her.

"What did Lillian Cummings tell you? What had she seen?" He was talking slowly, a further attempt to disguise his voice.

When Beth tried to answer, her speech was muffled by the horrible hood. "She didn't get a chance to tell us anything. When we came back to ask, she was dead."

"You will tell me the truth. Now or later." The whisper was close to her ear. She knew when he backed up slightly. Without sight, she had become super-sensitive to the very motion of the air around her.

Then he was back. She felt something cold on her arm.

"Do you know what this is?" he asked.

She was afraid that she did, but she kept silent.

He made a small prick on her arm. She felt the blood.

"You're a pretty girl. I would think you would want to stay that way," he said.

Then Beth felt the slash, through the hood, on her cheek, and the oozing of the blood. A small sound escaped her, unbidden.

"This is only a sample, little lady. Next time, I'll take an eye. That won't be a bit pleasant. Think about it. I can make you into a monster." His whispered voice sounded pleased with the idea. It sent chills down Beth's spine.

Her breath caught in her throat. She had convinced herself that she was immune to threats, but what brave and foolish nonsense that had been. C.J. never wanted her either deformed or dead—she had always known that. She hadn't realized what a safety valve it was.

She heard the footsteps walking away, heard the door screech open, a funny sound, like metal. Where could she be, with a door made of metal?

"I don't know anything," she called out as the door closed and a lock was bolted.

She had to get out of here. She had to. Beth tried to pull at her arms and faced the pain of nerves newly awakened. There was something holding her to the chair as well, so that she couldn't stand up. But now she squirmed and finally managed to loosen what bound her to the chair. It was tape, she could hear it tear. Her arms ached with pain, but she was able to put some weight on her feet, a half stance, that eased the pressure on her arms. She wiggled frantically, and the chair moved lower on her torso. She kept up the movement and, finally, the chair was down at her ankles.

Now that she was standing, and relieved from the pressure of her straining arms, she was able to move her hands against each other, feel the tape that bound them. She eased the fingers of one hand along the tape on the other hand, searching for an edge, an end to begin pulling. She finally found it. Her fingernails had grown since she had arrived in Beaumont. She worked one nail under the little end bit, pulling it away, little by little. It seemed like she picked at the tape for hours, but at last she was able to make a little pull, and then another, and another.

Beth had her first doubt about her captor. The fact that she could do what she was doing—that didn't seem like Colonel Crowell. He would do a better job, wouldn't he?

She got one hand free and tore off the disgusting hood. She could breathe again, but with a gasp of pain. The fabric of the hood had become imbedded in the cut. She had torn the cut open even more.

Looking up, Beth could now see that the tape still attached her other arm was wound several times around a pipe—a really sloppy job. She couldn't manage to do anything about the hanging tape, so she continued to try to find the tape end on her right hand. It was hard to see what she was doing, craning her head up as she had to, in the dark room and at the awkward angle at which her right arm remained, above her head.

Finally, she found a gap in the tape. After that, it was

easy. She ripped the tape off and was free in a matter of minutes.

Beth ran toward the door. Then she stopped. It bothered her how easy it had been. And something else was bothering her, too.

When she got to the door, she stopped and flicked on the light switch that was next to it. She was in some kind of metal storage shed. She took a minute to look around. The shed was empty except for groups of boxes along the walls. Her captor might be coming back at any second, yet it seemed important to see this place. Over by the chair she had just escaped from, in plain sight, she spotted something. She walked over and picked it up. It was a torn piece of camouflage fabric. *Interesting.* After looking at it for a minute, she tied the fabric around her wrist, not having any pockets in her nightshirt, opened the steel door—*unlocked? why?*—and dashed out into the night.

She had no idea where she was, but she was breathing in fresh air, and it felt magnificent. It was dark. She didn't know what hour of the night or even what night it was. But she was free. She ran, and her legs gained strength and the muscles that had been so cramped from being in one position finally began to function without pain.

It felt exhilarating, putting one foot in front of the other. Gaining distance. It was much like that original escape from Philadelphia. *Distance, distance, distance.*

Finally, Beth slowed down, out of breath and out of endurance. She didn't know how long it had been since she had eaten. The terrible thirst was still with her.

Now she was barely walking. She stopped and listened. Nothing was coming up behind her, yet she constantly looked back. She sat down on a tree stump. She had no idea if she was moving in a straight line or not. Maybe she had just circled around and was close to where she had been held. Maybe she had been running farther and farther away from any help. There were whole areas of desolation around here, areas where nobody ever went.

Beth got up again out of sheer nervousness. She walked, slowly now, looking around at the blackness. All she could make out were trees and bushes, undergrowth—wild land. She kept walking.

Stumbling more and more, she came to a place where there seemed to be only emptiness before her. She stopped. It was the lake. No lights showed along the shoreline in any direction. So it must be the middle of the night. The people were all sleeping, snug in their beds. Even their automatic outdoor lights had turned off. Perhaps dawn wasn't too far away.

If she followed the shoreline, she would come to something. She waded into the water. The coolness helped keep her awake, helped her keep going forward. She walked and walked and walked. If she were to come to a dock, she'd go up and knock on someone's door. But along this part of the lake, there didn't seem to be any docks.

Finally, Beth came to a wide beach. No dock but, as she sat down on a rock to rest, the moon showed itself briefly and she saw a path leading up the hill. It had to lead somewhere.

She followed it up, expecting to see a house of some kind. But there was nothing. The path ended in a field, a huge field, empty acres extending forever in front of her. It was too much to deal with. Beth sank down, hardly aware of the hard earth as her head lolled onto the ground.

Her dream was crazy: soldiers, a group of them, complete with weapons, standing over her. It took her several minutes to realize it wasn't a dream.

"She's hurt," one of them said.

"We need to get her help," said another.

"I'll go get the truck," said yet another.

"Don't be stupid," said a very large soldier who had

been standing behind the others. It was Tico Zane. He didn't let on that he even knew who she was; he simply scooped her up and carried her as if she were a baby.

"You're one of these guys?" Beth asked him, softly. She was so confused. These should be the last people she would want to see, and yet she didn't feel the fear she should have, especially with Tico. She trusted Tico. She knew she shouldn't, not this tattooed giant, this person who freely drifted over the criminal line—yet she did. He had helped her when she needed help. He was helping her now.

But she felt ridiculous, being carried like this.

"Where are you taking me?" she asked in a louder voice. The others seemed surprised that she could speak.

"For help. Your face is bleeding," said Tico.

"It's not far," said another. "Just hang on."

"We'll get you to a hospital," said a third.

She tried to tell them she could walk, she tried to ask them questions, but they were marching forward in some sort of formation of which she was the center, more of an object than a person to be listened to.

Finally, they came to a small log building, surrounded by tents.

"Colonel," they yelled, and Colonel Crowell appeared

at the door of the building.

"Oh, no," Beth exclaimed. He was still wrapped up in the frightening figure that had captured her. And yet…

"Bring her inside," commanded the colonel. There were lights on in the building.

"Put her down here," the colonel said, once she was inside, and she was lowered onto some sort of camp bed.

Once she heard his voice, Beth was no longer afraid. The feeling had been growing on her, and now it was a certainty. It hadn't been the colonel. That piece of fabric was overkill on what was already forming in her mind. It was the "little lady" the whisperer had used. Only one person had ever called her "little lady" —the same person who spoke too formally, who spoke in a way that worked in speeches, but not in conversation, and certainly not in whispers. And Beth listened carefully to the way people spoke and the words they used, more so than most. She noticed.

She lifted up her wrist with the fabric tied around it. "Does this belong to any of you?" she asked.

They shook their heads, looking bewildered. "But it wouldn't be hard to come by," said one of them.

"Where did you find her?" the colonel asked his men, and they had a quiet conversation among themselves. She wanted to tell them she was capable of speech, but she also wanted to hear what they were saying.

The colonel knelt down beside her and turned her head toward the light. "Nasty cut," he said, "but not too deep. What happened?"

It all came out in a jumble—about waking up in a dark place and the scary man who came and threatened her. "I thought it was you," she said. "Until he called me 'little lady.' That's when I kind of knew it was the mayor."

"Maxwell Cummings?" The colonel let a hearty one-note laugh. "I'll be..." He stopped, looking at Beth again. "Where is he now?"

Beth tried to explain where she had come from, but she really didn't know. She described the room where she had been, the steel door, and how far it had been from the lake.

"Get Chief Winters on the phone. Get him out here. No, wait. Have him meet us at the hospital," he said. "The rest of you, get a search party formed and try to find this place. Keep in radio contact and call Chief Winters if you find it. Tico, you come with me. Get her into my car."

His car was a huge Humvee. It was not the smoothest ride she had ever had, and she could feel her cheek start to bleed again. While they were driving, she told the colonel and

Tico of the threats the mayor had whispered to her.

"That…" Again the colonel stopped what he was about to say. "He'll pay for this," he finished, flushed with anger. Beth wanted to tell him that she had actually heard a great deal of swearing since she had started going to school, but she was aware that he was showing her some kind of respect, and she rather liked it. So he wasn't a good tipper; still, she was beginning to like the guy anyway. But then there had been that brief period after the award thing, where she had tried to like the mayor. She had tried to push away her basic instincts and accept him for who he pretended to be. She hoped she wasn't making that kind of mistake again.

The colonel had been right, the cut wasn't too deep. She left the small surgery room with seven stiches and a big white bandage. It had taken them longer to pick the lint from the hood out of the cut than to do the actual stitching.

Dee had been called and was standing in the waiting room with Chief Winters and Colonel Crowell when Beth came out.

"Everyone's looking for our illustrious mayor," said Dee, giving Beth a gentle hug.

"The Sheriff's Department and the State Police are in on this," said the chief. "I don't think he knows you're gone yet or that you identified him. That's going to make it easy."

Beth's cheek had been numbed for the stitches, and now it was hard for her to talk. But the colonel was only too happy to repeat what she had told him in the car, about the threats, about the questions.

"I know what this is all about," said the colonel.

Chief Winters gave him a look, skeptical, but willing to listen.

"It's all about the land, Lillian's land, what we now use as our camp grounds," the colonel started. Now Josh was paying attention.

"Lillian gave a big portion to us. But Bert Floyd talked her out of a little piece of it and then decided to hold us up for his part. We do need those acres. They're right in the middle of our piece. It was a handshake deal. Floyd did a lot of that. I guess a lot of people around here do."

Now the chief was really listening. "Why haven't you told me about this before?"

"It's all come to the surface just now, since Floyd died. I paid him some money. He was going to deed over the land. So where is the money? Where is the deed? I needed that guy alive and with pen in hand."

The chief put his hand to his head. "I liked this place

411

better when it was boring," he said. "And the land thing explains some of it, but not all, not the questions he was asking Beth."

"I think he was just trying to make me think he was Colonel Crowell," said Beth. She showed the chief the fabric. "It was too much in plain sight," she said "Too obvious, don't you think? He didn't kill me, and he killed the others. I don't think he ever meant to kill me. Just scare me and make me accuse the colonel."

"Do you think Lillian saw her husband doing something with Floyd's body?" Dee asked.

"We'll never know, will we? But the rest of it makes an awful lot of sense," said Josh.

"But he must have thought Lillian saw something, or why would he kill her?" asked Dee.

"Again, for the land. It's all his now," said the colonel.

Beth had been thinking about all this. She had a different idea. "I think it was all a plan and that she was the one he wanted dead to begin with—everything else just fell into place. That's part of what gave him away. Even when he was asking me questions, it was like he didn't care about the answers, only about hearing himself ask the questions. It made me begin to think something was fake."

"Then why the cut?" asked the colonel.

"To make *you* look really bad," said Beth. "So people would be all too willing to get *you* in jail fast and not care about the fine details. He's a psychopath, just like someone else I know. That's why I always distrusted him. He reminded me of someone else." Beth had only recently heard the word *psychopath*. It explained C.J. It explained a lot. She was finding it so amazing and so wonderful that there seemed to be a word for everything; every feeling, every situation, every person. "What I can't figure out," she continued, "is why he killed Slim."

"That was one great kid," said the colonel. "Way too idealistic. We fought all the time, but he was a great kid. He scared me—he would never survive a battle. He'd be the first one to jump up to save the others. I was trying so hard to disabuse him of that sort of thing."

"So his being killed could be blamed on the two of you not getting along?" Dee asked.

"Maybe. In some twisted mind, maybe," said the colonel.

Beth had one more thing to say. "Did you shoot at us the night of Lillian Cumming's funeral?" she asked the colonel.

"The night..." Crowell was thinking. "There was a

target practice going on at my place that night. I wasn't there, but I heard about it. Some heads rolled over that one, believe me. We've got some hotshots in the group that we've been thinking of getting rid of. It's going to be a much more responsible group under my direction."

Beth had been standing up all this time. She couldn't stand any longer. She made her way to a chair and collapsed into it.

Immediately, both the chief and the colonel came over to her.

"I'm so sorry," said the colonel. "How inconsiderate we've been. You're exhausted. You need to be home and in bed."

"I don't know what's the matter with me," said Josh. He turned to Dee. "Can you get her home? And Colonel, can you meet me at the station? We have a lot to talk about." Finally, he turned to Beth, "Get some sleep and take some aspirin. Your face is going to be sore." He hesitated for a moment and then went on, "You're a pretty girl, Beth. Don't worry about having a scar. At your age, it will disappear very soon. And you could have Doc Purdy look at it. He knows a really good plastic surgeon. But I don't think you'll need anything like that. I'm just mentioning it because my daughter would be thinking of nothing else right about now."

Beth followed Dee out of the hospital and fell asleep on the way home.

Dee saw her up to her apartment.

"Why isn't this door locked?" she asked as she opened it.

"I left in a bit of a hurry," said Beth thinking about her rush into the woods.

"Yeah, but Molly was here checking on you. I'm surprised she didn't lock the door." Dee was fiddling with the knob. "I think this had been tampered with," she said.

Beth bent down and looked. There did seem to be scrapings by the lock.

They tried the door several times. Sometimes it locked, sometimes it didn't.

"You be sure to double check this," said Dee.

And Beth did as soon as Dee left. She already had her eye on her pillow, but she knew she had to shower—she was filthy and her nightshirt was damp and dirty. As soon as she was dry and in a clean T-shirt, she aimed for the bed and sank into it.

There will be no more murders in Beaumont. The town was safe now. No one would be looking at Holt with suspicion;

he could get on with his life. And so could she. That was the last conscious thought she had.

It was a sound that woke her. Beth was groggy with exhaustion. She could not have been asleep for long.

Something told her not to open her eyes, some inner feeling that she wouldn't like what she would see. Or maybe it was the smell—familiar—clothes that smelled of cigarette smoke.

She couldn't stand not looking. She opened her eyes to mere slits.

It was her horror, her nightmare, her deepest fear. C.J. stood at the foot of the bed, smiling.

Beth felt herself begin to tremble. She was cold, even under the blankets.

C.J. laughed. "You see me. You know you can't fool me. Why would you try?"

C.J.'s voice sent waves of repulsion through Beth. She was not going to allow fear to control her. She was not. Yet she couldn't stop trembling.

She opened her eyes fully and sat up in the bed. No point in pretending. C.J. was right. There was no fooling C.J. Ever.

Maybe it was being in the bed, raised up slightly, but as Beth looked at C.J. standing there, she had a sense of.—something. C.J. had always loomed so large. But the woman who stood at the foot of the bed was short and stout and small.

The fierce glare that was aimed toward her seemed more ridiculous than frightening. Yet Beth knew better than to underestimate her. This woman was dangerous. Beth had the scars to prove it.

"Did you really think you could escape me?" C.J. asked.

"How did you find me?" Beth asked.

"You led me right to you. I knew you would. Footprints, remember? You're fool enough to have your good deeds all over the television, and you ask me such a stupid question? But if not that, I still would have found you. No escape for you, except the same escape that Jack endured."

Beth felt so cold. She held her teeth tight together so they wouldn't chatter.

"Get up out of that bed," said C.J. The expectation of instant obedience was clear and, without thinking, Beth got up.

"I was here before," C.J. said, taking look around the room. "The night you were running through the woods like a crazy person. Turned off those ridiculous fairy lights you had all over the place." C.J. turned as though to look back at the window. "So you got a couple of extra days out of your shenanigans."

They were both standing at the end of the bed. For the first time, Beth realized that she was taller than C.J. Had she simply not observed that fact before, or had she grown in the brief weeks she had been gone? Somehow, it made a difference. Yet Jack had been much taller than either of them, and it hadn't made a difference for him.

"What's that?" C.J. demanded, looking intently at Beth's face. She reached out and ripped the bandage off. Beth gasped at the pain. Some of the stitches must have torn; blood was oozing out again.

"So you're not even pretty anymore," said C.J., with smug satisfaction. She laughed the horrible laugh that filled Beth with dread. "Turned into a little Frankenstein's monster, have you? I was always careful about your face. You don't know how good you had it."

Beth suddenly wasn't cold anymore. The fear was receding. She was angry, a hot piercing kind of anger.

As always, C.J. had her big purse over her shoulder. She usually carried a knife in there. Beth wondered what would happen if she just grabbed the purse and flung it away.

If she hesitated, she would never try. If she was going to die anyway, what difference did it make? And death would be better than returning to life with C.J. She reached out and flung the purse toward C.J.'s head. Then Beth ran, jumping over the footstool, which gave her a brief advantage.

She dashed out the door and clattered down the stairs, calling out as she ran. "Help! Help!"

C.J. was right behind her.

"Stop," C.J. ordered. And there was something terribly twisted in Beth that made her almost do just that. But she didn't. She kept running, yelling at the top of her lungs as she ran.

"Help! Holt! Somebody, help me."

She aimed toward the house, not daring to glance back.

Holt was coming out the door as she tried to go in. They crashed into each other.

She dared to turn then. There was nobody behind her.

Holt put an arm around her to steady her.

"What's happened?" he asked anxiously.

"She found me. C.J. found me," was all Beth could say. "Don't let her get me. Please." There was so much explanation necessary, and she was not capable of even beginning the long and involved story.

"I don't understand..." he began.

"Go after her. Find her. Call the police. Find her," said Beth. She knew it had to end here and now. Whatever the consequences, it had to end. She sank to the ground. She knew C.J. would come back, but Beth felt a sense of relief. It was all going to be out in the open. She wasn't going to hide anymore.

"Who am I looking for?" he asked.

"C.J. Short, she's actually really short. Heavy. Her hair all tight in a bun. She doesn't look it, but she's dangerous. She has a knife." Beth could hardly breathe.

"Get in the house. Have my Mom call Josh. Can you do that?" Holt asked. But he was already heading toward the woods, after C.J.

Molly was right there in her robe. She grabbed Beth and led her into the kitchen and sat her down.

"Call the chief," Beth said. But Molly already had the phone in her hand. After she called Josh, she put the tea kettle on to boil.

The tea tasted good to Beth. Molly allowed her to be silent, even though she was very curious. They hadn't finished their first cup before the room was full of people. Holt had come back alone, and then the chief arrived, along with one of the sheriff's deputies. They had been searching for Mayor

Cummings when they got the call. The deputy couldn't seem to understand that this wasn't about the mayor. After all, it was the same girl.

When Beth finally started to speak, the others were silent, listening, expressions of horror on their faces. She couldn't get it out fast enough, and it came out all jumbled and out of order.

She had seen C.J. burying Jack's body. She had seen Jack, all blue and terrible, his throat slashed. That had been it. She might never have left if she hadn't come across that horrible scene. She had to stay a couple of more days, until C.J. wasn't watching her every move. But she knew right then that she would leave, dead or alive, that she could not be there anymore.

C.J. was sure that she had frightened Beth enough so that she wouldn't leave. She told Beth that she had planted evidence on the body: Beth's hair, complete with follicles. C.J. had even put some of the hair under Jack's fingernails, she had told Beth proudly. Then there was Beth's blood, taken after a punch to the nose had caused a nosebleed. That was dribbled on Jack's clothes. No one would ever believe Beth. C.J. knew how to talk to people. Did Beth think for a moment she would be believed after C.J. told her story?

"Jack was the only person who had ever been kind to me," Beth said. "Why would I kill him? And there were others there. There were others before Jack and me. There were other mounds out there. Before that night, I never questioned what they were. But they were in a row. A neat row. C.J. always does everything neatly. I don't expect you to believe me. I don't even care anymore."

The chief sat down next to Beth. He took her hand in his. "Of course we believe you, Beth. We know you. And we'll find this C.J. Don't you worry about that."

She didn't have to tell them the whole story that night. She knew she would, eventually. She'd tell them about the sessions—sometimes cuttings, the sometimes burnings, the sometimes being locked away without food or water. She'd tell them about the constant fear, the constant turnarounds, being told to do something one way one day and being punished for doing it that way two days later. The never knowing. She would show them the scars. The cuttings and the burnings were never life threatening, never serious enough to require medical help. It was just that C.J. took such pleasure in the punishments. That was the frightening part, the pleasure on C.J.'s face.

That night, after the officers left, Molly insisted that

Beth sleep in the house. That was fine with Beth. C.J.'s presence in her apartment had spoiled it for her. She would never forget C.J.'s face at the end of her bed, Beth's nightmare turned true.

In fact, she slept with Molly. And that was fine too. She felt safe.

The next morning they heard the news that Maxwell Cummings had been found. They had been waiting for him when he came home. He would become the county's problem, or maybe even the state's; they were arguing among themselves about that. But Maxwell Cummings left Beaumont that very day and would not be returning to the town he thought he owned. He exchanged his expensive suits for a prison jumpsuit, his mayoral title for a ID number. Tico mentioned what would happen to Cummings in prison. Tico knew people there.

But C.J. Watson had disappeared. And Beth never wanted to be alone again. She would be sleeping at Molly's until Dee's house was ready. She would be watchful and wary, and she would try not to be afraid. *Try.*

41

During this commotion, Stan Jones arrived in Beaumont. His first stop was the police station. Leroy was the only one in the office and was dismissive of the detective's request to see the chief.

"I can help you with anything you need," Leroy informed Stan. "Although, frankly, I don't believe we'll have much time to help a *private detective*." He said the words with disdain. "We're pretty busy around here."

Stan tried several times to state his case, but Leroy seemed more interested in talking than in listening. Stan was about to give up when the chief came in the door. Josh immediately invited Stan into his office and closed the door.

The chief apologized for Leroy. "He's not going to be around here much longer. Hiring him was a favor for the mayor, who's now in jail. I keep trying to give Leroy one more chance, but none of it takes. The town council never allocated money for an officer before the mayor insisted on his nephew.

Now I want the officer, but not the nephew. It's a slippery slope, if you know what I mean."

Stan smiled sympathetically and laid a folder on the chief's desk. The two men had reached a rapport even before they realized they were both looking for the same person. Now, they put their heads together and studied the material.

"It's a woman?" Jones asked. "I always pictured a man. That gruff smoker's voice, I guess. And the cruelty. I still have illusions about women, I guess—the gentler sex. At least I want to think so."

"Yeah," smiled the chief, immediately picturing Molly Floyd. "Sometimes they really are."

"She won't have left here. She's waiting," said Stan. "This is one determined woman."

"So how can we keep Beth safe?" asked Josh.

"That's going to be my job. Beth doesn't know me. She won't notice me, and I can stay close, wait and watch."

"I'm going to take you up on that," said Josh. "Of course, I'll be checking you out."

Stan smiled. "Wouldn't expect anything else," he said. "It's all in there, my information." He shoved the folder across the desk.

Josh looked briefly at the contents. "So Beth's story is

true. Locked in the closet and all that," Josh asked.

"I'm afraid it is. I can take almost anything else, except hurting a kid," said Stan.

"You and me both," agreed Josh. "We'll find this C.J. Watson, don't you worry about that."

42

Beth never had an inkling that Stan Jones was following her. He spent the night parked down the road from Molly's house, and several times each night he walked the woods.

On the fourth night, at a little before two o'clock in the morning, he sat down on a stump where he could see both Molly's house and Beth's apartment window, figuring that C.J. wouldn't know Beth wasn't there anymore.

Suddenly, he was grabbed from behind. Stan had been a policeman for many years. He still kept himself in shape. It was an automatic reaction to grab and bend the little finger on his assailant's hand, turning him around in the process. He put a chokehold on him, quick and firm.

He had expected a short, stout woman; instead he was holding a tall, thin boy.

"Let me go," the boy cried out.

Stan grabbed one of the boy's arms, let go of the chokehold, and twisted the boy's arm behind him, this time turning him so that they were face to face, close up.

"Who are you?" Stan demanded.

"Who are *you*?" the boy shot right back, groaning with pain. "And what are you doing watching Beth's window?"

"Name. I want a name," Stan said in his best policeman's voice.

"Tony Grimes. Let go of me."

"So, Tony Grimes, what are you doing here?"

"Watching you stalk Beth Waterman," said Tony.

Stan eased up on his hold. "Why?" he asked.

"Because I don't want her hurt," said Tony.

"Don't try to run," said Stan. He let go of the boy's arm.

Stan hadn't been able to get his flashlight out of his belt before. Now he did. He shone the light in the boy's face. The kid was trying to put on a brave face, but he was scared and he was rubbing his little finger. Stan shone the light up onto his own face.

"Stan Jones. I'm trying to see that Beth doesn't get hurt as well," he said.

"You've been out here all night?" Tony asked.

"No. Once before, about midnight."

"Somebody was out here earlier. I heard them," said Tony.

"Then let's you and me watch together," Stan said. It would be a way of keeping an eye on both Tony and on Beth.

They moved farther into the woods and they watched silently. After about an hour, Stan said, "I don't think we're going to see anything more tonight. Go home, kid. I've got this covered. Tell Chief Winters what you saw and heard. That's what you should have done in the first place."

"I'm not thick with the police," said Tony.

"Thick or thin, it's what you need to do."

"So, she *is* in danger, isn't she?" Tony asked.

"Yeah, she is."

"Nobody else thinks so. Mayor Cummings is in jail. They think everything is over. But I've seen a car following her around."

"That might have been me," said Stan. "But the person she was running from in the first place is here now. And believe me when I tell you, Beth had good reason to run."

"So, who are you?" the boy asked.

Stan explained, briefly, how he had been hired to find the girl, but had become less than trusting of the person doing the hiring.

"I needed to get to her first," he said. "I didn't know about all the other stuff happening around here. But you can help. Watch out for her at school. Look for a woman, short, a bit heavy. Just get Beth away if you see her. This woman is dangerous. Don't try anything on your own."

"Like I couldn't take some short woman?" Tony scoffed.

"It's not about that, believe me. Help Beth by using your head, not your fists. Get her away and then get help." Stan gave Tony his cell phone number. "I won't be far away."

Stan felt a little better after that. The kid looked like trouble, but he reminded Stan of himself when he was young, with the tough act and all. And Stan had been worried about Beth when she was out of his sight at school. Now somebody would have her back even there.

Beth wasn't sure how the kids at school would react to all the news that was flying around. Nobody except Molly and Dee and the police chief knew the whole story, and they never told anyone the details. But the fact that there was an arrest warrant out for C.J. Watson was known, and it was for child abuse and murder. And it was now known that Beth Waterman was really Beth Watson. What they didn't know was that she had no intention of ever going back to that other name.

When she did go back to school, it was her face that

intrigued everyone. After the stitches were out and the bandage removed, there was a swollen red welt that ran down her face. Some people stared. Others made a point of not staring, which was even more obvious.

Lindsey and the other Queens tried to make fun of Beth's face and were seriously condemned for their efforts. The Queens were totally shocked by their peers' reaction, and it would probably not have happened if it hadn't been for Beth herself. She didn't care. It didn't seem to bother her a bit. She never asked Doc Purdy about that plastic surgeon; she simply didn't care.

In fact, if the truth was known, she liked the idea that this latest injury showed. It was out in the open, honest. All the other scars, hidden away as they were, seemed shameful. There was nothing to be ashamed of here. This one didn't make her a victim—she was here and the mayor was in jail. She was the victor.

At the Friday assembly that week, Sidney and Samantha had saved a place for Beth in the middle of the third row, a prime location. Everyone stood to let her pass, and Lindsey called from further back, "Poor thing, so sad, so pathetic. Nice to let her sit with you. And she used to be so pretty."

Beth turned and smiled. "I'm going to call it a sign of character," she said in a loud, strong voice.

Everyone laughed—with her, not at her. Holt Floyd called out in an equally loud voice, "Like she's still not pretty?"

The compliment made Beth blush. She supposed she appreciated it, but she looked quickly over to Samantha to see how she was taking it. Samantha was looking down at her lap like she hadn't heard. But Beth knew that she *had* heard, and Beth hated the fact that Samantha felt uncomfortable.

The idea that everyone was siding with Beth and not the Queens was very satisfying. It was even more than that. Beth knew she belonged here now—she was a part of this school. People liked her. She liked them. She eased down in her seat and listened to the glee club perform a couple of songs. But she couldn't stop thinking about Holt. He kept telling her he had broken up with Samantha. He had approached her a couple of times with the suggestion of a movie or a hamburger. But she didn't feel right about it. She felt disloyal to Samantha. Sidney told her she was crazy—they had broken up, and Holt was free for the taking. But something made Beth hold back. Samantha would be hurt. It would be a betrayal.

That weekend, Beth and Dee moved into Dee's new

house. Dee was as excited as a kid with a new toy. It was a small Victorian house. There would be a lot of fixing up to do. But what entranced Beth was the turret on the side of the house. When Dee told her to pick any bedroom she wanted, Beth didn't hesitate: she chose the turret room. It was the smallest bedroom by far, but Beth now not only knew what a circular room looked like, she lived in one. It made placing the bed and other furniture a challenge. But she felt a bit like Rapunzel, without the long hair. The row of windows let in lots of light but were too close to the neighbors' house. That was okay—Beth didn't want to see any woods at night, not ever again.

Beth thought it would be easier to not run into Holt all the time. But it felt more like a hole in her stomach. She missed him, missed talking to him, missed the quick smiles he would give her in passing.

He started coming into the diner more often—to see his mother, he'd say. But the minute he entered, Dee and Molly would look toward Beth. Then they'd manage to get very busy so that Holt would end up talking to Beth. It was obvious and embarrassing. And there was the Samantha issue. Holt would again mention going to a movie in Keene or something. Beth would again put him off.

But one night, when she and Dee returned home from the diner, Holt was waiting for her.

Beth started to make excuses. But Dee chimed right in: "You finished your homework. Talk to the kid for a minute." And she went into the house and closed the door.

There was a swing on the large porch. Beth went over to it and sat down. Holt sat beside her. That hadn't really been her intention.

For a few minutes he talked about school and the last football game. Then he started telling her about a conversation he had had with his mother.

"I hear you knew about it—the money my Dad left."

"Yes. I seem to overhear a lot of stuff," said Beth, defensively. She gave him a quick look to see how he was taking it.

"Mom thought I'd be mad. But I'm not. One more sorry thing he did. And he never got to enjoy one minute of it. I almost feel bad for him. Now, I can go to college without worrying about a scholarship or anything else. He'd hate the fact that we're going to use it, and enjoy it, Mom and me. And it makes me so relieved, knowing Mom has some money. She deserves it."

"I'm glad she told you," Beth said. There was a silence between them.

Suddenly, Holt grabbed her face awkwardly and turned it toward him. "I can't stand this," he said. And he bent down and kissed her very gently.

It took her breath away. She was kissing him back. She didn't want to do that. Yet it took all her effort of will to pull away.

"This isn't right," she said, her words stumbling out.

He looked at her with such disappointment. He got up slowly and walked down the steps of the porch without looking back.

43

Beth should have been safe. Stan was watching her, the chief was aware of her danger, Tony was keeping an eye on her at school, and Holt had always looked out for her.

But sometime between the last bell at school on Thursday and when Stan belatedly noticed that Beth's car was the only one left in the lot, something had happened. Stan had been held up in town when the chief stopped him and gave him an update on the legal proceedings against the mayor. The metal shed had been found. Traces of Beth's blood had been collected. Things were not looking good for the ex-mayor of Beaumont. All of which was good news, but it had made Stan late.

Beth knew it was a crazy thing to do. But she had seen C.J.'s car parked at the edge of the student lot. There was no mistaking that left bumper that Jack had damaged long ago. C.J. had refused to fix it so that he would constantly remember his offense.

There was nobody in the car. Beth looked around carefully, at the corners of the building, the shady spots, the milling students. C.J. was not visible, but Beth knew she was watching and waiting somewhere.

Then she saw C.J. talking to a teacher—Mr. Glazier. If C.J. was asking him about Beth, C.J. was out of luck. He still hadn't learned her name.

She thought about running and getting someone, but she knew that C.J. would escape. She thought of just calling out but, again, C.J. would disappear before she could make anyone understand.

C.J. was facing away from Beth. Mr. Glazier was ranting on about something and had C.J.'s full attention. Nobody else was looking at Beth. She opened the trunk of C.J.'s car and climbed in. This waiting and this fear of when C.J. would pounce would end now. Beth would be the tracker, not the other way around. She would find out where C.J. went, where she was staying—and she would have the upper hand, because she was angry. It was an anger that had been building since she left Pennsylvania, fed by the people she had met in Beaumont and by all she had discovered about what life should be for a young woman.

A child accepts the world he or she lives in, has no basis for comparison. But now that Beth had seen the world, she knew that she had been cheated out of a normal childhood, out of any loving or kindness, out of everything. And she was very angry. She had no real plan as to what she would do. She only knew she would not be hunted. She would do the hunting.

She held her hand on the trunk lever, afraid that if it closed all the way, she would be locked in. The trunk's musty smell made her gag. When the car finally started, Beth braced herself with her legs and wondered why she wasn't more frightened. Things were about to happen—she had started something that couldn't be stopped.

Beth could tell when they left the paved roads and moved onto the dirt roads. The car jerked and jostled and threw her one way and then another. She had no idea of direction, little idea of time. She was uncomfortable, cramped up in the small space, unable to move her arms and legs to any real extent. There was the fear of discovery, but even that didn't erase the feeling of finally getting to the end of all this. One way or another, this was going to be over.

Beth had no idea what she was going to do; she couldn't see herself physically doing battle with C.J. But she had to stop her somehow.

Finally, she felt the car slow and then stop. How long should she wait before easing open the trunk and peering out?

She held her breath, then she counted—first to ten—then to one hundred, the numbers coming faster and faster in her anxiety. Now she opened the trunk a few inches. She saw hard dirt. She opened it a few more inches. Something about the nothingness she saw looked familiar, a ragged fence and a field of weeds behind it.

First one leg, and then another. Was C.J. standing there watching? She quickly got out of the trunk and turned in a full circle. No C.J., but she couldn't believe where she was. Tico's motel. Yet, it made sense in a way. Of course, C.J. would aim for the cheapest place to stay. She would not be intimidated by Tico. She would have put on her fake charm.

The sun was shining brightly. The light called attention to the shabbiness, the peeling paint, and the sign with the missing letters.

So which room was C.J. staying in? There was no way to tell. Beth considered going and asking Tico, but maybe C.J. was in the office. There was no window to look into.

She waited. If C.J. came out, what would she do? Grab her? That wasn't any kind of a plan.

But what was she thinking? Beth wasn't all alone in this

world anymore. She marched up to the office and opened the door.

No C.J., but no Tico either. She called out his name.

At first there was nothing, no sound. Then, suddenly, he appeared at the door to the inner room. She had not remembered his size—it came as a shock with each encounter. But to Beth, right now, it looked totally reassuring.

"A woman is staying here." Beth tried to describe her, but in her haste, her words were falling over each other.

Tico held up one of his big hands to stop her. He nodded.

"Mrs. Watkins," he said. "Not a real name."

"She's my…" What exactly was she? Beth had always denied she was her mother, at least to herself, and C.J. had never claimed she was, never allowed Beth to call her anything but C.J.

Having told the story once, it was easier this second time. It poured out. This time, because Beth had admitted the anger to herself, there were tears as she told the tale, even before she got to the part about Jack. She hadn't expected a second release, but it was there, a loosening of the tension of her muscles in her jaw, in her shoulders.

Finally, Tico held up his hand again. "Knew there was

something wrong about her," he said in his low, rumbling voice. "Let's go visit her."

They walked out and down the line of doors. Beth was about to confront C.J., and yet she had never felt more safe. With Tico looming in front of her, she felt strong.

Tico stopped at the room right next to the one Beth had stayed in. She knocked softly. He was having no part of that. His fist rocked the door.

"Open up. Now," he yelled.

And suddenly C.J. was standing there. She looked first at Beth, then up at Tico. She took a step backward.

He pushed his way in, taking Beth with him. He pulled out a cell phone and called 911, asking for immediate help.

"We wait," he said.

C.J. looked around the room, sudden panic in her eyes. Beth smiled. That look was the best revenge there could be. How often had C.J. caused that same look in Beth's eyes?

Tico had not touched C.J. He didn't have to. He just stood, towering over her. Finally, she sat down on the bed.

"You mistreated this girl?" Tico asked, finally.

C.J. looked away.

"What is she to you?" he asked.

Again C.J. was silent. That too, seemed wonderful to

Beth. Silence had been *her* only retreat for so many years.

When they heard the siren, Beth was almost disappointed. She could have stayed there, in the safety of Tico's presence, and stared at this woman and the fear in her face, forever.

There were so many things she wanted to shout at C.J. So much she wanted explained. But there was no place to begin.

It was a county sheriff's deputy who came. He looked like he was going to put the handcuffs on Tico at first. But finally Beth found her voice.

"No, no. It's her you want," she said, pointing to C.J.

"She can tell you some stories, this girl," said Tico. "Big-time child abuse and, I think, a lot more."

As she was led away, C.J. turned at the door and smiled her really frightening smile. "You've forgotten what I told you," she said. "You'll be the one in jail, not me."

Beth had already told Chief Winters about the evidence planted on Jack's body. He had reassured her about that. Not that the smile still didn't have power. It always would.

In the weeks and months that followed, Beth didn't see C.J. again. She wouldn't until the trial. There were many interviews with Chief Winters, and he accompanied her to other interviews with prosecutors, lawyers, and state officials. She felt comfortable when he was there.

Law enforcement officers took pictures of the knife wounds on her body, scarred over now, but still visible. They had found Jack's grave, and two others as well, in the backyard of C.J.'s house. There had been DNA testing, and Beth was so grateful that she was not a match with C.J. The police were pursuing missing children, looking at those who disappeared sixteen to eighteen years ago, since Beth didn't remember ever being anywhere else. But Beth no longer cared about that. She had her family, she had her home now. If she found more family, that would be fine. "Family" now held a whole new meaning.

One day after school, Samantha came up to her and said she wanted to talk. They sat in Beth's car.

"You can have him," Samantha said.

"What are you talking about?" Beth asked.

"You know good and well—Holt. All he ever did was talk about you, anyway. I was never very much at ease around him, never. Not even last year. He thought I was dumb, and I acted dumb around him because he made me nervous. What I liked was walking down the hall with him, having people admire us as a couple. That's not exactly love. And guess what? I'm not even mad. I'd rather have you as a friend than him as a boyfriend, and I actually don't have a choice in the matter. He's fallen for you big time."

"I think you're imagining things."

"So maybe you like Tony Grimes better?"

"Don't be silly."

"Well, I find him kind of fascinating, although I'm really sick of the goo-goo eyes he has for you."

"Please, not him. He's bad news," said Beth.

"Well, if not him, somebody. I can get a new boyfriend. And once people start seeing you and Holt together, the boys will start asking me out."

Beth was embarrassed by this whole conversation, but elated. She had been feeling very guilty about Holt. There had been that kiss that she had tried so hard to push away but had enjoyed so much.

"I owe you, anyway," said Samantha. "Lindsey and Laura and Jenna are *so* yesterday now. I love the group we're in. We actually like each other. Don't you think that's rare?"

"That friends like each other?" Beth looked to see if Samantha was making some sort of joke. She wasn't. There was still a great deal about this world that Beth would simply never understand. But here, in Beaumont, with people she had grown to love, she would learn. And maybe Samantha was right—it *was* rare. And she had been lucky to find it.

About the author

J.D. Shaw is the author of six adult mysteries, including the *Ask Emma* series and her previous young adult mystery for Tiny Satchel Press, *The Secrets of Loon Lake*. A married mother of three, Shaw lives near Philadelphia, Pennsylvania.

other books from

Tiny Satchel Press

www.tinysatchelpress.com

Also by J. D. Shaw:

The Secrets of Loon Lake

Sarah Ramsey's summer at Loon Lake won't be like any of the other summers spent at the isolated lake where her parents grew up. Sarah's parents are barely speaking and her pretty and popular older sister is getting all the attention.

Sarah enlists her two best friends, Jake and Rob, on an excursion to the forbidden Big Island. There they discover a pile of old bones in tattered clothes half-buried near a small bungalow. Jake and Rob don't want trouble, but Sarah's curiosity won't let it go. She begins to investigate and uncovers another mystery: a hotel that burned down in the 1920s, killing several people. A fire that was no accident.

In an era of cell phones and Internet access, Sarah has to dig through old newspapers and talk to the great-grandmother of neighbors to glean facts. The revelations stir up something evil. Sarah is threatened, her sister mysteriously disappears, and Sarah must find answers before something terrible happens.

ISBN 978-0-9845318-0-6

Praise for J.D. Shaw's

The Secrets of Loon Lake

"In this debut young adult novel, J.D. Shaw doesn't simply tell us what it's like to spend summers on a mountain lake, she puts us in a canoe, shoves an oar into our hands and sends us down the rapids. A fast, suspenseful read, *The Secrets of Loon Lake* has the perfect heroine in fourteen-year-old Sarah Ramsey—she's smart, caring, gutsy, and very much her own person." —Elena Santangelo, author of the Pat Montella *Possessed* mystery series and winner of the 2009 Agatha Award for *Dame Agatha's Shorts*.

"J.D. Shaw has crafted a coming-of-age novel in the tradition of Stephen King's *Stand By Me*. A compelling and engaging read for all ages." —Joanne Dahme, author of *Tombstone Tea, Creepers*, and *Contagion*

"J.D. Shaw has written an intelligent mystery featuring a young sleuth who has all the smarts of Nancy Drew, plus the added charm of being fully human. The setting is so real I could almost hear the mosquitos buzzing and the water lapping on the shore of the lake." —Sandra Carey Cody, author of the Jennie Connors mystery series

Taken Away by Patty Friedmann

It's the last week of August 2005, and Hurricane Katrina is about to hit the Gulf Coast—hard. As the storm comes closer and threatens to destroy New Orleans, 15-year-old Summer "Sumbie" Elmwood's two-year-old sister Amalia undergoes open-heart surgery. She survives the surgery, but when New Orleans is evacuated, Amalia disappears from the hospital. With the city deserted and destroyed and no food, water, electricity, or phone service available, the Elmwoods are forced to leave New Orleans without Amalia and go to Houston to stay with Sumbie's aunt. The FBI and others search for her missing sister, but thousands are missing and the little girl is no one's priority. Sumbie's parents begin to suspect that Sumbie did something to Amalia. With the aid of two would-be boyfriends, Hadyn and Robert, Sumbie tries to find her missing sister and prove her innocence in the chaos left by the killer storm. Will she succeed? Or will she become the FBI's prime suspect?

"Patty Friedmann is one of the finest writers in Louisiana. Not only did she stay in New Orleans throughout Hurricane Katrina and its aftermath, she ended up being rescued twice! No one knows New Orleans better and no one is better qualified to write about that period." —Julie Smith, Edgar Award-winning mystery author

ISBN 978-0-9845318-2-0

Sorceress by Greg Herren

Seventeen-year-old Laura Pryce has just completed her junior year of high school. Her parents were killed in a car accident weeks earlier, and she is moving from Kansas to California to live with her great aunt Melisande LaValliere, whom she has never met. Sad and depressed, Laura finds herself drawn to Jake, Melisande's handsome young handyman, himself the victim of a horrible family tragedy.

Melisande's estate is huge, Laura can't help but notice there are a number of paintings of women who look just like her hanging on the walls, each from different periods in history. Melisande explains that a genetic quirk leads to a girl in each generation being born with the "LaValliere face," which leads to a wholly unpredictable life, including visions.

Laura finds herself having nightmares about magical rituals and reliving episodes from the lives of the LaValliere women whose portraits hang in Melisande's house. When Jake begins to share her visions of these ancestresses, Laura begins to question where to turn and just what moving to her great aunt's home might cost her...

.

"*Sorceress* is a delightfully creepy thrill ride. Filled with twists and turns, it will have you jumping at every bump in the night and leave you afraid to close your eyes." —Michael Thomas Ford, winner of the American Library Association Award for Young Adult Fiction

ISBN 978-0-9845318-1-3

From Where We Sit:
Black Writers Write Black Youth

Thirteen established and emerging African-American writers present a range of compelling and provocative stories in this exciting collection, with a wide range of dynamic characters, divergent styles, and compelling issues. Jewelle Gomez, acclaimed author of *The Gilda Stories,* offers a new episode in her historic series. Harlem native and award-winning writer Mecca Jamilah Sullivan, romance writer Anne Shade, short-story stylist Craig L. Gidney, actress and playwright Ifalade Ta'Shia Asanti, noted children's author Becky Birtha, and award-winning novelist Fiona Lewis each explore what it means to be black in America today as well as in America's historic past, addressing issues not only of race, but also of class, gender, sexual orientation, and religion. Filmmaker Lowell Boston details the multi-faceted complexities of racism in America for young black men, while emerging writers Lisa R. Nelson, Guillaume Stewart, Misty Sol, kahlil almustafa, and Quincy Scott Jones take on different aspects of urban life: Nelson presents a young girl who wants to escape her middle-class neighborhood, Stewart writes provocatively about missing fathers in black America, Sol explores the impact of gun violence and no-snitch rules, almustafa details the day-to-day suspicion young black men face, and Jones places a young black man in white academe in a dazzling display of wordplay.

ISBN 978-0-9845318-3-7

Dreaming in Color by **Fiona Lewis**

Carlene—her friends call her Cee-Cee—came to the U.S. from Jamaica to be reunited with her mother, who has been working to make enough money to send for her. But for Cee-Cee, life in her new country is hard. She misses her island home, the friends she left behind who don't even Facebook her anymore.

High school is a minefield of bullying. It's not even October and talk of homecoming and parties has Cee-Cee super depressed after the boy she likes plays an ugly trick on her. When a group of mean kids, led by one of the most popular girls in the school, targets Cee-Cee, taunting her for her accent, she turns to art as a refuge.

Then Cee-Cee meets Greg, another teen from Jamaica, who plays saxophone and has his own secrets. Greg and Cee-Cee stand up to the bullies, but then events take a devasting turn.

"Fiona Lewis grabs a handful of issues in her new novel and tosses them back out on the table with sensitivity, wisdom and clear-eyed vision. And you can't put the book down!" --Jewelle Gomez, award-winning author of *The Gilda Stories*

ISBN 978-0-9845318-5-1